What the critics are saying...

ꟸ

EROTIC INVITATION

"Delightful. Decidedly wicked. Completely wonderful!" ~ *The Romance Studio*

"Cheyenne McCray has turned this erotic novella into a sexual paradise. The no holds barred sex scenes make this one hot read…" ~ *Love Romances*

"Ms. McCray has truly created an erotic story with a fulfilling conclusion and brings the true nature of romance back to its fantasy roots as well as allowing our sensual nature to shine through." ~ *In the Library Reviews*

EROTIC WEEKEND

"…I was drawn in by the masterfully penned white-hot eroticism of the BDSM lifestyle that most of us only fantasize about…" ~ *eCataRomance Reviews*

"Erotic Weekend is like a decadent sweet. It is short, delicious, and oh so satisfying." ~ *A Romance Review*

"Erotic Weekend is Cheyenne McCray's best work to date. The storyline had this reader mesmerized from the first page to the last." ~ *Enchanted in Romance*

EROTIC STRANGER

"Erotic Stranger is a rare and special experience that no one should miss!" ~ *eCataRomance Reviews*

"...both characters have depth and literally come alive, stepping right from the pages and into your wildest imagination. Once again this author has impressed me with her writing style and with each story the heat radar peaks a little higher." ~ *Coffee Time Romance*

"The raw sexual energy pulsated off the pages...I was spellbound until the end of the story." ~ *Erotic-Escapades*

EROTIC INTERLUDES

CHEYENNE McCRAY

USA Today Bestselling Author

An Ellora's Cave Romantica Publication

www.ellorascave.com

Erotic Interludes

ISBN 9781419954931

Edited by Heather Osborn and Patricia Haley
Cover art by Darrell King and Syneca

Trade paperback Publication March 2006

Content Advisory:

S - ENSUOUS
E - ROTIC
X - TREME

Ellora's Cave Publishing offers three levels of Romantica™ reading entertainment: S (S-ensuous), E (E-rotic), and X (X-treme).

The following material contains graphic sexual content meant for mature readers. This story has been rated E–rotic.

S-*ensuous* love scenes are explicit and leave nothing to the imagination.

E-*rotic* love scenes are explicit, leave nothing to the imagination, and are high in volume per the overall word count. E-rated titles might contain material that some readers find objectionable—in other words, almost anything goes, sexually. E-rated titles are the most graphic titles we carry in terms of both sexual language and descriptiveness in these works of literature.

X-*treme* titles differ from E-rated titles only in plot premise and storyline execution. Stories designated with the letter X tend to contain difficult or controversial subject matter not for the faint of heart.

Also by Cheyenne McCray

Blackstar: Future Knight
Castaways
Ellora's Cave Tales of the Temple III (*anthology)*
Hearts are Wild *(anthology)*
Seraphine Chronicles: Forbidden
Seraphine Chronicles: Bewitched
Seraphine Chronicles: Spellbound
Seraphine Chronicles: Untamed
Things That Go Bump in the Night 3 (*anthology*)
Vampire Dreams with Annie Windsor
Wildfire
Wildcat
Wildcard
Wild Borders
Wonderland: King of Hearts
Wonderland: King of Spades
Wonderland: King of Diamonds
Wonderland: King of Clubs

Contents

ജ

Dedication

ഇ

To Annie Windsor, Mackenzie McKade, Heather Osborn, Patti Duplantis, and all the ladies of the CheysFantasies chat group. You Rock!

Author's Note

ഇ

The stories found in Erotic Interludes incorporate only elements of Domination/submission and BDSM. It is not intended to accurately portray a true BDSM or Dom/sub relationship.

Erotic Invitation

Chapter One

ഗ

With a sigh of longing, Sheila Lane placed her elbow on her desk, propped her chin on her hand, and studied Nick Tarantino as he spoke with the company's Vice President. The two men were ensconced in conversation, unaware of her soulful expression.

Thank God. She'd die on the spot if Mr. Tarantino could read on her face how much she wanted him.

How much she loved him.

Not that it mattered now. She still couldn't believe it. Nick was leaving. The CEO, President, and owner of Tarantino Investments had sold the company and was turning over the reins to Derrick Macintyre effective today.

After three years of being Nick's personal assistant, Sheila found herself with a new boss.

And the man she'd fallen in love with years ago would walk out of her life…forever.

Not that he'd ever been more than professional with her. Not that he'd ever shown the slightest inclination that he might be interested in her personally.

On occasion he'd given her smiles of approval that had melted her heart, but that was it. Sometimes he'd lean over her shoulder to review her notes and she would almost moan out loud at the feel of his warm breath against her neck. When she'd hand him a document or a file, her fingers would lightly brush his and she'd feel a jolt of electricity from the roots of her hair to her toenails. But Nick never gave any sign that he'd felt anything at all.

Sheila sighed again as she continued to study his profile. Of course she likely wasn't his type, although she'd never met any woman he might be dating. Sheila was petite in height and had breasts so large she'd topple over if she didn't have a nice sized ass to keep her stable. She kept her wheat-blonde hair pulled back in a clip and she wore conservative business suits when she was in the office. She was working class…he was a god.

Italian by birth, Nick had lived in the U.S. most of his life. He still had the sexiest accent, and when he spoke her nipples went hard automatically and only her business suits kept him from seeing the taut buds peak against the soft fabric of her blouses. The man was a good six feet tall with broad, powerful shoulders. He was built like a pro basketball player, lean and muscular. A man built for speed…and sex.

So many times she'd imagined what it would feel like to be taken by Nick. Whether it was hard and rough, or slow and sensual, all her fantasies revolved around him. And all her fantasies involved him dominating her, mastering her like he mastered everything else in his business and in his life.

Like right now as she watched him, she wondered what it would feel like to be on her knees before him, his trousers undone and his cock jutting out in front of her. Her wrists would be tied behind her and his hand on the back of her head, forcing her to go down on his cock. She'd swirl her tongue around the head and then take him deep, to the back of her throat.

She clenched her thighs together at the thought and her clit ached as she imagined how he'd pump his hips against her face, fucking her mouth as he held her captive.

At that moment Nick cast a look at Sheila. Her face flamed and she felt like she could sink through the floor with embarrassment at being caught staring at him and fantasizing about him.

She quickly moved her hand from her chin to the file in front of her and dropped her gaze to the papers she was supposed to be going through. She felt the heat of his stare and hoped her cheeks weren't as red as they felt. After three years she should be an expert at hiding her feelings for the man.

While she pretended to study the file, she listened to his powerful voice and she almost teared up at the thought of never hearing that throbbing tone again. Her thoughts wandered and she imagined him taking her on his polished mahogany desk, her wrists tied above her head, his hands and mouth upon her body, and his cock sliding into her wet channel—

"Sheila?"

Her head shot up at the sound of Nick's voice so close to her, and her pulse pounded in her ears. He was standing beside her desk and studying her with his intense aquamarine eyes that gave away his Sicilian heritage. The heady masculine scent of him surrounded her, a combination of his light aftershave and the smell of pure male.

"Are you all right?" he asked in that deep penetrating voice that made her shiver and her panties dampen.

Sheila cleared her throat and nodded. "Yes, Mr. Tarantino." A very large part of her wanted to beg him to take her with him, wherever he was going. Hell, just to *take* her.

But she kept herself under control. "It's been a pleasure serving you these past three years. I—I," she faltered wanting to say *I'm going to miss you.* Instead she said, "I wish you well in your future endeavors." Her cheeks went hotter at the lameness of her words.

God, she was so pitiful.

A flicker of something crossed Nick's features and he gave a slow nod. "It has certainly been a pleasure, Sheila." He paused, those eyes never letting hers go. "You have been a most…efficient assistant."

Sheila's heart plummeted and she attempted to keep her voice steady. "Thank you, Mr. Tarantino."

He didn't even grace her with one of his rare smiles. He simply turned away and strode into his office.

One last time.

Nick shut the heavy mahogany door behind him and raked his fingers through his black hair as he ordered his cock to stand down. He wore his slacks loose because invariably the beautiful Sheila Lane would make him rock-hard with one demure glance, with one whiff of her light orange blossom perfume.

Oh, he'd recognized those glances for what they were, and although he'd wanted to take advantage of the delectable Miss Lane, he didn't believe in crossing the employer/employee line. He never mixed business with pleasure.

Well now there was nothing to stop him.

In a few strides he reached the floor-to-ceiling windows of his luxurious office and stared out at the Los Angeles skyline. The sky was a cloudless cerulean blue and a light wind caused palm fronds to wave to and fro below the ten story office building. Tarantino Investments occupied the entire top floor. What had been a venture capital start-up company had just sold for millions, and now Nick was free to move on to new and more interesting ventures.

Including the blonde beauty who had been his assistant for three years. Three years she had taunted him with her fine ass and luscious breasts, even though most of the time she'd hidden them beneath form-fitting suits. Occasionally she would take off her jacket and when she moved he would catch a glimpse of the curve of one breast through gaps in her conservative button-up blouse.

And that ass of hers. Often he had pictured her on all fours as he slid his cock into her slick core and spanked those cheeks until they were a fine shade of pink. As pink as her face had just turned when he'd caught her watching him.

She'd played the unobtainable Miss Lane these past years, now it was time to make her pay for all her teasing, intentional or no.

"Girl, you've got to get over Tarantino." Andi tossed her shimmering black hair over her shoulder and braced one hand on the copy machine as she watched Sheila. "That or proposition him."

"Humph." Sheila turned her gaze to the copier and watched the incandescent light flash with every copy the machine made. Her eyes were glazed and her heart heavy. "Three years, Andi." Sheila fidgeted with the top button at the throat of her blouse. "And all I could say was 'I wish you well in your future endeavors.' How lame is that?"

Andi snorted. "Well, honey, it was better than throwing yourself at his feet and begging him to take you right on the Berber carpeting in his office." Sheila cast her friend a glance as Andi continued, "Although that certainly would have caught his attention."

Sheila rolled her eyes and Andi said, "I would've asked him out for a drink."

The copier stopped and Sheila snatched out the original and grabbed the copies. "You've got guts. I'm just a wimp, plain and simple."

Andi shook her head, her long black hair sliding over her shoulders like a silken black curtain. "You've got to stop playing it safe and take chances. *Live*, girlfriend."

"I'm not you." Sheila strode out of the copy room toward her desk. "Besides, it's too late. He already left."

"It's never too late," Andi shot back as she rounded her cubicle and vanished from sight just as Sheila almost smacked into Kate Baron, Vice President and resident Bitch From Hell.

Kate smirked and raised a perfectly plucked eyebrow. "Nick Tarantino wouldn't waste his time with you."

Sheila's cheeks burned as she moved behind her desk and eased into her chair. "I don't know what you're talking about."

"Oh, I think you do." Kate laughed, a fake cultured laugh that grated on Sheila's nerves. Kate propped a perfectly manicured hand on her perfectly slim hip. "After all this time I'd think you would have realized that the last person he would be interested in is you. All these years you've made it only too obvious that you want him. And it's only too obvious he wants nothing to do with you. Except maybe a fuck if you do throw yourself at him."

Sheila's face burned hotter as she realized Kate must have been listening outside the copy room. "Is there anything I can do for you, *Ms. Baron?*"

The woman brushed a piece of imaginary lint from the sleeve of her perfectly tailored black suit. "Don't waste his time any further by making a fool of yourself."

With that the Wicked Witch of West L.A. turned on her heel and strode down the hall, presumably toward her own elegant office.

Sheila slid into her seat and clenched the copies in her hand. *Bitch, bitch, bitch!*

She moved her gaze to Nick's empty office. Tomorrow the movers would bring Derrick's belongings into the luxurious office and she would officially be his assistant.

Kate's words burned in her ears and she longed for a Q-tip to clean them right out. Rather than discourage her from contacting Nick, Kate's digs only pissed Sheila off.

Andi was right. She should contact Nick. She had his cell number and his home number. It wouldn't hurt a damn bit to ask him out for a drink. They'd been co-workers and friends long enough that she could simply say she'd like to get together for a farewell drink. If it led to more…

She stuffed the copies into a file folder and grabbed the cordless phone receiver before her nerves and self-doubt got the better of her. With shaking fingers she dialed Nick's cell number, a number she'd memorized long ago. Just as the phone started to ring, she spotted something propped up against a picture of her family.

It was an envelope with *Sheila* embossed in gold across the creamy white surface.

She dropped the receiver back onto its cradle and picked up the envelope. It was thick and heavy, obviously expensive stationery. Curiosity filled her as she turned it over. Gold wax sealed the envelope with a crest she didn't recognize. She broke the seal, slowly opened the envelope, and pulled out a single sheet of paper in the same heavy stationery. The paper was folded in half and when she opened it, her heart began to pound.

Across the white surface a single word was embossed in gold:

Tonight.

Chapter Two

ஐ

All the way home Sheila's mind raced and her pulse pounded in her ears. She barely kept her mind on traffic and her little Nissan in her own lane. When she reached her condo, she parked in the garage, snatched her purse off the passenger seat, and slowly went into the small house through the garage door.

Okay, nothing to get excited over, her calm, rational mind told her. It might be nothing at all.

The door banged shut behind her and she faced the tiny but cozy living room. "It could just be a party someone's holding," she mused aloud.

"Who's throwing a party?"

At the sound of Greg's voice, Sheila nearly jumped out of her skin. She held her purse tight to her chest and glared at her roommate who'd come up behind her. "I've told you a zillion times not to sneak up on me like that."

Greg gave her an unrepentant grin. "But it's so much fun."

"Get lost, surfer boy." Sheila turned her back on her too-cute-for-his-own-good friend and slipped into her bedroom.

Of course surfer boy followed her. "C'mon, give."

She set her purse on her vanity and tossed her suit jacket onto the bed. "It's Friday night. Don't you have a beach-volleyball-bonfire thing to go to?"

He hitched his shoulder against the doorframe. "So what's up?"

"I told you there's no party." Sheila pulled her hairclip out and let her long hair tumble over her shoulders. "Now beat it." She began unbuttoning her up-to-the-neck blouse in front of Greg. They'd been friends for so long that neither of them worried much about modesty in front of the other. As long as they had underwear on, what difference did it make?

Greg cocked an eyebrow as she slid out of her blouse. "You really should get rid of those granny bras and panties. Get something really hot from Victoria's Secret or Fredericks of Hollywood."

Sheila gave him a glare as she shimmied out of her past-the-knee skirt and flung it onto the bed with everything else. "Like anyone's going to see them but you. And you don't count."

"The only reason you haven't dated is because you've been lusting over one man and won't give anyone else a chance." He tossed wavy sun-streaked hair from his eyes and his voice grew softer. "So, was it hard with him leaving today?"

With a heavy sigh, Sheila peeled her nylons over her ample hips and down to her ankles where she stepped out of them. "It's hard to believe that I won't see him again."

"You should call him." Greg's expression was serious. "The man can't be blind. You're caring, sensitive, and well, you're pretty."

She smiled. "You're just saying that because you want me to spring for dinner tonight."

The corner of his mouth quirked. "Well there's that," he responded with a wink, then his expression went back to serious. "Call him. What can it hurt?"

"You sound like Andi." Sheila studied her reflection in the vanity. Her bra was heavy-duty and held up her large breasts but didn't show them to their full advantage. And she had to admit the cotton panties were a bit on the grandma-ish side. "Actually, I did start to call him, but then I found something on my desk."

She didn't know why she was telling Greg, other than the fact that he'd been her best friend and confidant since high school when they were both fifteen. And here it was, sixteen years later and they were living together, unattached and no serious prospects in either of their futures. Although Greg played the field, he never stayed with one girl for long.

They were truly pathetic.

"Well…what was it?" Keen interest lit Greg's warm brown eyes.

Sheila went to her purse, slipped out the envelope, and handed it to Greg.

A puzzled expression crossed his features and then he whistled. His gaze shot to hers and he tossed the envelope and paper onto her bureau. "I'll bet it has something to do with the package."

Before Sheila could ask "What package?" Greg tore out of the room. In a few moments he came back bearing a thick white box bound with a gold bow. A single long-stemmed red rose had been slipped through the bow.

He handed the package to her. "Some guy dropped this off about fifteen minutes before you got home."

Sheila's hands trembled with a combination of uncertainty, fear, and excitement as she took the box from him. After she set it on her vanity, she pulled the red rose from the bow and brought it to her nose. She inhaled the sweet scent, drawing it in and letting it seep through her being.

Greg punched her lightly in the arm. "Hurry up all ready."

With nervous anticipation, she set the rose aside and pulled at the bow until it fell away, and then she lifted the lid from the box and tossed it aside and caught her breath. On a bed of sapphire-blue satin was another creamy envelope with her name embossed in gold.

More quickly now she broke the seal and pulled out the heavy paper. It simply said, "7:00 p.m."

Greg snatched the paper from her fingers and let out another low whistle. But Sheila was too intent on exploring the contents of the box. She withdrew the blue satin and discovered that it was a strapless gown, simple yet elegant—although it looked like it would barely cover her breasts and was a little too short, even by her petite standards. Carefully she laid the dress on her bed beside her discarded work clothing, then returned to the box.

Inside it was an evening bag that matched the dress to perfection, a lovely strapless sapphire-blue bra, thong underwear, a garter belt, and sheer thigh-high stockings.

With every item she withdrew, Sheila's cheeks grew hotter and hotter. "Oh my God." She said as brought out a dainty pair of three-inch heeled sandals. Everything looked perfectly sized, as though the person knew her intimately.

"Shit." Greg tossed the second note on top of the first one. "The guy's got class, I'll say that."

Sheila turned her gaze to him. "I'm supposed to dress up in all this and be ready at seven for a man I don't even know?"

Greg shrugged. "I'd say it's obvious he knows you *very* well."

"A stalker?"

He rolled his eyes.

"Not your friends Devon or Terry."

"Hell no." Greg laughed. "They haven't got class enough to send a woman a box of chocolates much less go through all this trouble."

Sheila's mind kept going back to Nick Tarantino. "He wouldn't, would he?" she asked herself aloud.

"Ding!" Greg made his voice sound like a game-show host's. "Sheila Lane, if you're talking about your mega-rich ex-boss, you're tonight's winner."

"Wow." She shook her head slowly. "I mean no. He hasn't given me any reason, *ever*, to believe he'd do anything like this."

"He has plenty of reasons, but I'm not going to go into them now." Greg glanced at the clock on her bureau. "You've got less than an hour to hop in the shower and be ready in time."

Sheila gripped the shoes tighter. "I can't just jump because someone sends me a couple of notes and a box of clothes."

Greg backed out her door and grabbed the door handle. "Time to stop playing it safe and take a chance, hon," he said as he shut the door behind him.

She stuck her tongue out and glared at the door. Yeah, he and Andi would get along just fine.

Fifty-five minutes later, Sheila was dressed and ready. She stood in front of the mirror again, this time amazed at the transformation in her appearance. The sapphire satin clung to her curves and plunged low enough to show her generous cleavage. The lacy bra, thong, and garters felt sensual and wanton and the high heels made her feel extremely sexy. She'd put her hair up, but this time in a soft and elegant look instead of the usual business style she used at work.

Everything had been a perfect fit. As if the man knew her better than she knew herself.

Was it really Nick? Was this some sort of treat for being a good employee for three years?

Oh, yeah. That made perfect sense. What man bought a woman thigh-highs and thong underwear if he wasn't after one thing—sex?

Sheila shook her head. He'd never shown her the slightest indication that he'd been interested in her in any way outside of her job. But tonight…if he wanted a good fuck she'd be happy to oblige. After all wasn't that exactly what she'd fantasized about so many times?

That and him actually loving her as much as she loved him.

No, I'm not *going to allow myself to think that way.* Not after years of wanting him in every way a woman could want a man.

She loved everything about him, from his powerful presence to the way he made each employee feel important. He didn't tolerate incompetence, but he had a gift for hiring well-qualified and efficient employees and the company turnover had been practically nil. She also loved how generous he was with local charities from breast cancer research to homeless shelters. She only knew about his large donations because all correspondence crossed her desk. Nick was a very private man and she doubted anyone but her knew just how generous he was.

The doorbell rang, jolting Sheila from her thoughts and it was all she could do not to hide in her closet just out of sheer nerves. She took a deep breath, picked up the evening bag and the long-stemmed rose and walked to the living room. The air was cool on her bare shoulders, the satin dress rasped her nipples through the bra, and the thong snaked up her slit and pulled against her folds.

Greg had the door open and a man in a sleek Italian suit stood in the doorway, a strap of blue satin in his hands. The man was in his late thirties, she guessed, devastatingly handsome with sandy blond hair and ice-blue eyes.

Behind him in the darkness Sheila saw a long black stretch limo at the curb and her pulse picked up to an alarming pace. Her steps faltered as she felt a keen sense of disappointment. Was this blond man the one who had sent her the invitations?

Sheila raised her chin and walked across the room. When she stood directly in front of the tall and good-looking man holding the satin strip, he said, "Please turn around, Miss Lane. I've been instructed to blindfold you."

Chapter Three

ꟼ

Her jaw dropped. "Excuse me?"

Greg smirked but the man's expression remained stoic. "Blindfold you. Now please turn around if you will."

She glared at Greg. "Is this something you've done? Because if it is—"

"Not me, I swear." He held his hands up in surrender. "I'll check out the limo while you let robot-man blindfold you."

With a little shiver of uncertainty and yet excitement, too, Sheila turned her back to the handsome hunk of man. He carefully placed the blue satin over her eyes and tied it behind her head just snug enough to keep it from slipping. In the distance she heard the sound of a door being opened and Greg's voice, but she couldn't understand a word he was saying.

While she strained to hear him, the man carefully turned her by the shoulders so that she was facing the same direction from where she heard Greg speaking.

"Let me guide you, Miss Lane." The man held her by her upper arm, helped her over the threshold and down the sidewalk toward the curb. Her heels clicked against the sidewalk and the purr of the limo sounded louder now that her vision had been eliminated. Her steps were uncertain but the man strode confidently ahead, not giving her time to worry about tripping over her high heels and tumbling to the concrete.

The moment the man brought her to a stop, she felt her friend's hand on her wrist. Greg's lips brushed her forehead and she caught his familiar scent of testosterone, sunshine, and coconut suntan oil. "It's all right. Have fun, kiddo." And then he walked away.

Sheila took a deep but shaky breath and let the man help her into the limo.

Nick's gut tightened as he watched Greg Stuart kiss Sheila's forehead. Greg gave one more warning glance to Nick before turning away and sauntering back into the house.

In all honesty, Nick appreciated the fact that Sheila's friend had watched out for her, grilling him on what he intended to do with her. Nick had been polite but restrained himself from telling Greg that he intended to fuck the hell out of Sheila Lane.

That and win her heart.

He remained silent as the chauffeur helped Sheila into the limo and closed the door behind her, and he caught a whiff of her orange blossom perfume. Nick studied her petite form as she settled into the seat, the long-stemmed rose and her evening bag clutched in her trembling hands. The dress had been made for her at the finest dress shop on Rodeo Drive. It presented her mouth-watering breasts to perfection and clung to every curve. The color was perfect for her—it matched her sapphire eyes. Her hair was up in a softer, prettier style than she wore in the office, but he intended to set it free, to strip all of her bare.

Nick wanted more than Sheila Lane's body. He wanted her heart and soul. He intended to have all of her.

As soon as Dave Carson was in the driver's seat, Nick rapped his knuckles on the dividing glass, letting his chauffeur and friend know he was ready to leave.

"What—" Sheila started as soon as the limo went into motion, but Nick placed his hand over her lips, stifling her words.

"Shhhhhh," he murmured, "I want you to just listen…and feel. All right?"

Sheila nodded, her lips rubbing against his palm. His cock ached at the feel of those lips and he wished only to push up her dress, pull aside the thong he knew she was wearing, and slide his cock deep within her.

But that would be soon enough. First he'd tease her and bring her close to the brink again and again before he finally allowed her release, and before he allowed himself to have her. They had waited this long, and he wanted to make their first time more than memorable.

Sheila swallowed as she felt the limo move through traffic and as she felt the heat of Nick's body near hers. Even without her sight, anywhere, anyplace, she'd recognize the sound of his voice, his scent, his very presence.

But what was this all about?

He moved his hand from her mouth and placed it on her thigh. The warmth of his hand close to her center made her ache so badly it was all she could do not to squirm in her seat. "Mr. Tarantino?" she whispered. "What's going on?"

"No talking." Nick brushed his mouth over her ear and she shivered. "After being in my employ all this time, Miss Lane, you know I expect my orders to be followed without question."

Sheila parted her lips to argue but he put his finger to her lips and murmured, "Quiet, my sweet." He pried the rose and evening bag from her tight grip. "I plan to pay you back for teasing me all these years, Sheila, even if it wasn't intentional. And I do believe you are going to enjoy what I have in mind for both of us."

She made a sound of amazement and turned toward his voice, even though she couldn't see him. *Teasing* him?

"Oh, yes." He took her by the shoulders and moved her so that she was facing him as much as possible on the seat of the limo. Gently he brought her hands in front of her, lightly stroking her wrists before binding them with another piece of satin. "Did you think I never noticed the look in your eyes when you watched me? The way your tongue traced your lower lip when you brought files to me for my approval?"

Sheila made another sound, this time in protest, but he simply turned her so that now her back was to the luxurious leather seat, her hands bound in her lap. She felt the limo make a turn and she wondered where he was taking her.

"As much as I wanted you, there was nothing I could do about it as long as I was your employer." His hands cupped her breasts through the satin and Sheila moaned. "But now I intend to have you, Miss Lane."

Confusion and amazement coursed through her veins at the thought of Nick wanting her sexually all this time, the same way she wanted him. She'd thought she'd been so careful to hide her longing for him, but apparently she'd made it only too obvious. "Nick," she whispered, but he placed one hand over her lips again.

"This is my time, sweetheart." He slid his hand from her mouth, down her throat and settled at her cleavage.

Sheila sighed and arched her back, offering herself to him. He could have her any way he wanted her, and the sooner the better. Her thong was soaked and she could feel her juices sliding down her thighs.

She heard the soft intake of breath and his thumbs circled her nipples through the satin of her dress, bringing the nubs to hard, tight peaks.

In a slow and sensual movement, he pulled down the front of her strapless dress along with her bra, so that her breasts spilled out of their confines and into his hands. "Gorgeous," he murmured. "As lovely as I imagined so many times." And then she felt his warm breath fanning the soft skin of her breasts. "Yes, payback will be very pleasurable."

Oh, lord, she wouldn't be able to take much more of his payback if this was any indication of how he intended to extract his payment. What an incredibly erotic feeling it was to be bound and blindfolded, and totally at Nick's mercy.

Nick pushed her breasts up high and Sheila moaned again as his tongue slowly circled one nipple. His tongue was hot and wet and the light stubble on his face was rough against her delicate skin. She felt the brush of his soft hair over her breasts and then he turned to her other nipple, attending to it in the same manner.

She heard him draw a ragged breath as he pulled away. "Lay on your back, Sheila," he ordered at the same time he was turning her on the seat.

Her heart jumped in excitement. Was he going to take her now, like this?

When she hesitated, he said, "Would you prefer I lower the glass and have my chauffeur watch while I enjoy your pleasures?"

The thought of being watched was somehow thrilling, but she definitely wasn't into that, and she didn't think Nick really was either. But still she moved as quickly as she could, so that with his help she was on her back, her bound hands in front of her, her knees bent and her dress up around her hips.

The limo purred along as it made its way through L.A. Where, she didn't know and right now she didn't care. All that mattered was the man who was pressing her thighs apart with his big hands, exposing her to the warm air and to his gaze.

He groaned and she felt the brush of his knuckles over her pussy lips. "Already you're wet and swollen for me. And your scent…amazing."

Heat flushed through Sheila, a heady combination of embarrassment and arousal. She wished that she could see him, was allowed to speak to him, could touch him. Yet at the same time she enjoyed what he was doing to her and wanted everything he could give her.

Nick's cock ached so badly to slide into the little enchantress, and to fuck her until she screamed with her release. How easy it would be to take her now, and he knew she wanted him with equal intensity.

He had instantly been attracted to Sheila the moment he'd interviewed her for the administrative assistant position at Tarantino Investments. He had hired her for her extensive experience and her impeccable references. The fact that he wanted her never entered the equation. He had strict rules over employee fraternization, and that included himself.

She was an incredibly efficient assistant, firm and in control with clients and suppliers. When it came to her dealings with Nick she was equally professional, but Sheila tended to avoid his stare, lowering her gaze, and stealing glances when she thought he wasn't looking.

But he'd kept an eye on her, always wanting her. He hadn't been satisfied with any other woman since he'd known Sheila. He'd grown to appreciate her wit, her devotion to her friends, her smile.

She was made for him.

And now he had to feel her, had to taste her sweet pussy. With slow, deliberate movements he moved her thong out of the way with one hand and slipped a finger from his free hand into her hot center.

Sheila cried out and raised her hips toward him while he fucked her pussy with his finger, his knuckles pounding against her swollen folds and clit. The ache in his cock increased to massive proportions, but he concentrated on Sheila's pleasure. When her legs began trembling and he felt her close to climax, he withdrew from her soaked channel.

"No, my little tease. You may not come…yet." He slipped his finger into his mouth, tasting her juices and inhaling her scent. He closed his eyes as if savoring the finest of wines, the flavor, the bouquet. "You are delicious," he murmured and brought his hand to her nose. "Smell your desire for me."

In the soft lighting of the limo he saw her cheeks flush. Her expression was one of pleasure and excitement, if not some uncertainty. Once again he sensed her desire to be dominated, to turn over control of her pleasure to him. She was giving herself willingly to him in every way, and he intended to fulfill her fantasies—to fulfill both of their fantasies

"I have a couple of rules I'd like you to follow tonight." From a compartment in the limo he retrieved a highly sophisticated device that was about the size of a thin matchbook. It had a small clip on the backside, so fine that it could barely be seen. "Don't climax without my permission." He slipped the device inside her thong, against her clit, and clipped it to the damp material.

"Do you agree, Sheila, that if you don't hold back, you should be punished?" he asked as he reached into his pocket. "I promise you shall enjoy every minute of it."

Slowly she nodded and her voice wavered, "Yes."

"Good." Nick smiled as his hand found the remote and pressed the "on" button.

Chapter Four

ℬ

"Nick!" Sheila bucked her hips as her thong vibrated against her clit. Oh, God, she'd never be able to keep from coming. She was already so close to the edge and he was driving her mad.

"Remember, Sheila." He lightly stroked the outside of one of her thighs with his fingers, adding to the sensations that wanted to explode within her. "Don't climax without my permission, or you'll get a taste of the little punishment I have in mind."

"Punishment," barely registered in Sheila's mind. She gave a strangled cry and she clenched her legs together to keep from coming.

Nick placed his hands on the inside of her knees and pushed them back apart. "When we are alone, don't hide yourself from me. I want to see all of you."

Abruptly the vibrations stopped. Sheila sighed with relief, but at the same time almost cried from the need to come.

"Very good, my sweet." Nick slid his hands down her thighs and arranged her dress so that it covered her hips and garters, then helped her up to a sitting position. He gently slipped her bra and the front of her dress back over her breasts.

Why wouldn't he let her come, damn it?

"Tonight you'll be mine, Sheila Lane." He lightly stroked her arm. "I'm in command of your pleasure, and I will have you."

Tonight, Sheila thought, for tonight I'm his.

One night of heaven—she'd take it.

"Nick," she whispered. "May I speak now?"

"Not yet." His warm breath caressed her face and then she felt his firm lips against the corner of her mouth. He grasped her face in his hands as he flicked his tongue over her bottom lip then gently nipped at it. Sheila moaned and he bit her lip harder until she cried out. He plunged his tongue into her mouth, taking her deep as he held her face tightly in his grip.

Sheila returned his kiss, hungry for him, for this man she had wanted for so long. She wished her hands were free so that she could touch him, could wind her arms around his neck and slide her fingers into his thick black hair. She loved the taste of him, the way he took her so fierce and intense, the feel of his light stubble chafing the soft skin around her mouth. God, how he took control was better than she had imagined. She could almost come just from the thought of what he had done already.

Nick withdrew from the kiss and she heard his breathing, more ragged now, as if he'd experienced the same incredible sensations she had.

"Your lips are sweet and your taste exquisite. Not only your mouth but your pussy, too." He gently freed her hands, slipping the satin away, and massaging her wrists where the cloth had been firmly tied. "And your skin is so soft. I can imagine how good it will feel to have your naked body beneath mine."

Sheila tingled from head to toe at the thought. She couldn't wait to feel his cock deep inside her. Why hadn't he taken her already? Why was he driving her crazy like this?

When he finally removed the blindfold, Sheila blinked, her vision coming back into focus. Her eyes met Nick's intense aquamarine gaze and heat flooded her anew. Now that she could see him, it was even harder to believe what she had just allowed him to do to her. This was her *boss* for cripesake.

Make that her former boss.

Nick reached up and plucked the clip from her hair. Her heavy locks tumbled over her shoulders, caressing the bare skin. "I would love for you to always wear your hair down." He fluffed it out with his fingers so that her hair curled over her breasts and her back. "You are absolutely stunning."

His comment took her off guard. She'd never thought of herself as stunning, but coming from him she could almost picture it, as if seeing herself through his eyes.

"You may speak now." Fire still lit his gaze, but it was softer, warmer.

Sheila swallowed, now not knowing what to say. She knew she must look like a besotted schoolgirl the way she was staring at him, and she struggled to find something to ask him. "Nick..." She gestured to the limo and then her dress. "Why—why all of this?"

He gave her a sexy grin that made her want to melt into a puddle at his feet. "I have wanted you from the first day you began working for my company." He gently stroked a finger over her wrist, causing her to tremble. "Even though you were entirely professional, I could see the hunger in your eyes, the hunger that matched my own. I wanted to teach you not only the ropes of the business, but also the ways to pleasure me so that I might pleasure you in return."

His words seemed unreal, like she was in some sort of fantasy. She shook her head, her hair sliding over her bare shoulders and the tops of her breasts. "But three years? Why did you wait so long? And why me?"

"What would you have me do?" Nick skimmed the back of his hand across her cheek and she shivered. "Fire you so that I might fuck you?"

Heat rose again to Sheila's cheeks and her pussy ached even more at his words. She lowered her eyes, unable to meet his gaze.

"I needed time to get to know you, and you needed time to get to know me." Nick caught her chin in his hand and tipped her head up so that she was looking at him again. "I didn't want to take the chance of ruining the excellent business relationship between us. As my desire for you grew, it became harder and harder to keep my hands off you. When the time came for me to sell my company, I knew it was the right time to take you, too."

Sheila wasn't exactly sure what he was saying, but she knew one thing and it absolutely amazed her. He wanted her sexually as badly as she wanted him, and he'd wanted her for just as long.

Tonight. He wanted her for tonight.

Right now she'd take him any way she could get him. It didn't matter that she loved him with everything she had. She needed a piece of him to cherish forever.

He gave her a sensual smile. "Will you be mine, in everything I ask of you?"

Wild thoughts ran rampant through Sheila's mind. He was offering her all she had fantasized about and more. How could she refuse? She took a deep breath and nodded. "Yes."

Brilliant colors of L.A.'s city lights flashed by while the luxury automobile cruised the freeway. Her pussy still ached and she knew she didn't want this night to stop.

He smiled as he handed her the evening bag from where it sat on the limo's wet bar. "You might want to freshen up a bit. I seemed to have eaten off all of your lipstick."

Nick almost groaned out loud as Sheila worried her lower lip and dug into her sleek blue purse. That lower lip was still red from his bite and he imagined sliding his cock into her mouth and deep into her throat.

Soon. Soon he'd have her in every way.

After he used the intercom to let Dave know he was ready to take Sheila to the nightclub, Nick lowered a lighted mirror built into his limo. He silently watched as Sheila touched up her makeup from her eyes to her cheeks to her mouth. Her hands trembled as she applied it, and he wondered if it was from nerves or excitement, or perhaps both. As far as he was concerned she was beautiful without makeup, but he had a feeling she would feel more confident with it.

Especially since he was taking her out to claim her publicly. Later he would claim her privately.

Chapter Five

ꟾ

By the time Sheila had arranged her dress, hair, and makeup, the limo had arrived at the exclusive restaurant. Butterflies went berserk in her belly as Nick climbed out of the luxury vehicle, his movements as fluid and graceful as a panther. He helped her out of the limo then placed his hand at the small of her back as he escorted her to the famous restaurant and nightclub that Sheila had never dreamed she would ever go into.

"Mr. Tarantino," the concierge said as soon as they arrived within the establishment's foyer. "Right this way."

Sheila tried not to let her amazement show while they were led through a maze of tables alongside a dance floor. She felt completely out of place amongst so many famous people, from politicians and powerful businessmen to movie and television stars. Sequins and diamonds glittered all around her and she caught whiffs of expensive perfume that wove through the delicious smells of the restaurant.

When they reached a corner table with an incredible view of the nighttime Los Angeles skyline, Nick assisted her, pushing in her chair before seating himself. The concierge handed each of them a menu then bowed and left.

Nick sat so close to her, surrounding her with his unique masculine scent and his powerful presence. She could hardly catch her breath. To take her mind off him, she took a moment to gaze at all that was around her from beneath her lashes so that she didn't look like a star-struck kid.

The lighting was low and intimate and at the center of the room was the dance floor. Beneath the crystal chandeliers, couples danced to ballroom music performed by a live band.

The music flowed over Sheila and her years of training and love for dance made her want to be out on the floor with Nick.

When the waiter arrived, Nick ordered for them both and chose a fine Chardonnay to go along with dinner. He poured each of them a glass of the wine, and handed Sheila her crystal stem.

"To tonight." He raised his glass and lightly clinked it against Sheila's, his aquamarine eyes focused on her as if she was the only person in the room. "An evening with a most delightful woman."

Warmth flooded Sheila at the intensity of his gaze and his words. Her throat was dry and she barely managed to respond, "To tonight."

Just as Sheila took a sip of her Chardonnay, her thong vibrated against her clit. She almost spat her wine all over the fine linen tablecloth. "Nick," she whispered.

He slipped his arm around her and lightly stroked her collarbone with his thumb. "Yes?" he asked in a nonchalant tone as she clenched her thighs tight.

She could hardly speak from the sensations shooting through her body from the vibrator stimulating her clit. "I can't take much more."

Nick moved his mouth close to her ear. "You can."

"I'm too close to coming," she whispered in a hoarse voice.

Nick's tone went deep. "Wait until I tell you to climax, my sweet Sheila."

Oh, lord. He was going to kill her.

Even when the waiter arrived with their appetizer, Nick left the vibrator on. Sheila avoided the waiter's gaze, afraid he would see how hard she was fighting to keep from coming.

To her relief, Nick turned off the vibrator long enough for her to draw back from the edge, at least for a few moments. However, throughout dinner he continued to turn it on, driving her to the precipice of an orgasm and back again. Sheila's clit was so sensitive that she was going out of her mind with the need to come.

He spent the evening touching her intimately, brushing his fingers along her arm and stroking her face. His eyes seemed to hint at more than simple lust, but Sheila refused to allow herself to think beyond the moment.

For dessert Nick ordered a single slice of a decadent chocolate cake and insisted on feeding it to her. This time he didn't let up with the vibrator. In between bites of the dessert, when she'd managed to swallow the rich chocolate, she begged him to stop.

"I'm so close." She squirmed in her seat, but the movement only made her hotter. "Please, Nick."

He gave her an utterly wicked male smile. "I'll have to punish you."

At the thought of being erotically punished by Nick, Sheila's skin flushed and her pussy grew even wetter. The vibrating thong kicked up a notch and it was too much. She bit her lip, hard, as an orgasm ripped through her unlike anything she'd ever experienced before. It started low in her abdomen and expanded outward, a hot flush of pleasure reaching every part of her being. Her body jerked in her seat and she kept her eyes lowered, praying no one could see her flushed face and her body shaking with her orgasm.

Nick caught her chin in his hand and raised her face so that his gaze met hers. "Such a very bad girl," he murmured as tremors continued to run rampant through her body. The way he said *bad girl* made her even more on fire.

"Please…turn it off." She tried to catch her breath, to speak without a quaver in her voice, but it was impossible. "I—I can't take anymore."

He gave her a smile, slipped his hand into his jacket pocket, and the vibrator stopped.

Sheila almost wept with relief. Her body tingled and throbbed and she felt like everyone in the room must know she'd climaxed right there in the nightclub. The feeling of being watched only added to the aftershocks jarring her body.

"No one could tell." Nick dabbed a napkin at the corner of her mouth and brushed the back of his hand over her breast as he moved away. "Only I know how badly you've misbehaved."

By the deep intense tone of his voice she knew he intended to deal out her punishment soon and that she would enjoy every minute of it.

When they finished the dessert and Nick had paid the bill, he pulled out Sheila's chair and helped her to stand. Her legs trembled and she prayed she'd be able to walk after that incredible orgasm.

With his hand on her elbow, Nick escorted Sheila along the edge of the dance floor and then away from the crowd, the talking and the laughter. He led her down a long and richly paneled hallway lit by occasional brass sconces that gave off a soft golden glow. It became so quiet that she heard only the sound of their footsteps on thick carpeting and the pounding of her heart.

They finally reached a door where a man in an impeccably starched suit stood with his hands behind his back. "May I assist you, Mr. Tarantino?"

"Is this room available?" When the man gave an affirmative nod, Nick slipped out his money clip and handed the man a couple of hundred dollar bills. "See to it that we're not disturbed."

"Yes, Sir." The man gave a quick nod and the money vanished within his suit jacket. He immediately returned to his former position, hands behind his back and his expression stoic.

Sheila's cheeks burned as Nick led them into a luxurious men's bathroom. Without a sound, the heavy mahogany door closed behind them. The walls of the front sitting room were dark paneled and an opening in one wall led from the plush room to where Sheila presumed the toilets were.

The sitting room carpet was a thick, rich forest green and the countertops and sinks were obviously made of extremely expensive marble. Fine linen hand cloths were stacked beside the sinks and the room smelled faintly of cigar smoke and almond-scented soap.

"What's that man going to think?" she whispered as if the attendant might hear.

Nick led her to a marble countertop before a huge mirror illuminated by low, seductive lighting. "He probably thinks I'm going to fuck you."

She went even hotter all over at the thought of the man knowing what they were doing—if in fact Nick intended to take her right then and there.

"Brace your hands on the countertop," he ordered in a low, rumbling voice. "And widen your thighs."

Sheila found herself following his directions automatically. After she set her evening bag on the countertop she bent over and waited, her body trembling with nerves. "What are you going to do?"

"Mmmmm..." He pressed his hips against her backside and through his slacks she felt his hard cock along the cleft of her ass. She watched his reflection in the mirror while he reached around and lowered the bodice of her dress and her strapless bra so that her breasts were bared.

Her body throbbed as she watched him knead her nipples and felt his rough masculine hands against her soft nubs. "I've wanted to touch your breasts for so long." His voice was hoarse as he cupped them in his palms. "You will definitely need another little punishment."

She swallowed her fear and excitement as he leaned back and pushed her dress up over her hips so that her backside was bared to him. All she was wearing was the thong, garters, and thigh-high stockings he'd bought for her. She could just imagine how she must look to him.

"Damn but I love your ass." He rubbed her butt cheeks with his palm and she moaned aloud. "Do you know why you're being punished?"

"For climaxing when you told me not to." Sheila's voice trembled as her eyes met his in the mirror. "And for—for teasing you."

"That's right, my sweet." He raised his hand and swatted her. *Hard*.

Sheila yelped at the sudden pain. To her surprise the tingling melted into a feeling that made her wetter for him. It actually felt kind of good. But when he swatted her again, the pain was sharper this time. It hurt, but then she was filled with pleasure that made her pussy ache.

"Watch me spank you in the mirror." Nick swatted her again, the smack loud in the quiet room. "See how enchanting you are?"

Her eyes widened as she watched their reflections. He was so handsome, so big and powerful, and by the gleam in his eyes she knew he was enjoying this erotic punishment. When she turned her gaze to herself, she couldn't believe how seductive she looked with her breasts naked, her dress up over her ass, her eyes wide and her lips parted.

Again and again he spanked her, and she tensed before every swat as she watched his hand sweep down to land on her ass.

Her breasts swung with every slap of his hand and her nipples ached. Her pussy was on fire, her folds swollen and her clit throbbing. "Please may I come?" she asked as he landed another slap on her ass.

"No." He spanked her again. "You'll have to wait until I tell you it's all right, sweetheart."

She groaned, her ass burning and tingling from his punishment. And when he finally stopped, she breathed a sigh of relief. Much more and she would have come no matter his orders to the contrary.

"Stand and face me." He pulled down her dress over her stinging ass and she turned around.

Damn, he was so handsome she could hardly take her eyes off his face. That devilish gleam in his eyes only added to his incredibly sexy appeal.

He reached into his pocket and pulled out a fine strand of diamonds that sparkled in the room's low lighting. Before she realized what he was doing, he looped one end of the chain over one of her nipples and tightened it, then did the same with the other end. She gasped at the intense feeling, again of pain mixed with pleasure as her nipples engorged with blood.

"This nipple chain signifies you are mine," he murmured as he gently tugged at it. "Will you wear it?"

His...it mean she was his...at least for tonight. "Yes," she whispered.

"Good." He smiled and pushed down on her head, gently forcing her to her knees in front of his obvious erection. "Now for your second punishment."

Chapter Six

ꟾ

Sheila's knees sank into the plush carpeting and her skin prickled with excitement, knowing what he would want now.

"Unfasten my slacks." Nick kept his hands clenched in her hair. "I want your hot, wet mouth on me now, like I've imagined countless times."

She bit her lip as she undid his trousers and unzipped his fly, her hands trembling and fumbling with the fastenings. She pulled down his boxers, and his thick, long, luscious cock slipped out right before her lips.

"That's it, sweetheart." He gently pushed her head closer to him. "Take me in your mouth, my little tease."

She slipped his cock through her lips and sighed at the feel of his hard length sliding to the back of her throat. She swirled her tongue over the ridges and contours and reveled in his distinctly male scent and the tight curls at the base of his cock.

"Play with your nipples while you suck me." His tone was powerful and commanding as he kept his grip on her hair and thrust his hips toward her face.

Sheila brought her hands to her nipples and caressed the incredibly hard nubs and the rings that were taut around them. The diamond chain swung between her breasts, lightly bouncing against her soft skin. The ache in her pussy increased so much that she thought she'd come just from the feel of his cock in her mouth and her own hands on her breasts.

"You're so damn good." Nick thrust his hips a little harder. "So damn beautiful."

His declaration made her hotter than ever and more excited. She squirmed, wanting to climax but knowing she'd receive another punishment if she did. This was her second punishment, being unable to come while she pleasured him and herself.

And it was such incredibly sweet torture that she could hardly stand it.

"I'm about to come." His voice was hoarse and she could tell he was close as his cock grew harder and his balls drew up. "You'd better let me know if you'd rather have me come all over your breasts or in your mouth."

In response, Sheila sucked him harder. Nick groaned out loud and his hips bucked against her face as his warm fluid spurted down her throat. Sheila drank from him as he continued to pump in and out of her lips until he finally said, "Stop" and pulled her head away from him.

Sheila remained on her knees looking up at Nick as he tucked his still thick and moist cock into his boxers then zipped up his trousers. The entire time he kept his gaze on her, an intense look in his aquamarine eyes.

She fought to keep from squirming with her need to come. "Please may I climax now?"

"No." He extended his hand and helped her to rise so that she was standing before him. "You'll have to wait," he added with a smile that told her he had lots more erotic pleasures in store for her.

Nick palmed her large breasts and raised them at the same time he lowered his head. Sheila moaned and grabbed his shoulders as he sucked and licked one nipple, then paid the same attention to her other. "You are such a lovely woman," he murmured as he paused. "Inside and out."

The chain swung between her breasts and he lightly tugged on it with one finger as he sucked her nipples. If he didn't stop she was going to come just from him sucking on her breasts.

The need to climax was so intense that tears pricked the back of Sheila's eyes. She wanted to beg and plead, but she knew it wouldn't do any good. Finally he raised his head and arranged her bra over the nipple chain, then the front of her dress.

The corner of his mouth curved into a roguish grin. "You might want to freshen up your lipstick again. I seem to be wearing it on my cock."

Heat rushed to Sheila's face, but it was more a feeling of excitement. She touched up her makeup and her lipstick while Nick stood behind her and fluffed her hair over her shoulders. Her nipples were still swollen from the nipple chain and she could see they were obviously hard through the bra and satin of her dress.

Nick watched her like he couldn't take his eyes off her. "You are gorgeous in that color," he murmured. "Hell, you're gorgeous in anything you wear." His smile was sinful as he turned her around in his arms. "But I'll bet you're even sexier in nothing at all."

Sheila's cheeks were still burning as Nick led her out of the men's facilities. Blissfully the corridor was empty, save for the attendant.

The attendant simply nodded and said, "Good evening, Mr. Tarantino," and Sheila wondered if this wasn't the first time Nick had taken a woman into the restroom.

"Do you do this a lot?" she said as soon as they were out of hearing range.

Nick slapped her on the ass and she barely contained a yelp of surprise as her gaze shot to his. "I do believe you need another punishment for your impudence." A hint of amusement lit his eyes.

While Nick led Sheila to the dance floor, he couldn't believe how hard he was for her again. When she'd first taken him deep in her throat, it had taken all his power not to come at once. She'd looked so enticing, his diamond chain sparkling between her breasts while she rolled her nipples between her thumbs and forefingers, following his directions.

And hell, her mouth had been so hot and sweet it had driven him insane with need. Just seeing her looking up at him with those incredible sapphire eyes while he fucked her mouth nearly sent him over the edge the moment she slipped her lips over his cock.

A slow song was playing when he guided her onto the dance floor and brought her into his arms. She put her hands on his shoulders and he placed his at her waist, drawing her close so that his cock pressed against her belly. She felt so good in his embrace, her warm, soft body against his.

Sheila was petite, her head just reaching his chest, and Nick had to lean down to nuzzle the top of her head. He breathed in her soft, sweet perfume, a mixture of orange blossoms and her own unique womanly scent. He lightly rubbed his thumbs along her waist, enjoying the feel of her curves beneath his hands.

Despite the fact he knew most of the people patronizing the establishment, Nick ignored everyone around them and focused on the delectable woman in his arms. He loved the way she snuggled against him, her full breasts pressed against his abs. He could feel the nipple chain through the satin of her dress and it made his cock harder to know she was wearing his token of ownership, his staking his claim upon her.

In truth she owned him, heart and soul.

"You're the loveliest woman here," he murmured into her hair.

Sheila gave a sigh of contentment as they moved to the slow beat. "And you say the sexiest things."

He chuckled and slipped one hand from her waist into his jacket pocket and turned on the vibrator. Sheila's gaze shot up to his immediately, her cheeks turning pink and her body stiffening in his arms.

"Nick." She bit her lower lip and squirmed against him, pressing hard against his cock. "God, I can't take much more of this."

"You will, my sweet." He kissed her hair and smiled. He loved that the device was vibrating against her clit, making her wetter for him. He only longed to put his mouth there instead, to lick her folds and taste her thoroughly. "I'll have to punish you again if you come. Would you like that?"

Sheila moaned against him and dug her fingers into the jacket covering his shoulders. "I'm so close, Nick," she whispered. "I'm about to come."

In response he lowered his head and captured her mouth with his. Her body trembled and she moaned as he bit her lower lip. And when he thrust his tongue into her warmth she gave a little cry into his mouth and her body shuddered against his. He could feel the waves of her orgasm as he kissed her long and deep.

"Stop," she begged when he pulled away from the kiss, her body still trembling with aftershocks, one mini-orgasm after another. "Please. It's too much."

Nick gave her a mock reproving look as he reached into his pocket. "Now you have earned another punishment, my dear bad girl."

He shut off the device and she went limp against him and gave a little groan. "You don't play fair, Nick Tarantino."

Nick chuckled softly and leaned back so that he could see her flushed cheeks and her eyes that had that just-got-fucked look. Only he hadn't fucked her—yet.

"Let's go," he said, suddenly feeling an urgency to get her alone, *now*. "I've got to have you."

Chapter Seven

ꟷ

The urgency in Nick's voice thrilled Sheila to her core. The way he said *"I've got to have you,"* made tingles zip from her belly to her pussy.

If only he wanted *her* and not just sex.

But she wasn't going to think past tonight.

In record time Nick whipped out his cell phone and called his chauffeur to bring the limo around, and the next thing she knew they were slipping out of the nightclub to where the limo waited. The driver already stood at the passenger door, waiting to let them into the luxurious vehicle. As she slipped into its plush confines, Nick paused a moment to give the driver instructions, but too quietly for Sheila to hear.

Sheila's pulse raced and her heart hammered as Nick slid into the limo and the chauffeur closed the door behind them. The minute they were alone he took her face in his palms and kissed her with so much urgency and need that it robbed her of her breath. Lord that man could kiss. He nipped at her lower lip, drawing her mouth wide and open for him, and then he plunged his tongue deep inside.

When he finally broke off the kiss they were both breathing hard and she was barely conscious of the limo moving through Los Angeles traffic and the glitter of the lights zipping by.

"Damn but you drive me crazy, woman," he said in a voice rough with passion.

She drove *him* crazy? "Don't you think you've gotten enough payback, Nick?" she said, half-teasing and half-serious. "*You've* been driving me nuts all night."

"Hmmm..." He gave her a thoughtful look. "I believe you have a punishment or two still coming."

At the word *punishment,* a shiver ran through Sheila. Her butt still tingled from the earlier spanking, her pussy throbbed from the orgasm on the dance floor, and her nipples ached from the diamond chain.

How much more could she take?

He reached into a hidden compartment and drew out a black leather handle with long suede strips attached to it.

"Er, what's that?" Her gaze shot to Nick's.

He took it and gently caressed her cheek with the soft suede. "This, my sweet, is a flogger."

Sheila's eyes widened but she couldn't speak because now he was trailing the flogger over her breasts in a slow, sensual caress. With his free hand he tugged down the front of her dress and her bra, freeing her full breasts. The diamond chain glittered in the limo's low lighting and her nipples were dark purple and achingly hard.

"Take off your dress and bra." He slid the flogger down to where the satin material of her dress was now bunched. "Leave on the garters and the heels."

The words and act made it seem suddenly forbidden and exciting, as if he was still her employer and taking her the way she'd always dreamed. How many times had she fantasized about a moment like this? Hundreds of times, at least.

But this was far better than fantasy. And far better than being alone with her vibrator.

City lights shimmered outside the darkened windows as it ran smoothly through the streets. Nick pressed a button on a panel and a soft, seductive melody filled the back of the limo.

While she undressed, she couldn't help but think about the chauffeur and the fact that he must know what was going on in the back, much like the attendant at the men's facilities. Somehow the knowledge made her feel much naughtier. It thrilled her, in fact.

Nick watched as Sheila shimmied out of her dress, his cock hard and aching. Her breasts swayed as she worked the satin over her hips. She let the dress slide to the floor of the limo, and he almost groaned out loud at the sight of her clad in the blue garters he'd picked out for her.

Before he lost control and took her right then, Nick grabbed her by the waist. She let out a little yelp as he flung her across his lap, her ass sticking up and her upper half hanging upside down.

"What are you doing?" She said in a muffled voice. "Um, Nick?"

He lazily trailed the flogger over her ass cheeks and he felt her tremble. "It's time for a little more punishment."

Sheila swallowed, remembering all too well the orgasm on the dance floor. She felt dizzy from the rush of blood to her head as she hung upside down over his lap, his erect cock pressed into her belly. And she felt dizzy from excitement, too.

He slapped her with the flogger's straps, so lightly that it felt like a mere caress. "You must be taught a lesson, Sheila."

This time he brought the flogger down a little harder. And the next swat and the next were harder yet, but the little bit of pain turned immediately into tingling pleasure. It stung a little then it felt good, much like the spanking he'd given her earlier.

"Widen your thighs." He pressed apart her legs, pushed aside the thong, and slid a finger into her slick channel while he continued to lightly flog her. "Yes…that's it, sweetheart. You're soaking wet for me."

Abruptly Nick stopped, needing to taste his woman. He easily picked her up and laid her on her back on the limo seat, her hair splayed behind her and her thighs pressed far apart. The damn thong was getting in his way. He reached into another compartment and drew out a small knife.

"Hold still," he ordered and Sheila's eyes grew wide as he brought the knife close to her. In a couple of quick movements he'd cut the thong and flung it to the side, along with the tiny vibrator. He tossed the knife into the compartment and immediately turned his attention back to Sheila.

Relief filled her expression, but then he slid his palms under her ass and brought her up, and buried his mouth against her pussy. She cried out and squirmed as if fighting another orgasm. "Nick!"

He raised his head and gave her a warning look. "Don't come, sweetheart. If you do it's going to be a long wait until I fuck you."

Sheila almost wept with the need to come. Her ass still tingled and his mouth against her pussy was driving her wild. But she needed his cock inside her. She could wait, she could hold back. She gritted her teeth and clenched her hands into the fine leather upholstery, fighting off her orgasm with everything she had.

Just as she thought she couldn't take any more, Nick stopped. He was so large and powerful that in an easy movement he brought her into his lap in the center of the limo so that she was straddling him. The feel of his slacks between her bare thighs was wild and erotic. He was fully clothed and she was mostly naked, one of her favorite fantasies. It was like the man could read her mind or something.

"You've been a good girl by behaving in the limo, and you deserve a reward." He unbuttoned his slacks and released his cock from his boxers. "Now I'm going to fuck you."

Yes!

Sheila placed her hands on his shoulders and rose up, ready to take him after he sheathed himself with a condom. The limo purred along, city lights glittering like gems, yet she hardly saw them. She was so ready to be fucked by Nick.

But when he placed the head of his cock at her pussy, he only slid in a fraction before lifting her up again. She groaned, wanting him to drive into her with everything he had. Instead he held her completely still, his cock barely an inch inside her as he licked and sucked her nipples.

With a moan of frustration, she tilted her head forward, her long hair brushing her naked shoulders and forming a curtain around them.

"What do you want, Sheila?" he asked as he paused and looked up at her.

Her eyes focused on his and she had no problem telling him exactly what she wanted. "I want you inside me."

"Do you want me to fuck you?" He lowered her a little further down on his cock. "Is that what you want?"

Sheila nodded. "Yes. Please fuck me!"

He gripped her hips and brought her down hard, driving his full length deep inside her.

She cried out at the surprise of his fullness, the feel of finally having his cock in her pussy. He kept a tight grasp on her hips and raised her up and down along his length while his mouth ravaged each of her engorged nipples. An orgasm began rising and rising within her, almost too strong to fight.

"Don't come," he said in between suckling her breasts. "Wait until I tell you."

It felt so damn good to be inside his woman after all this time. Nick couldn't get enough of her and it was all he could do not to come immediately. But he forced himself to maintain control as he fucked her, drawing their mutual pleasure out as long as possible.

Slowly he slid her up and down his cock, watching her face. She was covered with a light sheen of sweat and she was biting her lower lip. Gradually he increased their pace, pounding harder and harder into her, causing her to cry out with every thrust of his cock.

When he finally couldn't wait any longer, he shouted, "Now, Sheila!"

She screamed as her body jerked and quaked against his. His own orgasm roared through him. Heat burned him and he felt like he was on fire. A fucking inferno was blazing within him.

When neither could take any more Sheila collapsed against him, her breathing hard and fast, matching his own.

"Miss Lane," he murmured as he tried to catch his breath, "you have most excellent qualifications."

Sheila rose up and gave him a sated smile. "Mr. Tarantino, you certainly have great benefits."

Chapter Eight

ꙮ

Monday morning Sheila sat at her desk, unable to concentrate on her work. She stared out the window, reliving Friday night, remembering every last detail of her time with Nick.

Thrills continually rippled through her belly and her breasts at the thought of their night and how many times he'd taken her in the back of the limo. She swore she could still smell his scent on her skin, the feel of his hands on her body.

He'd dropped her off at her condo at two in the morning and had given her an earth shattering kiss at her doorstep. That kiss had been deep and possessive, and she'd hoped that he would call her over the weekend.

But he hadn't.

While the low hum of voices hovered in the background, Sheila sighed and watched clouds drift lazily by. She was wearing Nick's diamond chain and she felt her tight nipples beneath her jacket. The chain kept her in a state of constant arousal and she wondered again why she had worn it to work.

Of course she knew why. The diamond nipple chain was a part of her wonderful night with Nick, his gift to her. It was part of the memories she would treasure for a lifetime.

Likely he had just been satisfying a sexual urge, and now he would leave her wanting him. Would she ever meet any man who would live up to Nick Tarantino?

The answer came easily to her. "No," she whispered.

She slipped out of her chair and walked to Nick's former office. Sometime today the movers would bring in Derrick

Macintyre's belongings, but for now she swore she could still feel Nick's presence, could smell his masculine scent.

Sheila leaned against the doorframe of his office and crossed her arms beneath her breasts, hugging herself tight. His huge mahogany desk and shelves were bare, his expensive décor gone. All she had left were memories, but lord, what memories she had now.

"You really should stop embarrassing yourself like this," Kate Baron's haughty voice came from behind her.

Straightening to her full height—which was about five inches shorter than Kate—Sheila turned to face the bitch. "Don't you have throats to slit or something?"

Kate narrowed her eyes. "You're just a little nothing. Now that your lord and master is gone, I can get your ass fired."

Sheila opened her mouth to tell Kate exactly where she could shove her threat, when she felt a familiar presence. Hands gripped her shoulders, forcing her to turn around. Before she realized what was happening, she was facing Nick. He looked both angry and possessive all at once. He cupped the back of her head and brought her mouth roughly to his. He gave her such a soul-searing kiss that her whole body went weak and she melted against his body. She felt him pull the clip from her hair and it all tumbled down in a mass around her shoulders while he worked his fingers through it.

When he drew back, his expression was intense, as if he was telling her a thousand things with that one look. "Good morning, sweetheart," he murmured. "I'm sorry I couldn't call you this weekend. I had a family emergency."

He draped a possessive arm around her shoulders and turned to Kate. "You will never speak to my future wife in such a manner again, Ms. Baron."

Sheila's head started buzzing with what Nick had just said. *My future wife. My future wife*, kept going through her mind as she stared up at him.

Kate raised her chin, incredulity in her eyes.

Nick turned his attention to the speechless Sheila. The next thing she knew he eased down onto one knee and looked up at her. From his pocket he withdrew a black velvet box and snapped it open. Inside was a sparkling marquis diamond—at least 2 carats—surrounded by sapphires.

He took her hand in his and her head spun, unable to believe what was happening.

"Sheila Lane, I fell in love with you long ago." His aquamarine eyes sparked with fire. "And now it's time to make you mine, for good."

Her lower lip trembled and her entire body buzzed. "I've loved you forever, Nick." She gave him a sudden smile as incredible joy filled her. "And you are mine for keeps."

Nick gave her that soul-melting smile she loved and he slid the ring on her finger. Like the clothing he had purchased for her, the ring was a perfect fit.

He rose up, towering over her, and cupped her face in his palms. His mouth met hers, this time gentle and sweet. A long, deep kiss that made her heart pound and her knees weak. She clung to the lapels of his suit, barely able to stand on her own.

When he finally drew back, she could only stare up at him in wonder and love. But then sudden applause broke out around them and Sheila flushed when she saw virtually the entire staff of Tarantino Investments smiling and applauding, including her friend Andi and Derrick Macintyre. The only one not smiling was Kate Baron who was still looking shell-shocked.

In one smooth, powerful movement, Nick scooped Sheila in his arms and she gave a little cry of surprise and clung to his neck. Derrick approached and said, "Looks like I just lost my office assistant."

Nick grinned and looked down at Sheila. "Looks like I just gained a wife."

They rode in the limo to his home in Beverly Hills, and Nick couldn't keep his hands off Sheila. He kissed her, touched her, held her tight. It was all he could do not to strip her bare and take her right in the limo. Again and again.

When they arrived at his mansion, Nick carried his future bride through the enormous home and upstairs to the master bedchamber. He carefully set her on her feet beside the bed. Her eyes were wide, her blonde hair tousled and her mouth red from his kisses.

"I can't believe this is happening." Sheila's throat worked and she laid her small hand on his chest. "I had no idea you felt the same way I do. Friday night…I thought you just wanted sex."

"How could you not know?" He brushed the back of his hand over her cheek. "Didn't you notice how often I made it a point to call you into my office to go over files that I could have reviewed alone? Or the times I leaned over your shoulder while you worked and breathed in the scent of you? It was torture having you near, but it didn't matter. I *had* to be close to you."

Sheila shivered as Nick slid her jacket from her shoulders and let it drop to the floor. He smiled when he saw how taut her nipples were through the fine fabric of her blouse, and the rough outline of the diamond chain.

"You wore it," he said, his tone one of pleasure and surprise as he unbuttoned her blouse and reached the nipple chain. He lightly tugged on it and she gasped at the exquisite sensation.

She caught her breath as his knuckles brushed along her skin and hovered at the pretty lacy pink bra she'd bought that weekend at a lingerie shop, along with matching panties. She hadn't known if she would ever be with Nick again, but she'd felt so risqué just wearing the lingerie beneath her clothing with the hope that he would see them.

And here she was, in his bedroom, after he'd proposed to her.

She was going to be Nick's wife.

Slowly he undressed her as if cherishing every curve of her body. When she stood naked before him she burned even hotter for him. "I need to see you, Nick."

He kicked off his shoes, then let her undress him. He couldn't take his eyes off his woman as she pushed his jacket from his shoulders and to the floor, then unbuttoned his shirt and discarded it just as easily. But when her hands reached his waistband, she trailed her fingers over the taut outline of his cock, looking up at him with a mischievous expression.

"You'd better hurry, sweetheart," his aquamarine eyes burned with desire. "I'm about to take you just as I am."

Sheila smiled and unfastened his trousers, enjoying the power she had over him.

When they were both naked, Nick carried her to the bed, his body hot against hers. He gently set her on the burgundy satin comforter and eased onto the bed beside her so that they were facing one another, his hard cock pressed against her belly and her nipples brushing his chest.

"You have no idea how long I've dreamed of this," he murmured as he lightly skimmed his fingers along her curves.

"I think I might." Sheila raised her hand to trace his lower lip with her thumb. "You have been the subject of every fantasy I've had since I met you."

"It killed me knowing I had to wait for the right time." With a self-deprecating smile he shook his head. "So many times I wanted to break the rules, to say to hell with it and bend you over my desk and fuck you. To mark you as mine."

Tingles skittered through Sheila's belly and she gave him a little grin. "That was one of my favorite fantasies. The spanking part, too. I loved that Friday night."

He rolled her onto her back and slid between her thighs. "I have a feeling you're going to be naughty and need lots of spankings."

She gave him a wicked grin. "I can be a very, very bad girl."

"Don't I know it." Nick dipped his head and flicked his tongue over her nipple. "But now I intend to make love to you."

A moan escaped Sheila's lips and she arched her breasts higher, wanting more from him. He seemed to read her mind, latching onto one nipple and sucking it and the loop that kept her nipple swollen and hard.

"You taste so damn good," he murmured as he began easing down her body, lightly lapping at her skin and erotically tormenting her.

When he reached her pussy he slid two fingers inside her, working them in and out as he licked and sucked her clit. Just as her body began to tremble with an oncoming orgasm, Nick rose up and placed his cock at her center. For a long moment his gaze met hers and she read his love as clearly as she felt her own.

He slid into her with one slow thrust and stopped, his arms braced to either side of her shoulders. Sheila whimpered at the feel of him and she squirmed wanting him to fuck her. But he kept his intense gaze on her, his powerful body still between her thighs.

"You're mine," he said, his voice filled with possession and power as he slowly began thrusting in and out of her pussy. "All mine. Say it, Sheila."

"Yes." She could barely speak as she lightly scraped her fingernails over his back. "I'm yours, Nick. Forever."

He gave her a look of extreme satisfaction and began moving in and out of her, harder and faster. Sheila met his every thrust, her passion building and building until she shook with the effort not to come.

"Now," she said, "come with me now, Nick."

He shuddered and cried out, "Sheila!" and she felt his hot fluid pumping inside her channel.

Her own orgasm soared through her, a maelstrom of sensation intensified by knowing that Nick returned her love. She felt his hard body pressed tight to hers, but her orgasm seemed as though it might never stop. As if it might rip her apart. Her pussy clenched and unclenched around his cock and waves of feeling kept coursing through her body.

Nick rolled onto his side and brought her with him so that they were face to face, her leg over his hip so that his cock was still inside her. Gradually their breathing slowed and the corner of his mouth turned up in a sexy smile. Sweat dripped from his hair and she smelled the scent of her juices mixed with his come. Nothing had ever smelled so good, and no one had ever looked so wonderful as Nick did at that very moment.

"You're hired, Miss Lane," he said in a teasing tone.

Sheila laughed. "I accept the position, Mr. Tarantino."

Erotic Weekend

ജ

Chapter One

ꟸ

She could do this. She could be a submissive for one weekend. Now she just needed to find the right Dom to rock her world.

In the shadows near the resort bar, Andi Kelly clutched her martini glass so tightly she was afraid the slender stem would snap. The cosmopolitan would hopefully begin its magic soon, allowing her to relax, at least a little. This was her fantasy. She could do it.

What a way to have great sex, too, without worrying about a relationship. She had a career to think about, and wasn't ready to commit to any kind of ties. Some men she'd met had wanted relationships—more than she'd been willing to give. That or they'd just wanted to fuck around and use her, and she wasn't a one-night stand kind of woman. So she'd gotten away from dating, and it had been way too long since she'd been laid.

Even though this retreat was all about sex, and she was going to be dominated, she'd still be in control. No strings, no attachments, and she'd be able to choose her Dom. Hopefully she'd find one she'd love to have mind-bending sex with.

Her gaze took in the room filled with seemingly normal everyday people—they could be lawyers, doctors, secretaries, construction workers, computer programmers, waitresses—just ordinary people with one thing in common…

They were all into kink—BDSM.

Andi took a bigger drink of her cosmo and the heat of the alcohol burned down her throat to pool in her empty stomach. Oh, she'd be feeling the buzz soon, all right. She needed it if she was going to go through with this.

The resort's dimly lit lounge smelled of cigarette smoke, beer and wine, along with the tantalizing aroma of the appetizers displayed on a table along one wall of the room. Hot wings, spinach dip, cheese and crackers... Andi's stomach growled and she hugged herself with one arm while she took another sip of her cosmo. She was hungry, but she wasn't sure she wanted to eat—she might throw up, as nervous as she was. Instead she closed her eyes for a moment, listening to the throb of the music, an alternative rock song that pounded in time with her pulse.

When Andi had told her friend Shelia Tarantino about her fantasy to be a submissive for a night, maybe even a few nights, Shelia had surprised—no, shocked—her by recommending a weekend away at a country club resort...but to its patrons it was known as the Bondage Club. Andi had asked Shelia how she knew about the Club, but her friend had just blushed and shrugged. Apparently Sheila and her new husband were into kink themselves.

Interesting.

Andi opened her eyes, took a deep breath, and glanced at the bartender before turning her gaze back to the room. So far she had escaped notice—or maybe her body language had been read loud and clear. *Don't come near me. I'm scared half out of my mind.*

Which wasn't like Andi at all. Because of her tenacity, her ability to close the deal like no one else could, she had recently been promoted to Vice President of Tarantino Investments. Known as a tough but fair boss, she could run circles around any man when it came to her work. Any man but Derrick Macintyre, that was.

Andi frowned at the thought of the ruthless investor. He was her equal at the investment firm, also a VP, but his dominating presence made her feel like a novice in comparison. Something about him always made her squirm in her chair at board meetings. She hated how just being in the same room with him made her nipples so taut they ached, and her pussy wet enough to soak her panties. Of course, the fact that he was one of the sexiest men alive might have something to do with that.

Shoving thoughts of Derrick out of her mind, Andi raised her chin and stepped out of the shadows. This was her weekend to find out what it was like to submit completely and turn over all control to a Dom.

Why the thought turned her on, she wasn't sure. Except that maybe she was tired of always being the one in control in her job, in her life. To turn that over to someone else, if only for a weekend, was a fantasy she'd had for a while. At night when she was alone with her vibrator, she would imagine what it would be like to be at a man's mercy—tied up and forced to do whatever he wanted…

A tremor of shock rolled through Andi and she froze. Across the room, a tall and powerfully built man stood with his back to her. He was talking to a diminutive blonde who was looking up at him with a sultry expression in her big green eyes.

Andi narrowed her gaze. It couldn't be—no. But that dark wavy hair curling just above the collar of his coal gray suit jacket, those broad shoulders and strong hands…

No.

Andi took another drink of her cosmo, finishing it off in one gulp. It couldn't be him. She set the empty martini glass on the bar and started to slink back into the shadows, but the man turned and his gaze met hers. Electricity zinged through Andi's body, straight to her pussy.

It was him.

Derrick Macintyre.

Derrick's blood seared his veins as his gaze rested on the beautiful, yet heretofore elusive, Andi Kelly. A slow smile curved one corner of his mouth now that he had her attention. Andi's almond-shaped brown eyes widened and her lips parted in obvious surprise. She had a deer-trapped-in-headlights look about her as her gaze locked with his.

Dismissing his former sub without a backward glance, Derrick strode across the lounge, past club members, and straight toward Andi. She took a step back, as if she was about to turn and bolt from the room. He caught her by one wrist, and pulled her to him.

Before she had a chance to speak, Derrick's gaze raked her from head to toe. He took in her shimmering curtain of black hair and could just imagine how it would feel sliding over his naked skin. The tiny black dress she wore left nothing to the imagination, including her erect nipples rising beneath the thin material, and the way it clung to the juncture of her thighs. His eyes traveled down long legs that wouldn't quit, to a pair of sexy high heels. He couldn't wait to see her in nothing but those heels.

When his gaze met hers again, Andi tried to wrench her wrist from his grip. "I see you're just as much of an ass out of the boardroom as you are in," she said, her head raised and a determinedly haughty tilt to her chin.

Derrick drew her to him with a jerk and she lost her balance. With a soft gasp of surprise she fell against him, her slender body flush with his. He kept her pressed to him by gripping her ass with one hand. His erection was hard against her softness, and by the color rising in her cheeks he knew she hadn't had a problem noticing.

"As feisty as ever, Ms. Kelly." Derrick lowered his head and drank in Andi's jasmine perfume and her unique womanly scent. He had always loved how she smelled. From the first day he had met her, she had driven him out of his mind. "I might just have to punish you here and now."

Another soft gasp came from Andi and she tried to pull away from him. When he wouldn't release her, she tilted her head further back, fire in her dark eyes. "Damn it, Macintyre." She stomped one high heel onto his shoe. "Let. Me. *Go*."

In a fast motion, Derrick released her wrist long enough to cup the back of her head. He clenched her silken hair in his fist and crushed his mouth to her soft lips, staking his claim, letting her know she was his.

Andi tried to fight Derrick, her head swimming with shock. But he was too strong, too powerful.

His kiss was hard, almost brutal. Complete and total domination that took her breath away. She was so surprised that she parted her lips and Derrick took advantage, thrusting his tongue into her mouth. He plunged hard and deep while he clenched his hand in her hair, a man in total control.

Without even realizing it was happening, Andi began kissing him back, letting her tongue dart into his mouth and then tangle with his. Her fingers scaled his broad chest beneath his suit jacket, and she rested her palms against him, feeling the flex of his hard muscles beneath her hands. His heat radiated through her and the image came to her of the two of them, hot and sweaty, slick flesh against slick flesh.

And she was moaning. Good God, she was *moaning*.

The fierceness of his kiss lessened, but he bit her lower lip hard enough to make her cry out. The pain quickly blended to a sweet kind of pleasure. Before she could recover from her surprise, he thrust his tongue deep inside her mouth again. He tasted of breath mints and the intoxicating flavor of pure male. His hand gripped her hair so hard she could feel it tugging against her scalp.

In that moment she could see herself submitting to Derrick. On her knees, doing whatever he willed. Her hands tied behind her back while he fucked her mouth with his cock. Him taking her from behind, or fucking her ass. Taking her any way he chose.

It seemed like the kiss lasted forever. When Derrick finally pulled back, her lips felt swollen and moist, her breath coming in soft gasps.

She couldn't take her gaze from his finely chiseled features, the arrogant way one eyebrow rose as he watched her with those incredible blue eyes. The deep and throbbing sound of his voice sent a gush of moisture between her thighs when he said, "You're mine for the weekend, Andi." His jaw tightened and his face hardened with absolute seriousness. "You'll do what I say, when I say, and follow my instructions to the letter."

Andi started to shake her head, but his hand clenched her hair too tightly. "You bastard," she said. Heat rushed through her in a hot blaze. Yet part of her realized that it wasn't only anger flooding her, it was intense desire. His words had turned her on beyond belief.

"That will earn you your first punishment." His gaze narrowed, his look turning darker. "Do you wish to add another?"

Andi's jaw dropped. She couldn't believe this was happening. Derrick, here, at this exclusive BDSM club, and treating her like he was her Dom. And exciting her like no man had ever done before.

Derrick spoke before she could respond to his punishment remark. "Would you rather be a sub to a strange Dom? Would you rather be fucked by someone you don't know, Andi?" He brought her even tighter against him, digging his fingers hard into one ass cheek while clenching her hair in his other hand. He had her pressed so tightly against him that her hands and her breasts were smashed against his chest. "I won't let that happen," he continued. "I've wanted you, waited for you, for far too long to let another man have you."

Andi gulped. He had wanted her? Had waited for her? He certainly had never shown it. "I—I don't know about this, Derrick. You—me—submitting..."

"Turn over control to me, baby." He relaxed his hold on her hair and ran his fingers through the shimmering waves. The feel of his fingers skimming through her hair sent tingles of pleasure through her. "This weekend has nothing to do with the outside world. It has to do with you living your fantasy. And you pleasing me in whatever way I choose."

Her eyes widened and her fingers clenched his shirt tighter. "How do you know it's my fantasy?"

"You're here." Derrick moved his finger to her lips, quieting her. "And it's obvious you've never been in a BDSM club before. You've stayed hidden in the shadows, clutching your drink like it was a shield. Admit it. You're here to experience what you've always dreamed about. I'm the man who's going to fulfill that fantasy."

Andi swallowed as she stared up at his blue eyes. Deep, endless blue, the color of the Caribbean. Between the cosmo and her desire for Derrick, she was thoroughly intoxicated. She said the only thing she could say.

"Okay."

Chapter Two

ᘓ

Derrick's smile was absolutely carnal as he slowly released his hold on Andi. She found that she could breathe again, but her heart was still racing like crazy.

"Um, where do we start?" If she was going to do this, she was going to do it right.

He rubbed his hands up and down her bare arms and goose bumps roughened her skin. "Jamie will prepare you for me."

"Jamie?" Andi took her hands away from Derrick's chest. "Aren't you—I—"

He gestured behind her and Andi turned and gaped at the sight of a plump and pretty redhead. The woman wore a tight red bustier with her ample breasts practically spilling from it. A short and snug red leather skirt molded her thighs, barely covering her mound, and she wore a pair of red high-heeled boots. But what grabbed Andi's attention was the red leather studded collar around her neck—and the leash loop attached to it.

"Master Derrick." Jamie gave him a deep nod, snapping Andi's attention back to him.

"Please take Andi and ready her for me." His gaze locked with Andi's and she gulped down a sudden rush of trepidation. "Put her into something tight and black that shows off her assets even better than what she's wearing." He reached up to trail his finger along Andi's jaw to her lips, never taking his gaze from hers. "But leave the heels."

Andi trembled, feeling aroused, excited, and frightened all at once. What had she gotten herself into?

Jamie bowed her head. "Yes, Master Derrick."

Derrick leaned over and murmured something to the redhead, then turned and strode away, leaving Andi alone with Jamie.

Andi watched him walk across the room, pushing his way through the crowd.

On second thought…

She took a step forward, feeling the sudden need to follow him. She had to tell him she'd changed her mind. She couldn't go through with this.

But Jamie reached out and took Andi by the hand. "Derrick is a good Master. You'll enjoy this weekend."

At that Andi's attention swung back to Jamie, a strange sense of jealousy surging through her at the thought of this woman being with Derrick. "Were you—are you—having a relationship with Derrick?"

Jamie laughed. "No. I have served only Master John for nine years. But you know how it is." She lowered her voice. "All the slaves talk. Derrick's got a reputation as a strict but fair Dom."

A sense of the surreal made Andi's head spin. This was a lifestyle for Derrick, not just a weekend thing?

"Let's get you ready." Jamie tugged at Andi's hand, escorting her around the corner from the bar, down a long, richly paneled hallway. The entire place was gorgeous, at least what she'd seen of it so far.

Andi allowed Jamie to lead her, not knowing what to say or do. *Crap, oh crap, oh crap. I don't know if I can do this.*

But she'd already told herself that she was going to go through with it. Too late to back out now.

Never letting go of Andi's hand, Jamie brought them to a stop in front of a huge mahogany door and rapped on it with her knuckles. When no one answered, Jamie ventured in with Andi in tow.

The door slammed shut behind them with a solid thunk. Andi's gaze took in a room that was as tastefully done as the lounge. It was a mixture of mahogany furnishings and walls and furniture with cushions and drapes done in royal blue and slate gray. It smelled of almonds and vanilla, and again Andi's stomach growled.

In the center of the room crouched three massage tables upholstered in deep blue leather. Along one wall stood three stalls with drapes in royal blue, and next to them a door opened into a large walk-in closet filled with clothing packed too tightly together to see exactly what was in there. Leather, spandex, and that shiny black latex stuff, were about all she could define. Along another wall were mahogany cabinets and shelves holding a variety of bottles, containers, and strange-looking devices.

Mirrors covered the other two walls and Andi's reflection stared back at her. A too-thin woman with small breasts, big brown eyes, and black hair in a wild mass around a pale face.

The redhead swept her hand out to encompass the room. "This is where new slaves are prepared for their Masters."

Andi jerked her attention from the room to Jamie. "Slave? I'm going to be a sub for the weekend, not a slave."

The woman laughed and pointed toward one of the curtained stalls. "Pick a changing room. Strip out of your clothing and put it into one of the bags. We'll have it sent to your room."

Andi could only stare at the woman, her heart beating faster than ever.

Jamie patted one of the massage tables. "When you're ready, lie down. You may wrap a towel around yourself if you wish."

You bet I do. "Is this all necessary?" Andi found herself twirling one of her fingers in a lock of her hair, something she hadn't done since she was a little girl.

"Sweetie, you're going to love it." Jamie took her by the arm and led her to the closest stall. "Just relax and turn over control. Stop worrying, and start enjoying."

Enjoy, enjoy, enjoy. God, the thought of turning over control seemed almost uplifting. She could do this. Right.

Andi slipped behind the heavy velvet curtain and into the dressing room. When she finished undressing, she shoved her clothing and heels into one of the fine cloth bags then wrapped a thick blue towel around her body.

When she reentered the room, Jamie stood before the shelves, her back to Andi. "Go ahead and lie down, sweetie."

Andi held the towel tight around her as she climbed up onto one of the leather tables, face down.

"Jasmine." Jamie returned, carrying a bottle filled with golden oil. "Master Derrick insisted."

Andi frowned as Jamie poured some of the liquid into her hand and set the bottle down. Andi hadn't heard him say any such thing, although he *had* whispered to Jamie. It was a scent she loved, that she always wore, so she wasn't going to argue.

The air filled with jasmine perfume as Jamie rubbed the oil between her hands, then began massaging Andi's back with an experienced touch.

Andi couldn't help it. She groaned at the sensation of the woman working the oil into her body and relaxing the tension from her muscles. As Jamie worked, she pushed the towel down as she went, until Andi was naked. "Hey—" Andi started.

But Jamie said in a no-nonsense voice, "Best get used to baring yourself, sweetie."

Andi gulped. "Okayyyy…"

While she massaged Andi's backside, Jamie explained the rules. "When you are in the same room as your Master, you must keep your hands behind your back, your stance wide, and your gaze lowered."

Andi buried her face in her arms as Jamie rattled off more "rules." Oh, Andi had done her research on the internet before coming to the Club, but the thought of actually going through with all this—with Derrick, no less—was scaring the hell out of her. This was no investment deal, nothing she was in control of.

As far as this weekend was concerned, she truly was going to be Derrick's slave.

Andi focused on the massage, trying not to tense up when Jamie kneaded her buttocks, then her upper thighs, nearing her folds. To her surprise, the intimate contact made Andi's pussy ache. When Jamie had her turn over, it was even worse. Jamie's hands were skilled, professional, but as she worked over Andi's breasts, belly, and upper thighs Andi thought she'd scream if she didn't have an orgasm.

She was relieved when Jamie finally finished the sensual massage. She would have been mortified if she had climaxed.

Boneless, Andi slid off the table with Jamie's help. She was entirely naked, but right now she didn't care. She felt too good, too relaxed.

"I have just the thing for you to wear for Master Derrick." Jamie bustled to the closet and rummaged through it. When she returned, she was carrying a little black leather outfit that didn't look like it would cover much of anything.

It didn't. When Andi finally squeezed into the tight outfit, she stared at herself in the mirror, wide-eyed. The black leather corset tied below her breasts, thrusting the small globes up and together so that she actually had cleavage. It made her breasts look like they were on a serving platter. The top of the corset barely covered her nipples, a hint of her pink areolas peeking above the black leather.

The skirt wasn't much better, barely hiding the curls of her mound and her ass cheeks. There was no underwear.

"This can't be all of it," she said through the curtained changing booth.

"Let's see," came Jamie's pleasant voice from outside the booth. "But don't forget the heels."

"Heels. Right," Andi muttered as she rifled through the clothing bag and pulled out the four-inch black stilettos. She took another look in the full-length mirror. Her nipples rose up so hard and taut they could be seen pressing against the soft leather. The areolas puckered around the diamond-hard nubs that were barely concealed. Her cheeks were no longer pale, but flushed with either excitement or embarrassment—probably both—and her eyes were big, the irises a deep chocolate brown. Her hair hung in dark waves over her shoulders, and she arranged it so that it spilled over her breasts, covering up what had been peeking out.

Damn, she looked hot. Talk about a sex kitten. Everything about how she was dressed and how she looked screamed, *fuck me, I'm yours*!

Her cheeks burned at the thought of Derrick seeing her like this. Maybe he'd take her right then and there and relieve the ache between her thighs.

"Come on out, sweetie." Jamie sounded a trifle impatient. "Your Master is waiting."

Andi shivered. *Master.*

When she pushed aside the stall's curtain and stepped out into the room, her entire body burned. "There has got to be a wrap or something for this thing. I can't walk out there like this."

"It's perfect. Only one more thing." Jamie turned and rummaged in a cabinet, and then brought out a long strip of silver-studded black leather. "This should do."

Andi gulped when she saw that it was a collar, much like the one Jamie was wearing. It even had the loop to snap a leash to. "You are *not* going to put that thing on me."

Jamie sighed, her green eyes flashing with impatience. "Perhaps Master Derrick would prefer to do it himself. Some of the Doms do, you know."

Andi didn't know any such thing, but she'd wait and argue the point with Derrick.

Jamie escorted Andi from the room, down to another hallway, to a common room filled with couples dressed much like her. Andi tried not to look as Jamie led her up a sweeping staircase to the second floor. The entire way Andi trembled, and every time they passed anyone, she flushed with heat. From the corner of her eye, she noticed that both men and women gave her appreciative glances as they passed. But Andi kept her head up and tried not to meet anyone's eyes.

They passed numerous doors as Jamie led her forward. Everything was done beautifully in mahogany and forest green, and the carpet was paisley, done in the same deep green as well as burgundy.

They came to the end of another corridor, this one taking up an entire corner with a set of double doors, obviously a suite. Jamie knocked on the immense mahogany doors, and Andi held her breath.

Chapter Three

ℬ

The moment Derrick heard the knock at the door his gut tightened. He had bided his time, waiting for his opportunity with Andi. At the investment corporation she was always so cool and aloof—untouchable. But now he was going to do more than touch. His cock strained against his leather pants, and he wondered how long he was going to last before he had to take her.

No, he was going to make her wait as long as possible.

With slow, even strides, he walked toward the door of the spacious suite, knowing that every moment of anticipation would heighten Andi's nervousness and desire. It was going to take all his strength not to fuck her the moment he saw her.

He didn't realize how true that thought was until he swung the door open and saw Andi standing in the hallway, her chin raised and her eyes flashing with the spunk and fire he had always admired in her.

Yes, this weekend was going to be interesting, to say the least.

"Master Derrick, her collar." Jamie handed it to him then bowed her head. "If you have nothing further…"

He waved her off, unable to take his gaze from Andi. "Thank you, Jamie."

The slave strolled away, leaving Andi and Derrick alone. Clenching the collar in his fist, he took a moment to drink in the sight of her, letting her nervousness build as he appreciated every damn inch of her. Jamie had picked out the perfect outfit, the tight leather skirt, so short it revealed Andi's mile-long legs, and the corset pushed up her luscious breasts in a way that made his fingers itch to touch them.

Derrick took Andi's hand and drew her into the room. Her fingers trembled in his grasp despite the composed and haughty expression on her face.

Oh yes, he was going to enjoy teaching her to submit.

When they were alone in the room, Derrick said, "I'm certain Jamie taught you the rules. You've simply chosen to ignore the first."

Andi bit her lip and he could see the war within her. A take-charge woman giving over control to a dominant man—she was obviously going to need to be taught a lesson. Likely several.

Inwardly he smiled at the thought.

When Andi didn't answer immediately, he said, "Is a second punishment in order?"

After a brief flare of defiance in her brown eyes, Andi lowered her gaze and bowed her head. "No…Master." She widened her stance and put her hands behind her back.

He slowly walked around Andi, trailing the leather collar over her shoulders and her back, admiring every beautiful inch of his woman. She smelled of jasmine oil and the rich scent of her desire.

He stopped behind her and skimmed the collar along the inside of one thigh, up and under the skirt toward her mound. Andi made a small gasp, but to her credit did not move. His hand slowly traveled up to her folds where he cupped her pussy, pressing the leather against her softness. He slid one finger into her silky heat and she shuddered.

"You are ready for me." He stroked her clit and Andi let out a small groan as more of her moisture coated his hand. "Would you like me to make you come now?"

Andi's voice was low and breathless when she responded, "Yes."

"Yes…what?"

"Yes, Master."

He paused for a moment, letting the anticipation build. "No, I don't think you've earned that." He slipped his fingers from her folds and brought his hand to his nose to drink in her heady scent. His cock twitched. Damn, at this rate, *he* wasn't going to last long.

When he finished circling Andi, and stood in front of her again, he said, "Raise your head."

Andi obeyed and thrust her breasts out so that they were displayed in a most tantalizing way. But still, her long dark hair obscured his view.

Desire seared Andi's veins as Derrick pushed her hair behind her shoulders. Her pussy still tingled from where he had stroked it, and she was just dying for an orgasm.

He looked so damn good in a black sleeveless T-shirt and tight leather pants that molded his athletic thighs. He smelled good, too. Of spicy aftershave and male musk.

After he pushed back her hair, Derrick used the black collar to trace the top of the corset, over each breast, stroking the dark pink of her areola that peeked above the material. He hooked one finger at the middle of the corset and Andi gasped as he tugged and her breasts popped free.

"Beautiful," he murmured, rubbing the collar from one taut nipple to the other. He lowered his head and flicked his tongue over each pebble-hard nub. Andi couldn't help the soft moan that spilled through her lips at the contact.

A knock came at the door and Derrick raised his head. His gaze locked with hers for one long moment. "Don't move," he commanded and turned on his heel.

Andi brought her hands in front of her and started to tug the corset up and over her breasts before he opened the door. Derrick glanced at her when his hand rested on the door handle.

"I told you to not move." He gave her a firm look as he stuffed the collar into a pocket of his leather pants. "You have earned your second punishment."

"But—"

"Do you wish to earn a third?" His gaze narrowed. "Don't speak until spoken to, and put your hands behind your back and keep your stance wide. Leave the corset under your breasts so that I can view them whenever I'd like to."

Andi thought about arguing, but wasn't too sure what he had in mind for her punishments. She decided to obey and put her hands behind her back and tilted her chin even higher.

When Derrick opened the door, he let in three men carrying domed platters. Andi thought she was going to die of embarrassment, standing there with her naked breasts on display. A swirl of air came in from the hall, brushing over her nipples, making them ache even more.

To her relief, the waiters didn't even look at her. They busied themselves with setting down the trays, lifting domes, and arranging food upon the large mahogany table at one end of the room.

Andi's stomach growled even louder this time as she caught the rich smells of lobster, shrimp, grilled salmon, clam chowder, and fresh baked bread.

To get her mind off food, and off her naked breasts, she gazed at her surroundings. It was an absolutely amazing suite with its richly polished mahogany furnishings and the cushions done in cranberry velvet. Vases of fresh flowers graced the tables, in what must be the sitting room. Andi caught the perfume of roses, orchids, and lilies mixed with the scent of lemon oil.

To the far end of the room was another set of double doors, and Andi imagined it led to the bedroom. Just the thought of going into the bedroom with Derrick sent more thrills through her pussy. God, was she really going to fuck her fellow VP?

When the men finally left with their empty platters and trays, the door slammed shut behind them. Derrick moved to Andi, his movements as lithe and graceful as a panther. She had never seen him in anything but his expensively tailored business suits, and she couldn't believe he looked even hotter in just a sleeveless T-shirt and those leather pants and black boots.

He paused at a wardrobe with two drawers beneath it, and a pair of doors that swung open when he grabbed the handles. Several shelves lined the right side of the wardrobe, an assortment of items littering each shelf. On the left side, a few outfits hung—very sexy-looking outfits from what she could tell.

When Derrick closed the wardrobe, he had a tube in one hand and something that looked like a black leather belt with a dildo and a butt plug on it…

Oh, shit.

Andi swallowed, hard. Her eyes widened the closer he came. "Uh, you're not—"

"Andi…" He frowned. "You know you are not allowed to speak without permission."

She swallowed again. "Yes, Master."

He stood before her and stroked hair from her face. "And no, you don't have permission." He knelt before her and pressed the inside of one of her knees. "Spread your legs wider."

Andi obeyed, half-afraid and half-excited about what she knew he was about to do.

"This is your first punishment." He used the gel from the tube and lubed the butt plug so that it glistened in the room's soft lighting. He pushed up her skirt, grabbed one of her ass cheeks with one hand. "You'll wear this belt until I allow you to remove it."

Andi held her breath as he placed the head of the plug at the puckered flesh of her anus. Slowly he entered her, gently pushing the plug up her ass, filling her deep. She had to bite her lip to keep from moaning with pleasure.

He leaned forward and sniffed the soft curls of her mound. His tongue darted out, snaking along her slit, and more moisture flooded her pussy as a thrill curled through her belly.

"You're so hot and wet for me." His voice held a note of satisfaction.

Yeah, definitely no need to lube the dildo.

Derrick thrust the rubber cock into her channel and Andi gasped at the sudden intrusion. She almost moved her hands from behind her back to brace herself against his shoulders, but managed to catch herself in time.

He fastened the leather harness around her waist that kept the dildo and the plug tight in her holes. She'd never felt anything like it in her life, and she thought she'd come if she took a single step.

As if reading her mind, his blue eyes met hers as he straightened and said, "You may not come without my permission. Do you understand?"

Well, damn. She hesitated, but he narrowed his gaze and she hurried to say, "Yes, Master."

Derrick turned and strode to the table laden with delicious-smelling food, and seated himself. She waited for him to tell her to sit down at the table, but instead he began filling his plate, ignoring her. She started to say something but snapped her mouth shut. Her stomach did the talking for her, growling so loudly she'd just about bet it could have been heard through the heavy doors and out into the hallway.

When his plate was full, he finally looked at her. "Stand here." He pointed to the carpet directly in front of him.

Andi kept her hands behind her back and followed his instructions. With the plug up her ass, and the dildo up her pussy, she felt like she was waddling. It was hard to walk in stilettos and look graceful when her orifices were stuffed with rubber.

When she reached him, he said, "Kneel."

She only hesitated a moment then knelt before him, feeling the shift and pull of the plugs within her.

He withdrew the studded black collar from his pocket and held it in front of her. "You're my slave for the weekend, Andi, and you'll wear my collar." The tone of his voice brooked no argument.

She gritted her teeth. "Yes, Master."

He simply took it for granted and adjusted her long hair so that he could fasten the collar around her neck. When he finished he caught her chin in his hand. "You belong to me this weekend."

Shivers of excitement at his tone and the look in his eyes shuddered through her. "Yes, Master," she whispered.

"However, you do need a safe word." His expression became serious as he spoke. "If anything I ask of you frightens you or is beyond what you are physically or mentally capable of handling, you'll say your safe word and the weekend is over."

Andi swallowed. *Safe word…safe word…*

"Portfolio," she blurted out.

For one second Derrick looked taken aback and then he chuckled. "That will work. After all, you're investing in yourself this weekend."

Andi hadn't quite thought of it like that.

Derrick turned back to his dinner. A champagne glass was set before his plate with chilled shrimp around the rim. He dipped one into the red sauce in the middle of the glass and brought the morsel to her mouth. "Eat."

She parted her lips and took a bite of the giant shrimp he offered her. The tang of lemon and the sinus-clearing taste of horseradish filled her mouth along with the succulent shrimp. Keeping his eyes fixed on hers, he brought the shrimp to his mouth and took a bite from it before dipping it into sauce and feeding it to her again.

While he fed her, he brushed the fingers of his free hand across her bare nipples. She moaned around the bite of food. God, she could climax between the plug in her ass, the dildo in her pussy, and the way he was feeding her, stroking her.

The bastard knew exactly what he was doing.

Chapter Four

ꟿ

With Andi on her knees before him, Derrick had a hard time not showing his satisfaction in her submissiveness. How many times had he fantasized about this moment? Countless, he was certain.

Every time Andi took a morsel of food from his hand, her soft mouth would suck lightly at his fingers and he had to fight to keep back his own groans. She looked so beautiful with her breasts on display, staring up at him with those gorgeous, deep brown eyes.

As far as Derrick was concerned, the meal lasted far too long. But he was pleased to see Andi squirming at his feet, and he had to remind her that she didn't have his permission to climax.

When he had fed each of them the last bite of dinner, he said, "Time for dessert, which I fully intend to enjoy." He pushed his plate away and reached for the slice of Key lime pie. He reached down to twist a finger in her hair and tugged at it. "You will, as well."

Andi gasped as he yanked her hair a little harder, drawing her closer to him, allowing her to feel the pain and the pleasure of his control over her. He widened his thighs and brought her so that her face was close to his crotch, where his cock strained to get through his pants.

When he had her where he wanted her, Derrick released her hair and unfastened his leather pants, zipping them all the way down. The pants had a zipper that went below his balls, allowing him complete and total freedom.

His cock and balls sprang out of the opening. Andi's eyes widened and her tongue darted along her lower lip. He stroked his erection in front of her mouth, the head of his shaft almost touching her lips.

Derrick picked up the dessert plate and held it close to her. "Take the pie filling and spread it on my cock with your fingers."

Andi's face flushed a pretty shade of pink as she dipped two fingers into the dessert and scooped out some of the filling. He released his erection and watched as she spread the filling up and down his length. Damn, her hand felt good on him and he couldn't wait to have her hot mouth sliding over his cock.

"Until it's covered," he said when she finished spreading what was on her fingers.

Andi scooped more pie filling out and concentrated on coating his shaft until no bare skin remained. His voice nearly came out in a growl as he said, "Lick it off."

Her tongue darted out as she flicked it over the head of his cock, and he almost shuddered at the pleasure of it. It was all he could do to not allow his eyes to roll back in his head. She continued, slowly swiping her tongue up and down his length, licking and sucking every bit of the Key lime pie filling. He was certain she was teasing him, taunting him, perhaps to get even for the dildos. She even went down to his balls and licked the sacs that were as hard as walnuts from wanting her so badly.

When she finished cleaning the dessert from his erection, he said, "Suck my cock."

Without hesitation, Andi went down on him. He clenched his fist in her silken black hair and guided her as she sucked him off. She made little humming noises that about drove him out of his mind. "That's it, baby," he said as she moved up and down, working his shaft with her hand while her tongue flicked along his length. "Don't stop for a second."

Damn. He wasn't going to be able to last. "I'm going to come in your sweet little mouth, and you're going to swallow every drop." Her eyes met his, and she gave him a questioning look as she continued to suck.

"Come on, baby." He massaged the back of her head. "You can do it."

Andi sucked harder at him. "That's it. Just like that." He fought to keep his eyes open so he could watch his cock sliding in and out of her mouth. He began pumping his hips in rhythm with her motions.

His climax built up within him, a raging inferno that took him like a firestorm. He bit the inside of his cheek to keep from crying out as his cock jerked and his seed shot into Andi's mouth. She didn't pause. Instead she sucked harder as she swallowed every drop of his come.

When he could take it no longer, he fisted his hand in her hair and pulled her away from him. His moist cock slid out of her mouth and he gritted his teeth to retain control.

Shit. He'd never had such a mind-bending blowjob in all his life. He could swear he'd seen stars behind his eyes.

Andi licked her lips, swallowing the last of Derrick's come. She'd never swallowed before and she was surprised to find she enjoyed it. It had been the connection between her and Derrick that made the experience even more intimate. He had tasted salty-sweet, mixed with the flavor of the delicious Key lime pie. She had enjoyed licking off every last bit of it.

She also loved the look in Derrick's eyes right now. Dark, and burning with passion. Her pussy throbbed and she wanted his cock there instead of the dildo. She wanted him to fuck her in the ass, too, instead of the butt plug that filled her up.

He stood and tucked himself back into his leather pants. After he zipped up, he held his hand out to her and helped her rise to her feet. Her bare nipples brushed his T-shirt and she felt the heat of him emanating throughout her body.

"Very good, Andi." He took her hand and led her to the double doors across the room. "You have a talented mouth."

"Thank you, Master," she murmured.

The dildo and butt plug stimulated her with every movement she made and she desperately hoped he was going to remove them and then fuck her out of her mind.

Her stomach fluttered as he opened the doors, revealing a huge four-poster bed, along with beautiful furnishings. The tingling in her belly grew even more intense as she thought about Derrick fucking her in that bed.

The plush burgundy carpet sank beneath her heels and a light breeze stirred by an overhead fan brushed across her skin.

When they reached the center if the room, Derrick stopped and released her hand. "Kneel."

Andi obeyed, but when he said, "Rest your face and forearms against the carpet and keep your ass in the air," she nearly balked.

His gaze narrowed and she quickly assumed the position. The plugs in her pussy and in her ass seemed to sink in even further and she bit the inside of her lip to hold back a moan. She could just imagine how she looked from behind, that little black skirt not hiding a damn thing.

She heard Derrick rustling behind her and then the next think she knew he was kneeling beside her, trailing a black silk scarf over her cheek.

"I'm going to blindfold you now, baby." His tone was low and sexy. She liked the way he called her "baby." It was such a sensual endearment coming from his lips.

Derrick slipped the blindfold over her eyes and tied it securely behind her head. She heard rustling again as he moved away from her, and all her senses heightened. She heard the sound of her own breathing, Derrick's soft footfalls on the carpet, and the gentle whoosh of air from the overhead fan. She caught the freshly shampooed carpet smell and the scent of her pussy juices flowing from between her thighs.

And when she heard Derrick moving back toward her, all her senses came on full alert. A tingling sensation skittered along her spine and she shivered.

Derrick's strong hands gripped each of her ass cheeks and she startled. He gently kneaded the flesh as he spoke in a soft, reassuring voice, but what he said didn't reassure her at all.

"Baby, you know I have to punish you now." He continued massaging her buttocks as he spoke, but her *this-is-scaring-the-shit-out-of-me* ratio doubled.

"With the dildos you've been punished for referring to me as 'bastard' earlier, instead of Master." She thought she heard amusement in his voice, but she was probably imagining it. "Now you'll be punished for moving when I instructed you to remain still. Do you understand?"

"Yes," she whispered.

"Andi…" he said in a warning tone.

"Master. Yes, Master."

He continued stroking her, and speaking to her in the patient *I-am-god* tone. "I'll be forced to punish you the next time you forget to refer to me as Master."

Andi dug her fingers into the carpet to keep control of herself. This was turning out to be harder than she'd imagined. "Yes, Master."

"Very good." He moved his hands away from her and she felt something gentle sliding over her skin. Different than the scarf. This felt like soft strips of leather that tickled her skin and made her shiver.

"Do you know what this is?" Derrick trailed it over her ass and down between her thighs, causing more moisture to gush around the dildo in her pussy.

She thought about it a moment, and then a bubble of fear rose up within her. "A—a flogger?"

"That's right." He continued to slide the flogger over her skin, up to her neck, along her spine, and down again to her ass cheeks. "You've been a very bad girl, Andi Kelly, and you must be punished."

Oh shit, oh shit, oh shit. What had she gotten herself into?

Her body was unbelievably tense as he continued to stroke her, drawing out the moment when he would extract her punishment. "I should punish you for teasing me all this time in the boardroom. For making me want you and never giving me a moment alone with you. Why is that?"

Andi swallowed and then her words came out in a rush. "I was afraid. Afraid you would see how much I wanted you…Master."

Derrick trailed the strips of leather down between her thighs again. "I see."

What did that mean?

But in the next moment all thought fled her mind as the flogger met her flesh in a hard swat. Andi cried out, but barely had time to register the first when the second swat fell. It stung. It hurt like hell.

But then the pain began to take on a pleasurable feeling. It started to blend with the sensations she was feeling in her ass and in her pussy. Every swat heightened her arousal and she started to squirm.

"Quiet, baby." He swatted her harder and she jerked forward. "I can't stop until you are completely silent."

Andi trembled and bit the inside of her cheek so hard she almost cried out from the pain of it. The metallic taste of blood filled her mouth, but she didn't care—it only added to all the other things she was feeling.

With the blindfold on, it intensified all the sensations, making everything seem so much more extreme. Her thighs trembled and her stomach clenched as she felt the beginning of a major orgasm coming on.

"Don't climax," he said, as if reading her mind. He swatted her again, even harder. "Hold back or you'll earn a more severe punishment."

Shit. What could be more severe?

She didn't want to know.

But he kept flogging her. Her ass stung and her cheek burned from where she was biting it. She started to see stars behind the black blindfold as wave after wave of pleasure soared through her, bringing her closer and closer to that brink she wasn't supposed to cross.

And then he swatted her hard enough to send her over the edge. Andi screamed. Her body jerked and she rolled onto her side. She was barely conscious of anything around her. It seemed like her entire world had exploded. Stars burst in her head. Her pussy throbbed around the dildo, and her anus kept contracting around the plug. Her entire body was one big massive orgasm, and she thought it would never end.

As she began to come down from the high, she heard Derrick sigh before he said, "Baby, you have just earned yourself one hell of a punishment."

Chapter Five

ꕥ

At that moment, Andi couldn't care less what kind of punishment Derrick had in mind for her. She'd just had the most amazing orgasm of her life. She had no other way to describe it. Just fucking *amazing*.

She was on her side, panting, aftershocks still clenching and unclenching around the dildos in her pussy and her ass. Her butt stung like crazy and her blindfold had scooted up so that she could now see out of one eye. Her leather outfit stuck to her skin from all the sweat and she felt a trickle of perspiration roll by one eye. She was so limp, so completely sated, that a truck could have rumbled through the room and she wouldn't have been able to move.

But then something—er, someone—more frightening than a Mack truck bent down in front of her with a *you-are-so-in-for-it-now* look upon his strong features. "Get up, Andi," he said in a calm tone, and he pulled the blindfold the rest of the way off so she could see him clearly. Damn, he looked *mad*.

She forced herself to a sitting position, which was no easy feat at all. Her limbs trembled and she just wanted to lie back in a puddle on the incredibly soft and deep carpet.

With some effort she managed to get to her feet and almost stumbled in her heels.

"Come," Derrick said as he turned and strode away from her.

Andi grinned behind his back. *I just did.*

She quickly smothered the grin and hurried to follow him. She just about moaned again as the dildo and plug moved within her still quivering body. Her ass wouldn't stop stinging, which didn't help the urge to have countless more orgasms.

He strode toward another set of doors and pushed them open to the poshest bathroom Andi had ever seen. Her own room at the exclusive resort was nice, but could have fit in that bathroom. Acres of beautiful Italian tile, more mahogany cabinets and marble countertops, and vases of fresh flowers. An enormous whirlpool tub occupied one corner of the bathroom and looked as though it could seat at least four couples. Around it plants spilled down ledges built into the wall so that it looked as if the spa was in a tropical forest.

Derrick walked around a marble wall that flowed from cabinets to spa and Andi saw it was a large shower with three showerheads. There were also large unusual-looking hooks built into the shower, away from the showerheads, and Andi wondered what they were for.

When she reached him, Derrick held out the scarf that he had used for a blindfold. "Put out your wrists."

"Yes, Master," she murmured as contritely as possible.

Derrick quickly tied her wrists and then forced her back against the wall, beneath one of the hooks. He raised her arms and caught the scarf on the hook so that she was practically dangling from it. Her breasts thrust up and obviously caught Derrick's attention at once. He pinched and tugged at both her nipples, and rolled them between his thumb and forefinger, hard enough to cause her to gasp.

"My naughty, naughty girl," he murmured, his blue eyes fixed on her. "What should I do with you?"

"Is that a rhetorical question, um, Master?" She bit her lip, hoping he wouldn't catch her slip at speaking without permission.

"Cheeky." He reached for the ties of her corset and began to unlace them. "This isn't the boardroom, baby. There are no negotiations here. You do as I say, you serve me and see to my pleasure. That's your goal. Do you understand?"

Andi nodded. "Yes, Master."

Derrick focused on unfastening her corset and tossed it aside, leaving her naked from the waist up. But then he unzipped her skirt, letting it drop around her ankles until she was clad only in the leather dildo harness and her stilettos, the leather collar still around her neck.

"You look delicious just like that." He ran his finger from between her breasts down to the harness around her waist. "But we don't want to ruin the leather or your shoes, so we'll just have to lose them."

He removed the collar, and Andi felt strangely naked without it—even though she was already naked. *Like that makes sense.*

His talented fingers roamed her body, teasing and tantalizing her as he slowly unhooked the harness. Andi almost cried out in relief. Yet she felt a sudden emptiness at the loss of stimulation when the dildos were removed, too.

Next he bent down and took off her stilettos, massaging each foot after removing the shoe. When he finished, she was dangling from the hook, her toes barely touching the cool tile floor. Her arms ached from being over her head. She felt suddenly small and vulnerable, the way he was standing there, fully clothed, and watching her with a dark look on his well-cut features.

Derrick folded his arms across his chest and studied Andi's delicious body. Her long black hair hung down her back in waves and her slim body begged for his touch. He'd once heard her say she was too skinny, but he thought she was out of her mind. She was perfect.

His gaze traveled over her small, firm breasts, down to her narrow waist, and on to the triangle of dark hair between her thighs. And damn, her legs—he'd always loved her long legs.

Yeah, he had her right where he'd always wanted her.

Derrick stripped out of his T-shirt, kicked off his boots, and shucked off his leather pants. All the while, Andi's gaze never wavered. Her eyes widened at the sight of his very erect cock, and it jerked against his belly when her tongue flicked out, moistening her lips in a deliberate and inviting way.

Yes, she was a very bad girl. And he was going to enjoy every minute of her punishment.

He brushed by Andi as he stepped past her into the shower and she gave a soft gasp as his arm roughened her nipples.

He ran the water until it was at a comfortably warm temperature, then unhooked the showerhead and began spraying Andi's skin with it, avoiding her hair, before setting the showerhead aside again.

Derrick grabbed a cloth and soaped it with jasmine-scented gel. "You have such a beautiful body," he said as he began washing her. He started at her neck and she tipped her head back and gave a soft moan.

Slowly he worked his way down her body, carefully soaping every inch of her. Andi moaned again as he washed her breasts and paid special attention to her nipples, making sure they were more than sensitized.

"Is this my punishment, Master?" Andi asked, her voice breathless as he reached the soft curls of her mound.

"Not even close." He slipped one finger into her folds and stroked her clit, and was pleased by her trembling response.

Andi knew Derrick was intentionally driving her crazy. God, it felt so good having him wash her body with such great care. She wished her hands were free so that she could touch him, and wash his powerful body the same way he was washing hers. She loved the way his muscles rippled across his back as he moved, the flex of his biceps, the concentration on his masculine features. Part of her still couldn't believe she was actually here at the Club, Derrick's slave for the weekend.

Boy, this ought to make for some interesting board meetings once they went back to reality.

When he finished soaping her body, Derrick set aside the rag and once again took the showerhead in hand. He rinsed away the soap, rubbing his palms over her skin as he went. He stopped to palm her breasts, and Andi squirmed from his sensual touch. But when he reached her still-sensitized clit, he stroked it even harder than before, and she nearly lost it.

"Spread your legs." He pushed at the insides of her thighs as he spoke.

"Yes, Master." Andi did the best she could, considering she was hanging from a hook and her toes barely touched the shower floor.

Derrick pulled apart the lips of her pussy with one hand and brought the showerhead between her thighs. Andi cried out at the feel of the pulsating jets of water against her pussy. She could feel another orgasm building, and she was willing to bet that it would be a powerful one.

As she started to tremble, Derrick moved the showerhead away from her pussy, and her body sagged at the sudden loss of stimulation.

"Andi…" His voice was full of reproach as he stood and forced her to turn so that her back was to him. Fortunately, the way he had knotted the scarf and placed it on the hook managed to keep her wrists from hurting. But her body was another story. She ached from hanging for so long and she was beginning to feel lightheaded.

"I love your hair," Derrick said after he turned her so that her back was to him. He sifted his fingers through her hair and Andi sighed at the luxurious feel of it. "Do you know how many times I've imagined you naked, astride me, with your hair sliding across my skin?"

Wow. She'd had no idea. "Really? I mean no, Master."

"I have, baby." He continued running his fingers through her hair in a way that made her want to moan. "But that's not all I've imagined."

He left her for one moment and in the next she heard the shower spray and warm water rushed through her hair. When it was wet, he began shampooing her hair, massaging her scalp as he did so.

"I've imagined you tied up in my bed while I fucked you out of your mind." His massage intensified at the same time Andi's pussy gushed with moisture from his words. "I've imagined you here, walking naked beside me through the resort while other men admired your body, knowing no one else would ever touch you but me…or anyone I choose to touch you."

Andi stilled. "You wouldn't make me do that, would you?"

"You have earned yourself another punishment, baby." He began rinsing the soap from her hair. "You spoke out of turn and you didn't address me properly."

Andi sagged against her bonds. "I'm sorry, Master."

"I can't let you get away with it. You do understand, don't you?"

She sighed. "Yes, Master."

"Good." He turned her back around and reached up to untie the scarf holding her to the hook.

When he released her, he massaged her aching arms down to her wrists and smiled at her. "It's your turn to wash me."

With pleasure. "Yes, Master."

She used the showerhead on him, enjoying how the water beaded and rolled off his tanned skin. When she finished, she soaped him thoroughly, exploring every inch of his sexy body. She wanted to fuck him so badly, to rake her nails down his back, and to sink her teeth into his shoulder. She wanted it hard and fast and wild.

When she reached his very erect cock, she was on her knees and she wanted to slide her mouth over him again, to taste him. But when she looked up at him, he shook his head no.

Andi let out a little sigh and continued washing his legs, then moved behind him to scrub his athletic thighs. After she rinsed him off, she washed his hair. It wasn't easy considering how much taller he was, but she managed.

When they finished showering, Derrick toweled them both off, then led her naked to a vanity in the bathroom where he proceeded to comb out her hair. Her cheeks burned with desire as she studied his nude reflection and the concentration on his darkly handsome features. It was such an intimate moment, with him combing her hair, and she felt a flutter in her heart.

Once her hair hung down her back, every tangle combed from it, Derrick raked his fingers through his own hair, giving it a sexy mussed look. When they were finished, he escorted her back into the bedroom.

"Tomorrow you will be punished for climaxing without my permission." He led her to the bed. For one moment Andi felt excitement at being able to cuddle up next to Derrick while they slept, but then he knelt down and pulled a trundle bed out from under the much larger bed.

Her heart fell and her gaze shot to Derrick's.

"I'm sorry, baby, but you've disobeyed me. You'll sleep here tonight, and tomorrow if you've earned it, you can sleep in bed with me."

Andi just stared at him. The bastard! But when his eyes darkened, she swallowed her anger and said, "Yes, Master."

She eased herself down onto the bed and beneath the covers. He knelt beside her and brushed a kiss over her forehead. "Don't try to climax tonight." He lightly stroked her shoulder through the blanket. "I'll know and you'll earn another punishment."

Andi nearly groaned as he moved away. There went that idea.

Chapter Six

ꟙ

Derrick woke to sunshine sliding through the wooden slats of the bedroom's mahogany blinds. Propping himself on one elbow, he peered over the side of the bed to where Andi was sleeping, and studied her.

What a beautiful woman. Her black hair was wild around her head, strands of it lying across her face and along the curve of her neck. Her eyes were closed, her lashes dark against her fair skin. The comforter draped over her hips, and his cock hardened at the sight of one breast and its puckered nipple. A slight sigh escaped her full lips and she stirred in her sleep, rubbing her thighs together as if to assuage the need there.

He smiled at the thought of what he had planned for her today. She might balk, but he was sure she was up for the challenge. She was spirited and fiery, and not one to back down easily. The fact that she was submitting to him was amazing in itself.

Derrick didn't know how long he had watched her, drinking in the sight of her, when her eyelids fluttered open. She looked slightly dazed and confused when she first looked up at him, but then the prettiest blush stole over her cheeks.

"Good morning, baby," he said softly.

She covered her mouth as she gave a little yawn. "Morning, Derr—um, Master."

"Good girl." He slid out of bed, letting the blanket and sheet slide down his nude body. Andi's eyes widened, her gaze fixed on his mammoth erection. This was going to be hell, making her wait, making himself wait. But it was going to be so damn good when he finally did take her.

Derrick went to the wardrobe as Andi pushed herself up in the small bed.

"I have something I'd like you to wear today."

Andi raked her fingers through her hair, her eyes still heavy-lidded from sleep. "Yes, Master," she mumbled as she eased to her feet and moved to him. She walked as though she ached and he swore he heard a small groan of desire. He barely kept from smiling. She was going to be so on edge today, that by the time he fucked her, it was going to be one hell of an orgasm for both of them.

When she reached him, Derrick asked, "Did you enjoy the harness yesterday?"

Andi tilted her head as she looked up at him. "Do you want me to answer honestly, Master?"

He nodded. "Of course."

"It drove me out of my mind, Master." She ran her hands down her waist to her thighs. "I need to come so bad I could just scream."

Derrick almost laughed. "That's the idea. Part of your punishment."

Andi sighed. "Yes, Master."

"My concern now," he said as he partially turned to the wardrobe, "is today's punishment for climaxing without permission last night."

A worried expression crossed Andi's beautiful features, but to her credit she didn't say anything.

He withdrew a lingerie box from the cabinet that contained something special he had purchased just for Andi when she'd arranged the weekend. When Shelia Tarantino had let it slip that Andi would be here, Derrick had made sure she would be his for the weekend.

He handed the elegant box to Andi. "I would like to see you in this."

Raising an eyebrow, she took the box then moved to the bed where she set it down and opened the box. Wrapped in tissue paper was a leather push-up bra, a leather g-string, and a diamond-studded leather collar—along with a leash.

Andi's heart sank as she pulled the leash from the box. *Oh. My. God.* He was actually going to leash her.

She cut her gaze to him and he gave her that devastatingly sexy smile of his. "Put on the clothing, baby."

"This is not what I call clothing," Andi muttered.

Derrick raised an eyebrow. "Excuse me?"

"Nothing, Master." Andi dropped her gaze to the clothing. "I'll just slip into these…things." She gestured to the bathroom. "I need to use the facilities. Can I just change in there?"

He gave a deep nod. "Don't forget the heels. They're still in the bathroom, near the shower. Feel free to use any of the supplies. They're here just for you."

Andi swore he was trying to hide a smile. The bastard was getting a kick out of this. She'd kick him…

Andi gathered up the box of leather nothings and scooted into the bathroom before he changed his mind. She closed the large mahogany doors behind her, then leaned up against it.

Oh, shit. She was in for it today, she just knew it.

After she finished with the facilities and freshening up, she used the brush Derrick had used on her hair last night to fluff it out. It hung in dark shining waves over her bare shoulders, and slid across her naked back like a caress. She found a new package of lip gloss and blusher sitting on the vanity, which was all she ever used anyway, and assumed that's what Derrick had meant when he told her to make herself at home.

When she finished touching up, she slipped on the miniscule leather g-string and cringed. Crap. He wasn't going to make her go out in public like this, was he?

Next came the push-up bra that made her breasts rise up so high and close that they looked like they were airborne. She found her heels exactly where they'd left them last night, and by the time she had them on she was sure she looked like a stripper, or worse yet, a hooker.

Lastly, she pulled the collar and the leash out of the box. They were made from the same supple black leather as the g-string and the bra, and felt soft against her hand. Taking a deep breath, she clenched both in her fist. Maybe if she gave him big puppy-dog eyes, he'd forgo the torture?

Yeah, right.

While Andi was preparing herself, Derrick dressed. Breakfast arrived and was set up in the suite. He smiled to himself as he remembered Andi's embarrassment the night before, when dinner was served and she was wearing virtually nothing.

Smells of sausage, scrambled eggs, and pancakes filled the room, along with Andi's lingering scent.

When she finally pushed open the bathroom door and slipped into the bedroom, Derrick just about came in his leather pants. Her chin was high, her black hair flowing about her shoulders, and she had a light tint of blush to her cheeks and gloss to her lips. But hell, it was her body that about made him drop to his knees. The g-string and heels made her legs look longer than ever, and that bra—God, he just wanted to rip it off and eat her up.

He gritted his teeth, trying to tame his erection and not having a whole hell of a lot of luck with it. He'd dressed in snug black leather pants and a leather lace-up shirt, both in the same soft leather as Andi's sexy outfit.

His voice came out gravelly when he spoke, and he mentally kicked himself. "The collar?"

Andi's expression fell as she raised her hand. "Here, Master."

He motioned to her to come to him and his cock ached at the sway of her hips and the bounce of her breasts in their tiny leather slingshots.

He slipped the collar from her hand. "Turn around, baby."

"Yes, Master," Andi said quietly as she obeyed.

He pushed her hair over one shoulder and wrapped the soft diamond and leather collar around her neck. When he turned her back around, the platinum D-ring glowed in the sunshine spilling through the blinds. He took the leash from her hand, and saw the glint of fire in her eyes as he raised the clasp to her neck. One cheek was sucked in, and he was certain she was biting the inside of it to keep from telling him exactly where he could put that leash.

"Do you know why you're being punished, Andi?" he asked, as he snapped the leash to the D-ring.

She closed her eyes for a moment then opened them to meet his gaze. "For disobeying you, Master. For climaxing without your permission."

He held the end of the leash in one hand and brushed his knuckles across her cheek with his other. She trembled beneath his touch. "You know I have to punish you. Remember that today."

Andi visibly swallowed. "Yes, Master."

He arranged her hair around her shoulders so that her breasts were clearly visible. "We're going to enjoy the amenities of the Club. I'll hold your leash and you'll walk so that it is neither too taut nor too loose. When in my presence in front of other guests, you must keep your eyes downcast. You must not look at anyone directly, unless I introduce you to them." He kept his tone intentionally stern and matter-of-fact. "When in the presence of another Dom, you must keep your eyes down and give the Dom a slight bow from your shoulders."

For a second he saw a glimmer of what looked like anger or frustration, but she bowed her head. "Yes, Master."

He hooked one finger under her chin and raised her face to look at him again. The glimmer was gone and her expression was resigned. "That's my baby." He brushed his lips over hers and she gave a sigh against his mouth. "Be a good girl and I won't have to punish you even more."

"Yes, Master," she whispered.

He gave her a wicked smile. "Good. Now let's eat breakfast."

Andi wasn't so sure what he had in mind, but she followed him to the table, the leash lightly pulling at her collar. Her ankles wobbled a bit in her stilettos, and she felt exposed and vulnerable in the skimpy clothing.

He seated himself at the lone chair before the table, which was situated so that it was somewhat sideways, facing her. He laid the leash across his lap, and gestured for her to kneel between his thighs. Andi held back a sigh as she knelt. *Here we go again.*

Only this time he immediately unfastened his leather pants and withdrew his erection. Andi's eyes widened.

He slipped his hand in her hair, forcing her forward so that her face was close to his cock. "I want you to suck me while I have my breakfast."

Andi's jaw dropped, and he took the opportunity to slide his length between her lips.

"That's it, baby." He kept one hand in her hair while he forced her head down as deep as she could take him.

At first she was too stunned to do anything, but when he said, "Andi…" in that warning tone, she started licking and sucking him in earnest. She used one hand to fondle his balls, while her other hand worked his cock. She found herself enjoying the feel of him in her mouth, the way his hardness slipped through her fingers, the taste of him on her tongue.

Derrick smiled as he took a sausage link in his free hand and bit into it. Damn, it felt good having Andi go down on him first thing in the morning. He kept his orgasm at bay while he ate. She made small mewling sounds and hummed along his length, which brought him closer and faster to climax than he'd intended. He clenched his hand around his orange juice glass and watched his cock move in and out of Andi's mouth. It was too much.

His climax burst through him as his come spewed down her throat. He ground his teeth and the juice glass rattled on the table as he gripped it, fighting to keep from shouting out.

When the last of his semen spilled into her mouth, he took her leash and pulled on it, forcing her to stop. Andi looked up at him, licking the come from her lips. He released his grip on the juice glass and brushed Andi's hair from her eyes.

"Did you enjoy your breakfast, baby?" he asked.

Andi gave him a teasing smile. "Sausage is always good in the morning."

Chapter Seven

ஐ

After feeding Andi scrambled eggs, sausage, and pancakes as she knelt before him, Derrick ordered her to stand. He tugged at her leash. "Now we'll go for a walk, baby."

Humiliation burned Andi's cheeks as Derrick led her from the room, into the hallway. God, she'd never been so embarrassed in all her life as she was at that moment. As he led her by the leash, she wanted to fall through the floor every time they passed other Doms and subs. None of the subs were on leashes like she was. She kept her gaze downcast as per Derrick's instructions, avoiding looking anyone in the eyes. That was one rule she was glad for. She'd surely die of embarrassment if she saw anyone at the resort who recognized her.

Of course that would lead to the question of why *they* were here.

Cool air swept over her nearly naked body. With the g-string, her ass was completely exposed, the front barely covering the triangle of hair between her thighs. The bra felt sensuous as it rubbed against her nipples, and her breasts seemed on the verge of exploding from their confines. Despite her nervousness, something about walking with practically nothing on past strangers was somehow exciting. Her nipples stayed hard as jelly beans, and her juices soaked the leather strip of her g-string.

Derrick led her down the sweeping staircase to the large and elegant common room. His boots rang against the marble floors, and Andi's stilettos clicked with every step. From the corner of her eye, she saw appreciative glances from Doms and a few subs. One Dom outright leered at her and his stare made her skin crawl.

She straightened, managing to keep her head high, but avoiding eye contact. Damned if she'd let anyone get to her.

They walked across the room, through the maze of lounge chairs, and people chatting. Subs in various states of dress and undress stayed close to their Masters. Andi didn't feel quite so bad about her own near nakedness, considering what some of the women and men were wearing—or not wearing.

She followed Derrick through glass and mahogany doors, and out into a beautiful paradise. Andi couldn't help but gaze in wonder. It was like what she would imagine a secret garden to be, with bowers of vines around and above them, intertwined with purple and pink flowers. A large fountain spewed jets of water into the air that pattered like rain upon the pool surrounding it. Sunlight dappled the flagstones, and cushioned chairs crouched around tables throughout the arbor. Men and women lounged throughout the area, touching, kissing, and more. Much more.

As they worked their way through the arbor, Andi saw there were private little corners where couples—or larger parties—could escape, and enjoy some of the resort's amenities.

It was one such hideaway that Derrick led her into, with three leather-padded benches in a U shape. He slid onto one of the benches and patted his knee, indicating he wanted her to sit on his lap.

Andi's face still felt hot from their trek from the room to the arbor, and she was grateful to finally be someplace private with Derrick. Nothing in the boardroom, the office, or her life, had prepared her for walking practically naked through crowds of people—on a frickin' leash, no less.

Derrick extended his arms. "Come here, baby."

"Yes, Master." Andi slid onto his lap. At first she was tense, but at his bidding, she relaxed against him. His butter-soft leather shirt and pants felt erotic against all her bare skin.

"Did you see how the other men and women looked at you?" He traced her lower lip with his index finger. "They wanted you, but you're all mine, and I'll do whatever I choose to do with you."

Her voice came out low and husky as she replied, "Yes, Master."

"You look so damn hot." Derrick trailed his finger down to the hollow of her throat and then over one cup of the leather bra. "I want to taste what others can only dream of."

Derrick tugged on the cup and her breast sprang free, the nipple tightening in the cool air. He lowered his head and slipped his warm mouth over her taut nub and she moaned at the exquisite feeling. While he suckled, he released her other breast, completely baring her. A part of her recognized that anyone could walk in on them, but right at that moment all that was important was his mouth and hands on her.

And when he slid one hand down her belly, she held her breath until he cupped her pussy through the soft leather. He hooked one finger under the strip covering her pussy and slipped the finger into her wet folds. Andi cried out as he thrust inside her, his finger entering her channel the way she wanted his cock to plunge into her.

"Damn," he murmured as he raised his head. He brushed his lips over hers. "I love how wet you get. I can just imagine how good it's going to be when I fuck you. Once you've earned it."

God, she wanted him *now*.

"What—" She moaned again as he thrust three fingers into her this time. "What do I have to do, Master?"

"Earn it, baby." His lips moved to her ear. "You have to obey my commands, follow protocol, do all I ask of you, and submit to me completely. And then you can have my cock inside you. I'll fuck you until you scream."

Andi shuddered from the combination of the erotic words, her breasts free in the cool air, and his fingers thrusting into her pussy. Her climax was building, coming on like a storm.

"May I come, Master?" she asked while barely being able to breathe.

"No." He didn't let up on his strokes one bit. "Part of your training is to learn to withhold your own pleasure for mine." His lips brushed her earlobe, and his voice was barely a murmur. "Your responsibility is to see that I'm thoroughly pleased. And right now it pleases me to touch you like this."

God, she was simply going to explode if he kept teasing her. She fought to hold back her release, her muscles tense and perspiration coating her skin. When he finally eased his fingers from her pussy, she sagged in relief against him.

He brought his hand up to his mouth and sniffed. "Damn, you smell good, woman." He slipped his fingers into his mouth and tasted her juices. "And you taste," he said after he withdrew his fingers, "so good."

Andi shivered. She could smell her scent mixed with his masculine musk and the sweet fragrance of the flowers above and around them. They were in a paradise and it was only the two of them.

She stilled as she heard voices and the sound of footsteps. A gorgeous man and two women rounded the corner and entered the little hideaway. Andi tried to turn away and to yank up her bra, but Derrick stilled her.

"Andi..." he said in that warning tone of his. "Do I need to punish you more?"

"No, Master," she muttered, keeping her eyes downcast and avoiding looking at the man and the women who reached them.

From the corner of her eye she saw the two women were on leashes, their eyes downcast, but without unhappy expressions on their pretty faces. Instead they looked appreciatively at Andi's breasts. The slaves wore matching metal-studded leather bustiers baring their tummies, skimpy panties, and thigh-high boots.

The man smiled, his eyes raking her form as Derrick slid her from his lap and forced her to stand in front of the trio, before moving to stand at her side.

"Derrick." The man reached out his hand and Derrick took it with a smile.

"Josh," he replied. "Just in time."

Andi's gaze shot up to look at Derrick. She quickly lowered her gaze again, her cheeks burning like wildfire.

Derrick turned his gaze on her. "Greet Master Josh, Andi."

She gave a bow from her shoulders. "My pleasure to meet you, Master Josh."

"Your slave is quite lovely." He reached out and tweaked one of Andi's nipples, twisting it between his thumb and forefinger.

Andi gasped and stepped back, her gaze shooting up to meet his. "Stop!"

Immediately she realized her error as Derrick and the other Dom gave her looks that told her she had just made a very big mistake.

The Dom twisted her nipple harder, then freed her as he looked to Derrick.

Andi lowered her gaze and he sighed. "Apologize to Master Josh."

She wanted nothing more than to slap the crap out of both of them and knock the domineering looks right off their faces.

Instead she kept her eyes downcast and muttered, "My apologies, Master Josh."

"Of course, punishment is in order." Derrick focused his gaze on Master Josh.

Josh turned to his two slaves. "Flogger." One of the women handed him a braided flogger with strips of leather that looked much more menacing than what Derrick had used on her.

"Turn around," Master Josh said. "Place your hands on the back of the bench and present your ass to me for punishment."

Andi trembled with indignation at the mere thought of the Dom whipping her. One look from Derrick and she knew she didn't have a choice.

Unless she wanted to shout out her safe word. Did she, though? Wasn't this part of her fantasy? Would this be the worst of it?

She slowly turned to face the bench and grabbed onto the back of it, and dug her nails into the padded backrest. Muscles throughout her body tensed as she waited for that first blow. Her naked breasts hung down, and the g-string presented her naked ass to the Dom.

She jerked when she felt a calloused hand rub her buttocks and she knew right away it was Master Josh. She couldn't believe Derrick was letting another man touch her.

"A beautiful slave, Derrick," the man murmured, and she heard the desire in his voice. "How about a trade? Lauren and Sara could both be yours for one night."

Andi's back went ramrod straight. He wouldn't dare!

"Perhaps," Derrick said, and Andi almost screamed at him.

How dare he even consider trading her for a night with the subs? Giving her away?

But in the next moment the lash of the flogger tore all rational thought from her mind. Andi cried out at the harsh sting, and tears formed at the back of her eyes.

"Not a sound," Derrick said in a warning tone.

There was a rustling sound and then Derrick moved a bright yellow ball before her gaze. "Bite this."

Andi hesitated only a second before sinking her teeth into the soft ball. A lash fell on her other ass cheek and she would have screamed again if it hadn't been for the gag ball in her mouth. The incredible sting of each lash fell with precision over her buttocks and thighs. To her surprise, the pain began to turn into a kind of pleasure. Amazingly, her pussy grew wet and her nipples tingled like her ass cheeks. And she was ready to come again!

The lashes stopped and she sagged in relief. She felt a hand caressing her buttocks, and this time she knew it was Derrick's touch.

He leaned close to her ear and murmured, "Very good, baby. Now behave and do what I ask you if you want to be in my bed and not Master Josh's."

He removed the ball from her mouth and took her by the arm, bringing her to a stand.

"Yes, Master." She was on the verge of either outright crying or climaxing, but she didn't want to give the safe word. She wanted to go through with this, but if he tried to give her away…

What's wrong with me? I thought I'd be here with a stranger, after all. It might be easier with someone I don't know. Hell. Master Josh might even fuck me and give me some relief!

But the thought really, really bothered her. She felt a new coolness toward Derrick. This was just a game to him. A conquest. She'd need to keep that in mind.

She did her best to keep the quiver out of her voice when she added, "I won't disappoint you, Master."

"That's my girl." Derrick turned her to face the Dom and his subs, and she kept her eyes lowered. "Now sit between Lauren and Sara."

The subs stepped forward and took Andi by her arms, positioning her between them on the middle bench. The subs were pretty, both with dark brown hair—they were twins, Andi realized. Every man's dream.

Derrick and Master Josh sat on the benches to either side of the women, across from one another.

"Look at me, Andi," Derrick said. She raised her eyes and met his. "It will please me greatly to see Lauren and Sara touch you."

Chapter Eight

ꙮ

Andi's eyes widened and she dropped her jaw. *You want what?* she almost shouted.

"Relax, baby." Derrick's beautiful blue eyes had a calming effect, like the ocean. "You need to learn to enjoy your body with no shame, no reservations."

Andi took a deep breath. She could do this. She wouldn't let him have the opportunity to punish her again. "Yes…Master."

Josh leaned back on his bench with his arms folded across his large chest and a very obvious bulge in his black pants. He had silver chains draping his pants and vest. Like Derrick, he was a powerful and good-looking man, but with blond hair and gray eyes. "You may speak at will," he said to his subs.

"Thank you, Master," Sara said with a smile lighting her pretty features. She raised her hand and stroked Andi's hair from where it had fallen across one breast. "She is a beautiful slave."

Andi wanted to scream *I'm not a slave*, but instead she found herself quivering at Sara's touch.

"She has a perfect figure." Lauren traced her fingers along the inside of Andi's thigh, and despite herself, Andi's pussy flooded with moisture.

Andi's gaze met Derrick's as the women caressed her, and she saw such fierce desire in his eyes that she felt even more turned on than before. Even the stinging on her ass added to her pleasure.

But when Sara's mouth latched onto Andi's nipple, she almost screamed in surprise. Before she had time to fully register what was happening, Lauren had begun suckling her other nipple, and Andi did cry out this time at the incredible sensations rippling through her body.

Her gaze shot to Derrick's and he smiled. "Relax, baby. Enjoy. Your pleasure gives me pleasure."

Andi gave herself up to the sensations of the women stroking her, licking and lightly biting her nipples. When they both slid their fingers beneath the strip of cloth covering her pussy, Andi thought she'd come unglued from both embarrassment and pleasure. Lauren and Sara stroked and fondled her, bringing her higher and higher to that peak, and she didn't know if she could hold back much longer. Her gaze locked with Derrick's and he slowly shook his head *no*.

Oh, God, he was trying to kill her.

In the next moment Sara's mouth met hers, and she slipped her tongue between Andi's lips. At first she was too shocked to move, but then she gave herself up to the kiss. Sara's mouth was softer than a man's, her taste different—sweeter somehow. Even the gentleness of her tongue was different than a man's. In the meantime, Lauren ran her tongue along the collar around Andi's neck, causing her to shiver.

Andi heard a soft purring sound, and realized it was coming from her. She was *enjoying* this. She had never fantasized about women, and here she was making out with *two* women, in front of two men.

Lauren slipped her hand from Andi's folds, then caught Andi's chin in her hand. "My turn." She pulled her away from Sara's kiss and locked her lips to Andi's. Lauren's kiss was fiercer, more intense, and Andi grew more aroused than ever. Lauren tasted different than Sara—of peppermint and iced tea.

Sara's fingers still stroked Andi's pussy and she continued to suckle one of Andi's nipples. Between Lauren's kiss and Sara's touch, Andi was growing wilder by the minute. She slipped away from the real world, their bodies twining on the benches and their hands everywhere as each one took turns kissing her. Lauren took one of Andi's hands, guiding it to her own pussy and pulling aside the material of the spandex suit she wore.

Shock rippled through Andi to feel another woman's folds, to feel her slick flesh beneath her fingers. Tentatively Andi began stroking Lauren's clit, then her touch became stronger the louder Lauren's moans became.

Sara guided Andi's hand to her pussy, and she found herself stroking two women at once.

Lauren gasped and said, "May I come, Master?"

"You and Sara both may climax," he replied.

Andi broke her kiss with Sara, and her gaze went to Derrick's. He shook his head. "No, you may not come, Andi."

She almost screamed her frustration and anger at the same moment both Lauren and Sara were shouting out as their hips bucked against Andi's hands.

Andi squirmed, fighting her own orgasm. Damn it, she wouldn't come without Derrick's permission. She wouldn't disappoint him in front of another Master and his subs. She had once, she wouldn't do it again. But *damn*, it pissed her off.

As she slipped her fingers from their pussies, the women removed their hands and mouths from Andi, and cuddled against her for a moment. Andi's body still throbbed and she was so sexually frustrated that she could barely think clearly.

She glanced from Derrick to Master Josh, and saw the satisfied, but almost pained expressions on both their faces.

"Master Josh needs relief." Derrick gestured toward the Dom. "Use that perfect mouth on him, Andi. Then let him come all over your beautiful breasts."

Andi gaped at him. He was going to make her suck another man's cock?

Derrick raised an eyebrow and Andi knew it was her choice. She could say her safe word now, and the weekend would end, or she could go down on Master Josh.

When her gaze locked with Derrick's, she saw how much the thought of watching her suck another man's cock turned him on. Would he want another man to fuck her, though?

It wasn't like they meant anything to one another, just a weekend of sex and then it was back to the real world. A conquest. A game. Yes, definitely, that's all it was.

Well, fine. If he wanted another man to get off with her, then she was going to give him a hell of a show.

Andi pulled away from the two women and approached the other Dom. "What would you have me do, Master Josh?"

"On your knees, wench."

Andi tensed at the word *wench*, but she obeyed, and kept her eyes fixed on the bulge in his crotch, avoiding his gaze.

While she watched, he stood in front of her, unfastened his pants, and pulled out his cock. It was not quite as long as Derrick's, but thicker, with a darker plum-colored head. He fisted his erection, running his hand along the length of it.

"Suck me, wench." The man was handsome enough to make a woman's heart stop, and his voice was deep and throbbing. "If I'm not pleased, I'm sure Master Derrick will find it fit to punish you again."

"Yes, Master Josh," she said.

He released his cock and thrust his hips forward. Andi lowered and flicked her tongue over the head. A bead of come was at the tiny slit and she tasted him, finding a somewhat different flavor than Derrick's. She was positioned in a way that she could see Derrick. The twins had moved to sit on either side of him. They had removed their bustiers so that they were naked from the waist up, and only wearing their skimpy panties and boots. Derrick had his arms around both of them and lightly stroked their shoulders as he watched Andi lave her tongue along Master Josh's erection. A spurt of jealousy surged through her at the sight of Derrick touching the other women.

Her eyes remained focused on Derrick and she thought she saw a flicker of jealousy in his blue eyes. But then Master Josh took her face in his palms and forced her to look up at him. "I want you to watch me while I fuck your mouth."

Andi obeyed, keeping her gaze focused on Master Josh's gray eyes, and a queer feeling tingled through her belly. He began thrusting his hips forward, fucking her mouth as Andi flicked her tongue along his length. She brought her hands up and began fondling his balls with one hand while wrapping the fingers of her other around his cock, working him in time with his thrusts. She couldn't believe how wet this was making her, how hard her nipples were. And what surprised her most was that her increased arousal was purely because she knew Derrick was watching—and she knew it was causing incredible sexual tension within him.

"That's it, wench," Josh said in a rumbling voice. "Suck harder."

Still watching the Dom, Andi increased the pressure of her tongue and her hands and applied deep suction.

Master Josh shouted and pulled his cock from her mouth. He fisted his length and pointed his cock at her chest. Come spurted out in jets over her neck and her naked breasts. The streams of his semen were warm, but quickly cooled against her skin.

When the last drop spilled from his cock, Master Josh gestured to Lauren and Sara. In a rumbling voice, still filled with the passion of his release, he said to the twins, "Clean Andi—with your tongues."

"Yes, Master," they said in unison.

Andi bit the inside of her lip as the two women came over, got down on their hands and knees, and began licking the come from her breasts.

Andi tilted her head back and allowed herself to enjoy the feel of their tongues and lips. She glanced at Derrick and saw approval in his eyes, and his erection looked even bigger, if that was possible.

When the women finished licking every drop of come from Andi's chest, Master Josh drew her to her feet and sat on the bench and brought her onto his lap. His still naked cock was erect again, and it dug into the crack of her ass cheeks. She clenched her fists, praying Derrick wasn't going to tell Master Josh that it was okay to fuck her now. No matter the freaking consequences, she'd be slapping the shit out of two Doms.

"Now," Master Josh said, "It's time for Lauren and Sara to see to Master Derrick's pleasure."

At Andi's startled look of jealousy, Derrick smiled. It pleased him that she didn't like the idea of other women having him.

She quickly hid her emotions by giving him a look of indifference, but he knew she was anything but.

Derrick settled back against the bench and let the twins unzip his leather pants down past his balls and free his incredible erection. Watching the twins all over Andi, then seeing her bring Josh to climax, had turned him on to the point that his cock had threatened to burst the seams of his pants.

As Sara slipped her mouth over Derrick's cock, Lauren began sucking his balls, drawing them one at a time into her mouth and applying light suction. The pressure she applied gave him a small burst of pain that enhanced his pleasure. But what made him even hotter was seeing the jealousy in Andi's eyes as she sat in Josh's lap. The Dom lightly stroked her nipples while she watched the twins suck him off, and he could tell that she was so on edge from her need to climax that she was ready to scream.

It turned him on, too, to know that Josh's naked cock was pressed to Andi's bare ass, as if poised to go into her back entry. Derrick wouldn't allow Josh to fuck Andi's pussy, but there was a good chance that Josh would be fucking Andi's ass at the same time Derrick was deep inside her. Even though Andi might not realize it yet, Derrick knew she would experience pleasure like she'd never had before, and that thought alone just about made him come.

He focused on the feel of the twins licking and sucking his cock as he watched Andi. Her nipples were taut, and Josh was moving her back and forth on his lap, rubbing his cock along her crack. He imagined that instead of the twins going down on him, that he was driving his cock deep within Andi's slick core.

Derrick came with a rumble that rose out of his throat in a near growl. He jerked his cock from Sara's mouth. He spurted onto Lauren's and Sara's faces and chests as they continued to milk his come from his body.

Josh squeezed Andi's waist and moved his lips near her ear. "Clean up the girls," he ordered. "Using your tongue."

Chapter Nine

ꟸ

A breeze rustled through the leaves and flowers around them, while everyone waited expectantly for Andi to obey. She swallowed past the sudden burst of shyness at the thought of having her tongue on the women. It was one thing to have their hands and mouths on her, another to be the one sucking and licking.

Master Josh slipped her off his lap, forcing her to stand. His cock slid across her bare skin and she couldn't help but imagine what it would be like to be with Derrick and Master Josh at the same time.

"Clean up the girls," he repeated, with a harder edge to his words, and she knew he was displeased that she hadn't answered yet. She certainly didn't want that flogger on her ass again.

"Yes, Master Josh." She wobbled in her heels across the flagstone to the twins, heat filling her as she thought about what she was about to do.

At Derrick's bidding, the twins moved to sit on the bench, and Andi knelt between Sara's thighs. The flagstone was hard against her knees, but Sara's thighs were soft around her waist.

Hesitantly, Andi leaned forward and flicked her tongue along a stream of come that was rolling down Sara's breast. The sub sighed and gripped Andi's hair in her hands.

Andi wanted to get this over with as soon as possible. She licked harder, with more purpose, and was amazed at how much she liked the taste of Derrick's come mixed with the salt of Sara's skin. Nervousness spiraled in Andi's belly as she licked one path of come down to the woman's nipple. Purely out of curiosity, she sucked the sub's nipple, drawing it into her mouth and lightly nipping at it. Sara moaned and thrust her breast further into Andi's mouth. Sara smelled of come and the juices between her thighs, and a light citrus fragrance that was pleasing to Andi's senses.

She found the feel of the nipple unusual in her mouth. Soft, yet hard, and the areola was puckered and bumpy to her tongue. Hardly conscious of anyone else, Andi moved her mouth to Sara's other nipple and sucked it despite the fact that there wasn't any come on it. After nipping at Sara, Andi finished licking the rest of Derrick's come from the woman's body. He had even come on Sara's face, and Andi licked it away, too. When she flicked a drop from the corner of Sara's mouth, the woman let out a soft sigh and turned her lips to Andi's. They kissed, a long and sweet kiss that made Andi's heart race.

"Lauren is waiting," came Derrick's voice, gruff and deep as if aroused beyond normal speech.

Andi broke the kiss, barely holding back a smile. She hoped Derrick's cock was so hard it was ready to burst through his pants.

She was certainly too hot for words. Actually licking and kissing women, going down on another man in front of her "Master," and being kissed and fondled by strange men and women, was unbelievably erotic.

She left Sara to kneel between Lauren's legs. The beautiful woman spread her thighs wide, and Andi smelled her juices. Before she had a chance to catch her breath, Lauren kissed her hard and fast. Andi sighed at the feel of the kiss, then moved her mouth away, licking at the drying come on Lauren's cheek. The sub pinched and pulled at Andi's nipples while she flicked her tongue along the trails of come, going over Lauren's collar, her neck and down to her breasts.

"That's it, baby." Derrick's voice was even huskier. "Clean her off."

Andi moved farther down, and Lauren eased her hands into Andi's hair. Andi enjoyed paying attention to the woman's nipples the same way she had sucked Sara's.

When she finished, she sat back on her haunches, her hands in her lap, and looked up at Derrick. "What would you have me do now, Master?" she asked, hoping he would allow her to come.

He stroked a strand of hair from her face and tucked it behind her ear. "I do believe it's time for lunch."

Andi was mortified. She sat at the luncheon table, alone with Derrick, her entire body burning with embarrassment as he forced her to eat lunch with her bra still under her breasts. Her nipples betrayed her, puckering to hard, taut peaks, and her pussy dripped with more moisture.

Damn it, how could he make her do this? Yet somehow it turned her on, and that thought embarrassed her even more.

Her only consolation was that many of the women and men seated at other tables were as bared as she was, if not more so. Around them were other couples, threesomes, and even larger groups. Open displays of sexuality were obviously the norm, as was nakedness and near-nakedness. Hell, once Andi's mortification lessened, she allowed herself to glance around and saw slaves of all shapes and sizes, and of both genders, who were completely naked. Many were on leashes, too.

Yet she still found her hands easing up to her breasts, wanting to cup them, hide them.

"Stop." Derrick placed his hand over hers and met her eyes. Electricity zinged through her at his touch. "You should be proud to display such beautiful breasts." His eyes narrowed with what appeared to be lust. "Right now I want to take you to our room, spank your ass, and fuck you until you can't walk."

Andi gulped. His words, the huskiness in his voice, the way he looked at her, all made her so hot she could barely stand it. Since she hadn't been allowed to have an orgasm today, she was so raw and horny that she was sure she could come with just a rub of her thong against her clit.

No. She wouldn't succumb. She wouldn't give Derrick the satisfaction of it, allowing him to punish her in lord knew what way he would come up with.

They were seated at a table in a beautiful courtyard surrounded by lush vegetation and a variety of colorful flowers. Afternoon sunshine warmed all her bared skin, and the air smelled good, of grilled chicken, fresh-baked rolls, and roasted meats. The additional scent of flowers and fresh air relaxed her. A little.

The waiter brought the meal Derrick had ordered for them, and Andi found herself avoiding his eyes, still embarrassed about her naked breasts. When she reached for her glass of Chardonnay, she felt the weight of the leash tug against her neck, and the soft leather collar seemed a little more constricting than it had before. Perhaps it was the fact she was having a hard time swallowing down her embarrassment—and her lust for Derrick.

Over the rim of her wineglass she studied him, admiring his profile as he said something to the waiter. Derrick's features were strong and masculine and she liked the way he focused on whatever task was before him, whether it was in the boardroom, or here at the resort, dominating her.

Her hand trembled as she carefully set the wineglass back on the table. Just the thought of what he might have in mind for her threw her off balance. *Jeez,* she told herself, *you're a Vice President of a major corporation, for Christ's sake.* She was confident, self-assured, in control of herself and her environment.

So why did she feel this way around Derrick? Like she could just let him take care of her, and do anything he commanded her to do?

When the waiter left, Derrick said, "Eat your lunch before I devour you in front of everyone." Those incredible blue eyes burned through her, telling her he meant what he said.

"Yes, Master," she managed to get out before focusing on the plate before her. She slowly ate her Atlantic salmon, bathed in capers and lemon butter. The broccoli, carrots, and yellow squash were crisp, the way she liked them, and the side of wild rice was cooked to perfection.

"That's my girl," Derrick said, and she was certain she heard humor in his voice. No doubt from the way she was devouring her meal. After all that sex—well, almost-sex on her part—she was ravenous.

When she had eaten her last bite of salmon, she glanced up to see Derrick watching her. His empty plate was pushed away from him, his arms folded on the tabletop, and he gazed at her intently. Andi's head swam, and she couldn't help but wonder if it was the wine, or the way Derrick affected her.

"Lean closer." He reached for his glass of Chardonnay, and held it close enough to his lips that his breath fogged the glass.

Andi's belly fluttered as she leaned closer to him, feeling his heat against hers.

Derrick sipped his wine, then set the glass on the table. He slipped his fingers into her hair and brought his lips to hers.

Andi opened for him, expecting the thrust of his tongue. Instead he fed her the wine from his mouth. Her world spun. The wine was so much more intoxicating coming from him, as the warmth of the fluid slid over her tongue and down her throat. She melted so completely against him that she lost track of herself and everything around them. He placed his hand against the small of her back, crushing her harder to him, smashing her breasts against his butter-soft leather shirt.

The last of the wine passed from his mouth to hers and his tongue replaced it, delving into her warmth as if to explore every bit of her. She clenched her fists in his shirt, her tongue meeting his. He tasted of wine and pure male, and he smelled of the clean scent of soap and musky aftershave.

She clung tighter to him, not wanting to break the kiss, not wanting to lose the precious contact between them.

But Derrick pulled away, leaving her panting, her breath coming in hard, hungry gasps. Her body trembled with need for him, for whatever he would give her, and her mind could hardly wrap around the unbelievable desire she felt for the man.

His eyes caught her, held her. "Your turn," he murmured in a husky voice that told her he was just as turned on as she was. For a moment she didn't know what he meant, but when he glanced at her Chardonnay she reached for it with a trembling hand. Her fingers barely held onto the glass as she brought it to her lips, and she felt a little of it dribble onto her chin as she took a mouthful of the wine and held it, not swallowing.

When she set the glass down, Derrick leaned close again. Instead of meeting her lips, he flicked his tongue out, lapping up the drops of wine on her chin.

He slowly moved his lips to hers and opened his mouth. She fed him the wine, letting it trickle from her lips onto his tongue.

Derrick groaned and smashed their lips together and clenched his hand so tight in her hair that the pain of it startled her, yet it quickly melded into a pleasure that joined the incredible kiss.

When he slipped his tongue from her mouth and raised his head to look into her eyes, he slid one hand from her hair to cup the side of her face. Andi leaned into his palm, feeling almost as if her muscles and limbs would no longer support her.

He touched the tip of her nose with one finger and gave her a sensual smile. "Did you know I've wanted to kiss you since the first moment I saw you?"

Andi's heart beat a little faster. "I thought you barely knew I existed, Master."

"How could I not notice you? You strode into the office with such confidence and grace you stole my breath away." He smiled as he traced his finger down her nose. "And now you are mine."

Her head briefly swam with his words, but she reminded herself how easily he had given her to another man. "For this weekend, yes…Master."

He just smiled. "Come on. I'll show you around."

Andi took a shaky breath and nodded. She didn't know what had just happened, but whatever it was, it scared the hell out of her. Even more than all the bondage and punishments he'd come up with so far.

ChapterTen

ꟗ

Derrick and Andi walked hand in hand around the lush resort. He held the leash, too, but needed the warmth of her small hand in his.

He couldn't get enough of her. He knew he never would. He enjoyed everything about her. The way she didn't back down in the boardroom when she felt strongly about an issue. The way she was willing to compromise. The way she treated her employees with fairness, yet with the firmness of a good manager.

From watching her all this time, he knew she was a good and loyal friend to her friends, and she would do anything for them. She was honest and forthcoming—you always knew where you stood with Andi.

And damn, but she was beautiful. Her gorgeous breasts, her long black hair, her soft curves, and long legs… God, he wanted to fuck her. It took a tight rein on his control to keep himself from taking her down to the grass and thrusting his cock into her slick warmth now, in front of everyone in the damn resort.

No. He would wait until they were alone like he had planned, and then he would have her.

He had always enjoyed watching his women being pleasured by other men and women in the past. Today, though, had been difficult. No matter how much it had turned him on, he'd found himself wanting to whisk Andi away and keep her all to himself.

Yet he was looking forward to tonight, in the dungeon. He couldn't wait to see her face while she was pleasured as she'd never been pleasured before.

But first he had to have her all to himself.

His steps became more urgent as they neared one of the themed cabanas, and he had to force himself to slow down. Andi tottered on her heels as she walked over the uneven lawn and he liked it when she slightly lost her balance and her nearly naked body brushed against his.

When they reached the elegant tent, Derrick pushed the door flap open and watched Andi's face as she took in the surroundings.

It was absolutely decadent, Andi thought as she gazed around the enormous room. It looked like a sultan's harem tent might look, filled with embroidered brocade pillows that covered every inch of the floor, and exquisite tapestries that hung along the walls. It smelled of exotic spices and light sandalwood incense. A tall golden pole at the center of the tent supported the ceiling which rose far above their heads.

Against one wall of the tent, she also saw what looked like two changing rooms. Next to them was a collection of whips, scarves, and floggers of different colors and sizes hanging from the dressing room wall. Andi bit her lower lip, wondering what Derrick had in mind. He was always surprising her.

She glanced up at him and met his blue eyes, and saw a wicked gleam mixed with lust.

"Get in here," he said. He tugged at her hand and she stumbled over a pillow, barely keeping her balance as he led her to the changing room. He pulled aside a drape and she saw a golden costume that looked like what a harem girl might wear. He slipped the garments from the hanger and handed the top and bottom to her. "Put these on."

She clutched it to her chest, the silky material sensitizing her taut nipples. "Yes, Master."

"Leave off your thong, and your heels, too." Derrick gripped her chin and trailed his thumb over her lips. "And don't make me wait."

Andi shivered from his touch. "Yes, Master," she said as he left, letting the drape fall shut behind him.

She turned and caught a movement out of the corner of her eye, seeing her reflection in the mirror that hung on one side of the dressing room. For one long moment she stared at herself, her eyes wide with embarrassment…and arousal.

Her long dark hair hung over her shoulders, looking tousled and windblown, and her naked breasts were lifted up with the bra pulled down beneath them. Her nipples were taut and her skin was flushed. She looked totally wanton, a woman who desperately needed to be fucked.

With a start she remembered Derrick's command to not keep him waiting. She stripped out of her thong, her bra, and her heels, and quickly slipped on the silk top with its sheer sleeves. The top didn't fasten, and with every move she made it fell open to reveal her breasts. The top of the pants was silk, but the legs were sheer, and she could see the triangle of curls at the apex of her thighs.

And they were crotchless.

A thrill skittered through Andi's belly, and she hoped this meant Derrick would finally fuck her.

"Andi…" came his voice from outside the changing room with a note of warning in his tone. She quickly pulled aside the drape and stepped barefoot upon one of the velvety pillows on the tent's floor.

Derrick's eyes flared and his jaw tightened, as if he was reining himself in. He looked absolutely gorgeous and her arousal deepened as she took him in. The muscles in his biceps flexed as he folded his arms across his well-built chest. His waist tapered down to trim hips and gold silk sultan's pants covered his long legs. His erection was a huge bulge against the silk.

She took a deep breath and put her hands behind her back, widened her stance, and lowered her gaze, hoping he wouldn't punish her for lack of protocol.

"Very good," he murmured and she shivered at his husky tone. "Come to me."

Andi obeyed, keeping her eyes downcast. The velvet and brocade pillows were both soft and coarse in texture beneath her bare feet, and she had to watch where she stepped to avoid tripping.

"On your knees, baby," he said in a voice hoarse with desire when she reached him.

Andi obeyed, feeling the softness of the pillows beneath her knees when she knelt. She watched as he rubbed his erection through his silk harem pants, then freed his cock through an opening that she hadn't noticed before.

He slipped his hand into her hair and guided her forward so that her lips were a hairsbreadth away from the plum-colored head. A drop of semen glistened in the low lighting, and she licked her lips.

"Suck me, my little harem girl," he said as his hand clenched her hair tighter, "I'll reward you well if you perform to my liking."

Her belly twisted with excitement and she started to reach up with one hand when he stopped her. "Use only your mouth," he said.

"Yes, Master." She crossed her hands behind her back, hoping she could please him using only her mouth.

With his hand still clenched in her hair, he pushed his cock through her lips as he thrust forward. Andi took him deep, feeling him at the back of her throat. She licked and sucked and found herself moaning as he fucked her mouth.

"That's it, baby." He groaned as he thrust harder yet, and the silk of his sultan's pants brushed her face as he ground his hips against her. "Now look at me."

Andi's gaze met his as he watched his cock move in and out of her mouth. Her breasts bounced beneath her gold silk harem top, and the silk rubbed her nipples until she thought she'd scream from the sensation. Her pussy ached and her juices dampened the material of her harem pants. She wanted to slip her fingers into her folds to assuage the need, to bring herself to what she knew would be a shattering orgasm.

Derrick groaned and she felt his cock tighten in her mouth. Just as she thought he was going to come, he pulled her head back and withdrew his erection from between her lips.

She watched as he closed his eyes for a moment and tilted his head back. She knew he was fighting to gain control and she felt a rush of pleasure that he had to fight so hard to keep from coming.

His voice was a low rumble when he released her hair to gesture at the tent pole. "Lay flat on your back, your arms above your head and to either side of the pole."

"Yes, Master." Shivers ran up and down Andi's spine as she settled against the pillows and raised her arms up. The harem top fell open and she almost grinned when Derrick gave a low groan, his gaze fixed on her naked breasts.

"Don't move," he ordered as he turned and moved to the wall of objects she had noticed earlier. When he returned he was carrying a gold silk scarf in one hand and his other fist was clenched around something she couldn't see.

He moved behind the pole where he was out of her sight, then took her wrists in his hands. Quickly he tied her to the pole, the bindings snug against her wrists.

When he returned to her, he knelt between her thighs, nudging them further apart so that she was splayed wide open to him. She felt the rush of cold air against her wet folds through the crotchless pants.

Derrick opened his hand and she saw two clamps with golden beads dangling from them. She caught her breath as he raised one to her nipple and clamped it onto the hardened nub.

The instant pain caused her to gasp, but then she was arching her back at the pleasure of it, her body begging for more. He smiled and clamped the other one to her bare nipple and she bit her lip to keep from moaning. The clamps felt tight, like

Derrick was biting her nipples, and the dangling beads lightly caressed the swell of her breasts. The pleasure and pain was incredibly erotic and she was even more turned on than she had been before, which was definitely saying something.

"You're so beautiful, baby." He cupped her breasts and massaged them, and she felt like blood was rushing straight to her head. "I can't wait to fuck you."

"Yes, Master." Andi raised her hips in a plea for him to take her. "Yes!"

Derrick groaned and grasped his cock in his hand. He brought the head to her folds, and rubbed it against her slick flesh. She pulled against her bonds, wanting to reach for him, at the same time, she squirmed with the need to have him deep inside her.

He stroked her clit with the head of his cock while he kept his gaze focused on hers. "Are you ready to be fucked hard?"

Andi almost screamed. "Yes, Master. Please fuck me. Fuck me as hard as you can."

Derrick gave a look of satisfaction the moment before he drove his cock inside her.

This time she did scream. It came out of nowhere, shocking her the same way her body was shocked at how he filled her and stretched her wide. She pumped her hips in rhythm with his. She tugged against her silken bonds, wanting to go wild beneath him. Wanting to scrape her nails along his back, down to his tight ass where she would clench him as he drove in and out of her.

He fucked her so hard her head banged against the pole and his hips bruised the inside of her thighs. The tent seemed to swirl around her, the bright colors blending with the incredible sensations she was experiencing. The clamps tight upon her nipples, the silk and gauze of the harem outfit against her skin. The feel of every thrust Derrick made within her pussy.

She was so close to coming, so close. Vaguely she remembered she wasn't supposed to come without permission and she barely kept from toppling over the edge before she asked him, "Please may I come, Master?"

"Not yet." Sweat rolled down his strong jaw and his dark hair was damp around his face. His arms were braced to either side of her head and his biceps bulged.

Andi moaned, so close to coming that she was certain she wouldn't make it a moment longer. And then he shouted, "Come for me, baby!" and her world spun out of control as she screamed. Her climax hit her so powerfully that her body bucked with one aftershock after another.

Derrick shouted and she felt his cock pumping within her core, his warmth filling her up.

He collapsed against her, just holding himself up enough that he wasn't crushing her. "My God, Andi." His breathing came sharp and fast. "What have you done to me?"

She was breathing so hard she couldn't have gotten a word out if she'd tried. Spasms continued to rock her body, her pussy clenching around Derrick's cock, still buried inside her.

He gave a low groan and brushed his lips over hers. "You're mine, baby. All mine."

Chapter Eleven

ဢ

After another erotic meal, a dinner that had left her beyond needing a climax again, Derrick led Andi by her leash to the dungeon. She wore only the g-string now, and her high heels. He had also insisted on protocol this time, and she walked with her eyes downcast, her hands behind her back, several paces behind him.

And her heart was pounding like mad.

Her heels clicked against stone as he led her down spiraling steps into the dark depths beneath the resort. Down, down, down.

The world slipped away when the steps ended at a darkened corridor that was a tunnel carved in stone. She became aware of the hiss and spit of torches burning in brackets, the only light offered in the dimness. Of the sound of her breathing, the feeling of cool air against her naked breasts and the dank smell of the tunnel. The clunk of Derrick's boots, and the steady drop of water in the distance.

Andi shivered and slowed as a moment of fear overcame her. *What am I doing?*

The tug on her leash brought her back to the moment, and Derrick narrowed his eyes as he glanced at her over his shoulder. "Do you require more punishment, baby?"

"No, Master." Andi lowered her eyes again and increased her pace to keep up with his. She had to remind herself that this was what she came here for. She *wanted* this. *Wanted* to turn over control. *Wanted* to pleasure and be pleasured in every way imaginable.

When they entered another corridor, it was exactly as she had pictured it. Very medieval, almost frightening. Wooden door after wooden door ran the length of the corridor. At each door was a small barred window. Some were closed, but others remained open—perhaps closed for privacy, or open so that voyeurs were free to watch.

She swallowed down another gulp of fear as sounds of screams, shouts, and soft cries met her ears. Chains rattled, whips smacked flesh and orders were shouted with answering cries of "Yes, Master!" or "Yes, Sire!"

"Shit," Andi muttered without thinking.

Derrick came to an abrupt stop and she smacked into him, feeling all that hard male flesh against her naked breasts, and the heat of him radiating through her body like a branding iron.

"You've broken another rule," he said, turning to her, his face as serious as if she had committed the worst of crimes. "You're not allowed to speak unless spoken to."

"Yes, Master," Andi whispered.

"Speak to me in a proper tone."

She tipped her chin up a notch, and raised her voice. "Yes, Master." Then she realized her mistake and lowered her gaze, but still looked at him from beneath her lashes.

No smile from him, only complete seriousness. "Another punishment is in order. See to it that you don't break any more rules."

Shit, Andi thought, this time keeping it to herself as Derrick turned and tugged at her leash.

This was it. She could scream her safe word and be out of here, or she could go through with what could possibly be the most erotic experience of her life.

At the very end of the corridor, Derrick paused in front of a huge rough-hewn wooden door. This one had a larger opening for a window, with thick iron bars. She waited with her heart in her throat as he tugged at the door. It creaked open, echoing eerily down the corridor.

He stepped into the dungeon room and pulled her leash, bidding her to follow. When she entered the room she came to a dead stop. Her skin flushed with heat and she grew lightheaded.

Master Josh stood nude in the center of the enormous room, whip in hand, his gaze centered on Andi. In those few seconds of recognition, she saw that Sara was naked, on her knees in a cage, her wrists bound over her head to one of the bars. Lauren was spread-eagle, her arms and wrists tied to the wooden arms of a St. Andrew's cross, and just as bare as everyone else.

Andi almost turned and ran. Derrick had something planned for her, and she wasn't sure she was going to like it. At all.

Derrick tugged at her leash again, and she turned her wide gaze on him. There he was, looking as incredibly handsome and dangerous as ever. Just how dangerous could he be?

He came up close to her so that she again felt his heat, and despite herself she wanted to melt into him. He reached up and unsnapped the leash from her soft leather collar. "Safe, sane, and consensual, baby." He let the catch on the leash trail down her shoulder. "Anything you can't handle, just say your safe word and this all ends."

At that moment, with him so close and making her dizzy with lust, she wasn't sure she could remember her safe word. *Investment? Stocks? No,* portfolio, *that was it.*

She hoped.

"Yes, Master," she said, and he smiled.

"That's my girl." His face again became a mask of dominance as he turned to Master Josh.

"Is the wench prepared?" Master Josh asked as he lightly snapped his whip.

Andi gulped.

Derrick gave a slow nod and glanced toward a pair of handcuffs dangling from a long, thick-linked chain. Andi's gaze traveled up the chain to see that it was attached to an iron ring secured in the stone ceiling of the dungeon.

"Stand beneath the handcuffs," Derrick commanded. "Your first punishment is to be bound and to accept whatever Master Josh and I choose to do to you."

She trembled as she walked past Sara's cage and tried not to look at Lauren's naked form across the room, where the woman was strapped to the St. Andrew's cross. Andi couldn't help but peek from the corner of her eye. Lauren's head was tilted to the side, her eyes at half-mast, and she looked as if she was in another world altogether.

When Andi stood beneath the chain, Master Josh took one of her arms while Derrick took the other and they fastened her wrists into the cuffs. Master Josh's cock brushed her thigh, and heat rose within Andi at the contact.

The metal cuffs were fur-lined, for which she was grateful as she dangled from the chain, the toes of her stilettos barely scraping the dungeon's stone floor. She felt strung out and lightheaded, her arms high over her head, and her body extending down as if she was being stretched like human taffy.

Derrick started to strip, pulling his soft leather shirt over his head and tossing it aside. His muscles flexed, his nipples hard, and the bulge beneath his leather pants told her how turned on he was.

Andi took a second to take in the huge room that looked as if it was from King Arthur's time. The walls were made of ancient-looking stone, crumbling in some places. The floor looked hewn from handmade blocks. But even though the setting looked authentic, it still appeared to be clean—as if all was kept sterile.

Her gaze tried to take in everything else in the room. Floggers, whips, chains, and other medieval-looking torture devices lined the wall across from her. Some of the warmth left her body. She didn't *even* want to know what some of them were.

To her right was a stockade next to a table with leather straps and metal stirrups. There was a leather swing in one corner, and what looked like a leather-covered sawhorse to her left. Her skin grew colder with every new discovery.

What *was* that damn safe word again? *Portfolio. Yeah, that's it.*

Master Josh left Andi's side to go to Lauren. He snapped his whip and it smacked against the woman's thigh. Her eyes flew open and she gave a small cry.

"Your punishment is to watch while the wench is pleasured, slave." His tone was firm and his eyes intent as he glanced Andi's way. Wildfire flared within her belly and heat flowed over her at his words. What was going to happen? Were they all going to watch as Derrick fucked her? The mere thought was heady, arousing, and confusing all at once.

Master Josh turned his gaze back to Lauren. "You have to learn that you're not allowed release with anyone but me, so long as you are my slave."

Lauren nodded and visibly swallowed. "Yes, Master. I'll never do it again."

Josh moved to Sara's cage. He snapped the whip and she jerked against her bonds, as if in surprise. "Your punishment is the same, slave," he said. "You and Lauren were very bad girls today, weren't you." A statement, not a question.

Sara licked her lips. "Yes, Master. We deserve whatever punishment you think is fit."

Master Josh gave one quick nod, the fierce expression still on his strikingly handsome features. He moved back toward Andi and her gaze flicked toward Derrick.

He was now completely and gloriously naked. Her heart pounded faster and her mouth grew dry as her gaze rested on his full and erect cock rising from its nest of soft dark curls. His balls were large and she imagined herself taking each one in her mouth and sucking before going down on his cock.

God, how she wanted him to fuck her again.

But then Master Josh pressed his cock against her thigh and stroked the leather strap of the whip over her breasts, scraping her nipples. She gasped. She tore her gaze from Derrick to Josh, her lips parting in surprise.

Master Josh dove for her mouth, his tongue slicing into her depths before she had a chance to realize what was happening to her. She didn't want to kiss him back, but the way he teased her with his tongue and nibbled at her lips caused her to moan. He was a damn good kisser, almost as good as Derrick.

She shuddered as Derrick rubbed his cock against her other thigh. He captured her face in his large hands and tore her from Josh's kiss to brand her with his own. Derrick was all heat and man. He still tasted of the wine they'd had with dinner and his unique masculine flavor.

He kissed her so hard her head spun with the wildness of it. She kissed him back, wanting him, needing him, wishing she could touch him.

Both men had their hands all over her body, touching her breasts, tugging at her nipples, and palming her ass as she continued to kiss Derrick.

"I caught Lauren and Sara fucking a Domme's slave," Josh murmured just before he bit her earlobe. "If that had been you, and I was your Dom, I would have whipped your ass raw."

Andi's eyes widened, and Derrick smiled against her lips. "If I ever catch you with another man without my permission," he said, "you can bet I'll find one hell of a punishment."

A game, Andi reminded herself, *this is all a game.* If she shouted her safe word, it would be over. And no matter what, when it was time to check out of the resort tomorrow, the game would end.

She wasn't sure how she felt about what was happening right at this moment, but when Derrick kissed her with fierce intensity, she didn't care about anything but his mouth on hers, his hands on her skin, his cock pressed against her. The feeling of having two men stroking her, kissing her, rubbing their cocks against her, was an experience she never would have imagined.

Yet here she was, and it was making her so wet she was afraid she'd come from the sheer pleasure of it.

As Derrick kissed her, she was aware of Master Josh dropping to his knees in front of her. He rubbed his nose against the small strip of cloth covering her mound and she shivered as he audibly inhaled. "Your wench smells sweet, Derrick." His voice was a low rumble. "I wonder how she tastes."

Derrick pulled away from Andi, his blue eyes fixed on hers. For a moment she thought she saw indecision and jealousy, but then his face became a mask of dominance again.

"Taste her," he told Josh while his gaze held Andi's, and her whole body went weak. Derrick was going to *share* her.

Again.

Just how far they would go, she didn't know.

Why should I care, as long as it feels good?

Derrick captured her mouth again with his, at the same time Josh caught her thong with his teeth and tugged it down. She felt the scrape of his teeth against the soft skin of her mound, and she groaned into Derrick's mouth.

In no time, Master Josh had her thong around her ankles and pulled it free of her heels. He used his hands to part her folds and at the first swipe of his tongue, she tipped her head back and cried out.

"I—I'm going to come, Master," she whispered.

"*No.*" Derrick took her face in his hands and forced her to look at him. "You will *not* come without permission."

She heard him, but her body didn't want to listen. Her thighs trembled on either side of Master Josh's head and her pussy flooded more of her wetness onto his tongue.

Derrick released her. He moved away and her body screamed for his warmth, his touch—even as Josh licked, sucked, and nibbled at her clit, much like he had her mouth when he'd kissed her. Damn, but that man knew his way around a pussy.

Her eyes were nearly crossing as she fought against an oncoming climax. Through her blurry vision she saw Sara and Lauren watching, pulling against their own bonds. Strapped to the St. Andrew's cross, in the torchlight Lauren's pussy glistened with her desire. In her cage, Sara's nipples looked rigid and she was biting her lip hard enough that a drop of blood beaded on it.

Andi twisted against her bonds, her skin slick with sweat, her head light from hanging from the handcuffs and from what the men had been doing to her. "Master, please," she begged, turning her gaze to where Derrick now stood.

Her body suddenly went cold when she saw the whip in his hand.

Chapter Twelve

ꟙ

Derrick must have seen the fear in her eyes because his expression softened. He held the handle in one hand and slid the long leather strap through the fingers of his other hand.

"Do you trust me, baby?" His voice was low, yet no less dominant.

Master Josh lapped her slit one last time then eased to his feet to stand before her as Derrick moved closer with his lithe, easy stride.

A wicked grin curved the corner of Josh's mouth and he swooped down to kiss her again. If these men didn't stop kissing her with such intensity, such passion, Andi was going to pass out. Josh's mouth was hot and he tasted of her juices.

But the heat and tenseness radiating from behind her was palpable. Without looking she sensed Derrick wasn't as cool about sharing her as he had appeared to be.

With a satisfied glint in his eye, Josh stepped back and folded his arms across his broad chest, never taking his gaze from Andi. His cock was large and erect, and she had no doubt he wanted her.

But would Derrick let him have her? Did she want him to?

She didn't have time to think anymore as warm breath stirred the hair at the nape of her neck, and the long leather strip of the whip caressed her flesh.

"I think you enjoyed Master Josh's attentions too much, baby," he said so low she was sure that only she could hear. "Just remember that you belong to me and me alone."

She couldn't get a word out at first and had to clear her throat. "Yes, Master," she finally got out. "Only you."

"Good." His voice held a note of satisfaction and she breathed a sigh of relief that she'd said the right thing. Maybe he would forget the punishment he'd promised her?

He snaked the whip around her body, gently caressing her with it as he moved from behind her to stand in front of her, blocking her view of Josh.

She trembled as he continued the slow and sensual movement of the whip over her body. He was all male…all intoxicating, hard, hot male. She wanted him so badly she didn't care who watched, and she wanted him now.

"What do you want, baby?" he murmured, mimicking her thoughts, then flicked the whip. It curled around her body like a leather lasso, suddenly capturing her.

She startled, even though there was no pain. Her answer spilled from her lips with no hesitation. "I want you, Master."

He snapped the whip again, and it curled tighter around her body. "Exactly what do you want of me?"

Andi groaned with need from him. The sting she felt from the whip this time did nothing but increase her desire for him. "I want you to fuck me…Master."

He gave a low growl of satisfaction and moved away. "I will…once you have been suitably punished."

Andi whimpered. She was afraid, she was excited, she was apprehensive, she was so crazy with lust she could barely hold back a scream.

Derrick stepped back and snapped his wrist. This time the whip stung every place it touched as it wrapped around her belly, her thighs, her calves, her ankles. She couldn't hold back her cry of surprise at the pain. She blinked back tears and was even more surprised to find the sting of the whip made her pussy ache more.

"You'll learn to obey me in every way." Derrick snapped his wrist again, and again the whip snaked around her body. "Isn't that right, baby?"

She nodded, fighting back more tears, determined not to cry. He wasn't really hurting her. Even though she was feeling pain, she needed him to fuck her more than ever.

Derrick smiled in satisfaction at the pink stripes wrapped around Andi's body like a candy cane. He was an expert with the whip and he would never injure her. He could bring her incredible pleasure with it, bring her to orgasm with it if he chose to.

God, she looked beautiful. She dangled from the handcuffs, the strong lines of her firm body taut as she stretched down to the floor. She was all curves and softness and pure woman. Her dark hair fell about her shoulders and her brown eyes glistened with moisture. Her lips were full and slightly parted and his cock jerked against his belly when she bit her lower lip.

Josh had moved to the side to watch while Derrick lashed the whip out again and again. The man's jaw was tight, his arms folded so hard against his chest that his elbows were white.

"I'm so close, Master." Andi's voice came out in a choked whisper. "I'm afraid I can't hold back any longer."

"You will." Derrick kept his voice controlled even though he wanted to wrap his arms around her and carry her to his bed. He didn't want to do what they had planned for her, but he intended to make Andi realize he was in control and that she would be his. And for this one night she would be pleasured beyond her wildest dreams.

He flung the whip aside and approached Andi. Torchlight flickered across her bare skin and he saw her tremble at his approach.

"The glass cock please, Master Josh," Derrick said to his friend, but kept his gaze on Andi.

Her eyes widened, then grew impossibly larger when Josh brought the clear crystal cock out of a freezer. The freezer was cleverly hidden in a cabinet that blended in with the room's realistic dungeon décor.

Andi shivered as her gaze darted to the thing Derrick called a glass cock as Josh handed it to him. It looked like a perfectly formed penis with a thick head and a shaft long enough to make her swallow, wondering if it would fit, and just how deep Derrick intended to shove it.

He reached her and brushed his lips over hers at the same time he slid the frozen phallus over one nipple and then the next. She groaned into his mouth and shivered. Her body still stung pleasantly from the whipping, and she was so strung out she was about to lose her mind. She felt almost high, like she could float amongst the clouds, yet grounded at the same time.

Derrick slipped the glass cock along the center of her belly, slowly traveling to her belly button, over her tight abdomen, and down to her moist curls. Shivers skittered throughout her body and she shuddered from his touch and the coldness of the glass.

"Do you want me to fuck you with this?" Derrick asked.

All that came through Andi's lips was a low moan. He cocked an eyebrow and she forced herself to speak. "If it pleases you, Master." She'd rather have his hot cock inside her, but right now she'd take anything to assuage the ache in her pussy.

He gave her a look of approval, slipped the ice-cold glass down through her slit and then shoved it into her channel.

Andi screamed. She pushed her chest out and tipped her head back, the sensation so intense that she couldn't control her reaction.

"That's it, baby," he murmured. "But don't come until I tell you. Remember that."

She whimpered again, and he thrust the glass cock a few times more, in and out of her pussy. Then he withdrew it and brought the still-cold glass to her lips.

"Lick it."

Andi kept her eyes focused on Derrick. Her lips trembled as he slipped the chilled head of the cock into her warm mouth. She tasted her essence again, but what turned her on even further was how hot Derrick's eyes were burning as he thrust the smooth glass in and out of her mouth.

He pulled it away from her and handed it to Master Josh.

Andi blinked. She'd forgotten about him, about everything but Derrick. Suddenly she was aware of the ache in her arms from being bound above her head, the fur-lined cuffs around her wrists, Lauren and Sara watching—everything.

She watched as Josh took a tube of clear gel and spread it over the glass cock. After he set the tube aside, he moved behind her.

Andi swallowed. Really hard.

Derrick palmed her breasts. "Relax."

She felt the cool head of the thick glass penis against the tight rosette of her ass.

"Don't clench, wench," Josh said in a deep rumble, his warm breath upon her skin causing her to shiver. "It'll go easier for you."

The glass felt slick and filled her, widening her as he pushed it up and into her ass. It was warmer now, her body having heated it, but it was no less stimulating as Josh pumped it in and out of her tight hole. The entire time he fucked her ass with the device, Derrick fondled her, his warm touch driving her to new levels of pleasure.

She sagged against her bonds when Josh finally pulled the glass cock completely out. He set it aside on a wooden table and returned to her.

Both men pressed up against her, Josh behind and Derrick in front of her. Andi went still. This was what they'd been leading up to all along. She'd known it.

She wanted it.

They reached up and unfastened her handcuffs. When she was freed, she went limp, her limbs refusing to hold her up. Derrick murmured soft words she couldn't comprehend in her muddled state of mind. She was crazy with lust, crazy with need and if she didn't get relief soon, she was sure she was going to die.

Derrick held her to him, smashing her breasts against his warm chest as he massaged arms that tingled from the rush of blood flowing back through them. Josh rubbed her muscles from behind and she was hyperaware of the two of them touching her, and then they began kissing her.

Derrick held her tight, his mouth hot on hers, his tongue delving into her. But then he withdrew and forced her head to the side where Josh waited. The Dom captured her mouth with his, his kiss harder and fiercer than Derrick's had been.

"Wrap your legs around me," Derrick commanded Andi as Josh broke the kiss.

She braced her hands on Derrick's shoulders, but she was still so weak from all that they had done to her that he had to help her wrap her thighs around his hips.

He moved his mouth to her ear, his breath hot against her face. "I'm going to fuck you, baby. Hard. Real hard."

The fire in Andi's belly grew to an inferno and she moaned at the erotic words. "Yes, Master."

From nowhere he produced a condom and rolled it down his erection with one hand. Then gripping her ass cheeks with both hands, he spread them wide. "Josh is going to slide into your tight ass and we're going to fuck you at the same time. It'll feel real good. You're going to love it, baby."

Andi swallowed, but there was no hesitation as she replied, "Yes, Master."

Josh pressed against her backside and rubbed his slick cock up and down her crack. She could feel the condom he'd slipped over his erection. She couldn't hold back another moan as he placed the head at the tight rosette of her ass.

"I've wanted to fuck you since the moment I flogged this sweet ass of yours," Master Josh said in a low rumble that sent impossible thrills through her belly.

At the same time, Derrick was palming her breasts and pinching her nipples so hard she had to bite her lip to keep from crying out at the sweet pain, and she clenched her thighs tighter around his hips.

All that male hardness surrounding her was so unbelievably erotic that she was flying high with sensations that were almost too much to bear.

And when Derrick placed the head of his cock at the opening of her channel, she thought she would fly apart into a million sparkling pieces.

"Fuck me, Master," she said, not caring that she was begging him.

He gave her a slow, sexy smile that she knew was only for her. "I'll share you this one time, but never again, baby. I want you to feel like you've never felt before."

Andi trembled and clenched his shoulders tighter as he spread her ass cheeks even wider.

Josh pressed the head of his cock against her hole and grasped her waist with one hand.

And then in perfect synchronization, both men thrust into her.

Andi screamed.

They held still for a moment as she felt herself expanded, filled, beyond belief. Two cocks were inside her. Two gorgeous men were about to fuck her senseless.

"That's it, baby," Derrick said as he began thrusting in and out of her pussy.

Josh thrust in tandem. "You're so damn tight," he said.

Andi could barely hear, blood was pounding in her ears so hard. Wave after wave of sensation rode through her, threatened to overcome her, to bring her to climax. Somehow she was aware that she couldn't cross that line, that she had to hold back. But her body didn't want to listen.

She fought to hold onto herself, but it was no use. She dissolved, becoming a part of both men as they thrust harder and harder. Their hands gripped her body, their cocks owned her pussy and her ass. Their sweat-slicked flesh slid together and her juices flooded, coating her thighs and Derrick's cock. The smell of sweat and testosterone and sex filled her senses. The men spoke words so arousing that her mind could barely bend itself around them.

It was all too much to bear. "I can't—" Her voice broke and tears blurred her eyes. "God, I can't hold back. Please let me come, Master."

Derrick thrust harder. "Hold on…hold on, baby."

And just when she thought she was going to explode, Derrick shouted, "Come now, Andi. Now!"

And then she did explode. Her body shattered like fine crystal smashed in an earthquake of massive proportions. Pieces of her seemed to fly throughout the room, her senses on complete overload. Her body quaked and quaked and quaked, and she thought her orgasm would never, ever end. She didn't want it to end. It was the most amazing orgasm, the most intense, that she had ever experienced.

Vaguely, she was aware of Derrick and Josh's shouts and groans as they came. She felt the throb of their cocks within her that only made her own orgasm pulse more.

Both men held her tight, their breathing heavy and matching the rhythm of her own.

At last Josh released her and slid his spent cock from her ass. Derrick eased his cock from her channel, then brought her up so that she was cradled in his arms.

Andi snuggled against his chest, unable to think, her breathing still ragged. Derrick brushed his lips over hers and she melted even further against him, totally sated, completely exhausted. And then her eyelids drifted shut and she passed into a deep and complete sleep.

Chapter Thirteen

Sunday morning, Derrick held Andi close in the bed in their master suite. Her body was spooned against his, and his erect cock pressed against her backside. Sunlight streamed onto her perfect features, illuminating her face so that she looked like an angel.

But still she slept, her breathing deep and even, an occasional soft sigh slipping through her lips.

Last night, after he'd taken her back to their suite, he'd allowed her to rest—she'd been so exhausted, it was as if she'd slipped into oblivion. If she hadn't been so tired, he would have made love to her again and again, branding her completely as his own.

She belonged to him.

He snuggled closer to her, enjoying the feel of her in his arms. His chin rested on her mussed hair, his arm cradling her slim waist.

The emotions that ranged through him surprised him with their intensity. He had shared women with Josh before, but this time had been harder. Andi wasn't just any woman. Sharing her had been Derrick's way of showing her that she was his to control.

But he realized the truth. *She* controlled *him*. She made him wild with need and lust…and maybe even love.

He pressed his lips to her hair, breathing in her jasmine perfume and her scent of pure woman.

Andi stirred and sighed again. Derrick propped himself on one elbow and traced his finger down her shoulder to her elbow and back, and she shivered in her sleep. Her nipples puckered against the silk sheet draped over her breasts and over the curve of her hip. Only her bare feet peeked out from beneath the cream silk.

He leaned down and blew into her ear. A soft smile curved the corner of her lips and then she opened her eyes, slowly blinking away the morning light.

"Derrick?" she murmured as she turned in his arms to face him. She frowned as if trying to remember something, and then said, "Oh. I mean Master."

He smiled and ran the pad of his finger down to the tip of her nose. "Let's just be Derrick and Andi today, okay?"

She returned his smile, only hers was so radiant it seemed to light up the already sunny room.

"All right." Her movement was bold as she reached up and pushed a lock of his hair from his face. "Does that mean I can do whatever I want to you?"

Just the thought of her having her way with him made him groan. "Baby, I'm yours."

She gave an impish grin and slid her hand over his stubbled cheek, down his chest and under the sheet. When she reached his naked cock, she wrapped her small fingers around his erection and he groaned again.

Before he lost all rational thought, he had to get something off his mind, something he'd wanted to tell her all weekend. He caught her errant hand and brought it to his chest, pressing it over his heart.

"We need to talk," he said.

Andi blinked. His face was so serious that for a moment she was afraid he was going to tell her their weekend was over already, and it was time to part ways. Why that bothered her so much, she wasn't sure, but she did know she wasn't ready for the weekend to end.

But come Monday—

Derrick grasped her hand tighter in his, his penetrating blue gaze focused on her. "I'm falling in love with you."

Andi's eyes widened. Her heart raced and heat flushed straight to her head, making her dizzy with it. "You—"

"I'm serious." He released her hand to cup the side of her face. He rubbed his thumb from her lips, across her cheek and back. "I can't get enough of you, Andi. I don't think I ever will. I can't imagine not waking up with you every day of my life."

She closed her eyes and took a deep breath. This was not happening. She did not want this.

But her heart ached at his words, a desire rose up even fiercer than sexual need. The desire to be with Derrick—maybe even to love him one day.

"Talk to me, baby." His voice was low, almost hesitant.

Andi opened her eyes to meet his straightforward gaze. She knew that with Derrick there would never be falseness or lies. He was a good and honest man.

"This is nuts," she said. "You can't love me."

"Why not?" A sexy grin curved the corner of his mouth, and she melted at the mere sight. "I've admired you from the moment I met you. And I've always wanted you."

Andi looked up at him from beneath her lashes. "I've wanted you, too. But love…"

He moved his hand from her face to her long hair and wrapped it around his fingers. "All I ask is that you give us a chance. Give what we have a chance to grow and we'll go from there."

She took a deep breath and slowly released it. Wow. He wasn't asking for commitment. He was just asking for her to give them time to build a relationship—if that's what she really wanted.

Somehow with Derrick the thought of a serious relationship didn't cause her to want to run the other way. Somehow it felt right. It felt good.

Warmth spread through her and she felt it radiating from her soul. She couldn't help but smile. "Maybe I'm falling in love with you, too."

Derrick's smile was so devastatingly sexy that it nearly caused her to melt into a pool of lust and need, and maybe even something deeper, that love thing they were talking about.

"But no pressure, okay?"

"No pressure," he said, but he had a wicked gleam in his eyes. "Just know that I don't intend to let you go."

Andi shivered at the note of possession in his voice. Before she had a chance to respond, he caught her mouth in a hard, fierce kiss. She couldn't believe how much she wanted him, how much she wanted to love him.

All conscious thought left her mind as Derrick eased between her thighs. She moaned and arched her hips up to meet him, enjoying the press of his cock against her belly, the feel of his weight, his hot flesh, his warm breath feathering across her lips.

Derrick kissed his woman, knowing that he could never let her go. He would give her the time she needed to realize she was his, and that she loved him.

He eased down Andi's body, brushing his lips along the line of her jaw and down the curve of her neck. She made sweet little moans as he kissed and licked his way to the valley between her breasts, tasting the salt of her skin and breathing in the scent of her. She was soft and warm, sweet and pliant.

Even as he thought that, she became wild and demanding beneath him. "Suck my nipples and fuck me," she said in her low, breathless voice.

He chuckled against her breast and licked a path to her nipple. He sucked, hard, and she cried out and squirmed beneath him. "Yeah, like that," she cried, and he moved his mouth so that he could bite her other tight bud.

She clenched her hands in his hair, pulling at it so that he felt it all the way down to the roots, so hard it was almost painful. He liked it, liked the way she was losing control beneath him, thrashing and crying out.

He wanted to drive into her now, but he held back, teasing her by slowly moving down the line of her belly and to her mound.

"You are so damn sexy, baby." He fanned his breath against her belly button, and she cried out. He smelled the flood of her juices, the scent of their sex.

He nuzzled her soft curls and groaned. His cock was beyond hard, but he had to taste her, had to give her pleasure.

It was a need that gripped him and wouldn't let go. It wasn't about him. This was about *her* pleasure, making Andi feel how much he cared for her.

He lapped at her clit, tasting her sweet cream, and groaned.

She clenched her hands impossibly tighter in his hair and he licked her harder.

Andi couldn't believe that she felt even hotter than she had the other times they'd fucked. But the fact that he'd told her he was falling in love with her made every one of her senses seem more alive than ever before.

Maybe this was what making love was like.

His stubble scraped the inside of her thighs and the lips of her pussy as he laved her over and over. He plunged his fingers into her slick core as he licked her clit, and she pumped her hips against his face.

"I'm so close to coming, Derrick," she said, barely able to breathe.

"Come for me, baby," he murmured against her pussy, then nipped her clit.

Andi cried out. She arched up off the bed with the force of her climax. It rushed from her belly through every part of her body.

She was almost sobbing from the impact of the orgasm when Derrick rose up, braced his hands to either side of her head and plunged his cock inside her.

Andi shouted again, more aftershocks causing her pussy to clench around his cock. He held himself still for a moment just staring down at her. His dark hair fell across his forehead in a sexy, disheveled look. The angular curve of his jaw was tense and his blue eyes were dark with his desire for her. He was so sexy, so gorgeous, that he took her breath away.

He rose up and hooked his arms under her knees and put her ankles to either side of his neck. He planted his hands beside her head and began to rock, thrusting his hips up hard but slow. So deep, he felt so deep, and he touched a spot far down inside her that had never been reached before. Every thrust of his cock caused her to tremble and squirm and pulse around him.

Derrick looked down between their bodies and her gaze followed to see his cock sliding in and out of her pussy. The sight was so erotic she climaxed again, her hips bucking and trembling.

"That's it, baby." He rocked harder, drawing out her climax, waiting for his own release.

And when she came yet another time, he finally shouted with an orgasm that was so powerful his entire body shook against hers.

He braced himself above her for a moment, his head thrown back, looking like a god in the throes of passion.

Slowly, he eased her legs down and rolled to his side, bringing her with him. His cock slipped from her core and she instantly missed him inside her.

They cuddled together and she melted into his powerful embrace, enjoying the strength of him against her. Their bodies were slick with sweat and their juices and the scent of sex surrounded them. Andi had never felt more content or more loved in her life.

Derrick smiled and kissed her softly. "You're mine, baby. You know that, don't you?"

She couldn't help a smile of happiness. "I'm all yours."

Erotic Stranger

ꙮ

Chapter One

ꟿ

Teri tossed her briefcase on the hotel bed and barely resisted throwing herself on it as well. God, she was tired and uptight. "Your problem, Teri Carter," she said with a sigh, "is that you *really* need to get laid."

Did she *ever*. It had been ages since she'd had a man, but her advancement in her career as a corporate lawyer had really put the skids on her sex life. She didn't have time to date, was never in one place long enough to really meet anyone that met her strict criteria—a good bank account so that he wouldn't live off of *her*, decent looks, great sex. A real man's man. Someone who could hold his own, especially with her. So far she hadn't dated any man who really could.

Ugh. Wimps.

Teri rubbed her temples with her fingertips. Her head and back ached and her shoulders were tense from yet another long flight. She traveled so much it was a wonder she even remembered what city she was in.

She kicked off her flats and padded over the plush carpet to the expansive window of the executive suite. She drew open the curtain to reveal an incredible view of the Golden Gate Bridge and Alcatraz from her San Francisco hotel. She could just imagine being out on the wharf now, breathing in the salty, briny smell of the water, feeling the moist air upon her skin, hearing the screech of gulls and the bark of sea lions.

A tired smile touched her lips. Too bad she was only here for business, not for pleasure. Her intense schedule didn't give her any room for relaxation.

Teri let the curtain drop and turned away from the view. She unbuttoned her silk blouse and the material slide down in a cool and sensual whisper against her skin. She was so tired she didn't bother to pick it up. Instead, she left a trail of clothing from the bedroom into the bathroom as she stripped from her bra, her slacks and her panties.

When she was naked, she paused at the mirror and studied her reflection. Her features were tight and drawn, her makeup barely concealing the shadows under her eyes.

She reached up, took the clip from her hair which tumbled to her shoulders in a long, brunette mass. After tossing her clip to the marble countertop she ran her fingers through her hair and massaged her scalp. The movement caused her breasts to rise and her gaze dropped to her nipples that were the color of pink carnations.

Slowly, she moved her hands from her hair and lowered them to her breasts. Her breathing quickened as she pinched her nipples between her thumbs and forefingers. The erotic feeling made her nubs tighten and she grew damp between her thighs.

Teri watched herself in the mirror, her eyes growing heavy-lidded as a fantasy weaved its way through her mind. She imagined a stranger pressed up against her ass, his erection firm against her backside. His hands pinched and pulled at her nipples, his touch made her pussy wet, craving his cock.

She slid one hand slowly from her breast, down her flat belly to the trimmed curls between her thighs. She cupped herself as the stranger would, before slipping a finger into her moist folds.

While she rubbed her clit, she never took her gaze off her reflection. She saw the flush steal over her skin as she drew herself closer to climax. Watched the way her hand moved against her mound and how her other hand continued to roll and pinch her nipple.

She imagined the stranger's warm mouth between her legs now, the feel of his tongue against her folds, his head between her thighs. The image was so powerful that her finger circled her clit faster and faster.

Teri came with a jerk of her hips against her hand and a rush of heat through her body. She continued fingering her clit as waves of pleasure washed over her. She had to move her other hand from her breast to the countertop to brace herself. Still she watched while her body trembled as her orgasm continued on, and she bit her lower lip as she met her green eyes in the mirror.

When the last pulse of her climax eased away she slipped her fingers from her pussy, brought them to her nose and inhaled. Sex. The smell of sex was so good. Even better when mixed with the musky scent of a man.

Teri placed both hands on the countertop and this time closed her eyes. What would it *really* be like to lose all inhibitions and have sex with a stranger? She wouldn't even have to know his name. He'd just have to fuck her good and hard and leave her satisfied.

She sighed, opened her eyes and pushed away from the mirror.

Did she dare make her fantasy a reality?

After taking a shower, putting on fresh makeup, fixing her hair and taking care of a few necessities, Teri headed to the hotel's bar instead of dialing up room service as usual. She could use a good drink more than a good meal. Rather than dressing casually, though, she had slipped into a little black backless cocktail dress with a halter-top and a skirt that reached mid-thigh. She always traveled with two evening dresses in case she had dinner appointments with clients or if she had business functions to attend. One cocktail dress was fairly modest, but this one was a little more daring.

In a tiny black purse, Teri had her room key, credit card, lipstick, cash and a small package of condoms she'd purchased in the hotel gift shop. A girl had to be prepared.

Her skin heated at the thought of her plan for the night. She couldn't believe she was going through with this. She intended to have a drink or two in the hotel lounge, then find out where one of the local hotspots was. She had every intention of making her fantasy come true.

Sex. With a stranger. Tonight.

When she reached the lounge, her gaze scanned the crowd. Businessmen in suits and ties, other men in casual slacks and polo shirts, none of them remotely interesting. Teri didn't even bother looking at the women in the room.

She found herself a small table in a dim corner of the lounge and signaled for the waitress. As she settled back in one of the cushioned chairs, she tried to relax. Her skin tingled all over from the warm shower she'd taken and she could smell the light scent of her orange blossom perfume. She barely had anything on beneath her tiny black dress—just a skimpy lace bra and a thong—and with every movement she made, the silky material of her dress slid across her skin and made her pussy wetter.

She'd finished two cosmopolitans to shore up her courage before heading to a nightclub…when she saw *him*.

A man straight out of her fantasies.

He walked into the bar with confidence—perhaps even arrogance—in his expression and in his stride. Immediately she had no doubt he was a man who knew what he wanted…and got it.

The man had blond hair that curled slightly at the nape of his neck, and he was dressed all in black from his T-shirt to his jeans. God, she loved men in black, and she loved the way his jeans molded his ass. It struck her as extremely sexy that he wasn't wearing slacks like the rest of the men in the bar. He looked rougher. Edgier.

He was handsome in a powerful sort of way that made her mouth dry. Those firm lips. That sexy mouth. She could just imagine…jeez. What *couldn't* she imagine with this man?

Her fantasy reached the bar and casually leaned against it. After he got the bartender's attention and placed his order, he turned slightly and his gaze raked the room. Her heart pounded a little harder as she focused on him, waiting for him to look at her. She didn't intend to play coy. She wanted this man.

The moment their eyes met, she felt a jolt from her nipples to her pussy. She couldn't have looked away from him even if she wanted to.

Josh Williams studied the brunette. She had large, beautiful green eyes and full lips, and her black dress was revealed just enough to entice. Her fingers slowly slid up and down the stem of her martini glass as she focused on him, and he could easily imagine that small hand stroking his cock.

As a Dom, Josh had more than enough experience in self-control, but at that moment his cock chose to ignore him and to harden painfully against his tight jeans.

This woman was going to have to pay for arousing him with a mere look, a mere movement. In that moment's perusal he had no doubt she wanted him, and she'd desire all that he could teach her, do to her, and more.

He had just ended his Dom/sub relationship with twins Lauren and Sara. He needed something more than a playful relationship. Something that he couldn't quite define. He'd decided to remove his collars from both women. They'd begged, pleaded that he remain their Dom, but his gut told him it was time to move on.

With practiced ease, Josh kept all emotion from his expression as he studied the green-eyed brunette. The bartender set the beer bottle on the counter beside Josh, and he turned away from the woman just long enough to pay. He held the cool bottle in his hand and without hesitation strode through the maze of tables filled with bar patrons, and headed straight for the woman.

Her eyes never left his, but her tongue darted out to lick her lower lip in a nervous movement. Yet her chin was raised and she had an almost haughty look on her face. He would break her of that—and she would love just exactly how he was going to do it. His experienced gaze saw her quickened breathing, the flush in her cheeks, the taut nipples against the silk of her dress. She hadn't even met him, and she was primed and ready.

When he reached her table, he didn't bother to ask if the chair next to her was free. He slid into it, close enough that his jean-clad thigh brushed the wispy softness of her dress. He set the beer on the table and studied her. She was gorgeous, and he could just imagine how all that soft pale skin would look with his brand upon it. He caught her scent of orange blossoms and woman and he couldn't wait to taste her.

A blush tinged her cheeks, and he knew in that moment that this was something she had never done before. "I'm Teri," she said in a soft voice that caused his balls to tighten.

Yes, she was going to pay for the reaction his body was having to her, and she was going to enjoy every minute of it.

Teri held her breath as she waited for the man to respond. This was crazy. What was she doing?

"Josh," he finally said. His voice was deep and sexy enough to make her toes curl. "Tell me about yourself, Teri."

A small shiver raced down her spine at the sound of her name on his tongue and the intense look in his gray eyes. His words weren't casual. No, they were commanding. A demand, not a request.

If she were at work, she'd use her tongue like a whip and bring the man to his knees with her frosty attitude. But she wasn't working right now…

Instead of putting her off with his domineering attitude, Teri wanted to squirm in her chair from the ache his request caused in her pussy. His musky male scent and the clean smell of aftershave made her want to wrap herself around him.

"Tell me, Teri," he commanded again, this time with an almost disapproving look in his eyes.

She didn't know what compelled her most, but perhaps it was the incredible desire burning inside her at just being near this stranger. "I'm a corporate lawyer," she said with a tilt of her head, challenging him. "I don't take orders well."

A slow smile curved one corner of his mouth. He reached up and gently stroked her bare upper arm. Goose bumps prickled her skin. "I can teach you how to take orders and love every minute of it, Teri."

She tilted her head to one side and did her best to sound casual. "How?"

"First tell me about you." He leaned closer to her, one forearm braced on the table. "What makes you tick, Teri?"

She raised her chin a little higher. "I'm a Harvard graduate, VP in charge of corporate negotiations—"

"*You*, Teri," he said more firmly, his gray eyes snapping with something electric. The way he kept repeating her name unnerved her. Like he was interrogating her, expecting her to cave and spill her guts. The bug under the microscope trick. She almost laughed. She knew that ploy well. Yet she didn't find it offensive. In fact, she found it stimulating.

All right, if this was how the game was going to be played. "I live in Los Angeles by myself. I don't even have a cat because I travel so much."

He slid his fingers along her forearm. "That's not who you really are, Teri."

What did he want? Her panty size? "My favorite color is yellow," she tossed out. "I like to jog, to go sailing and to spend time with my sister's kids when I can. Which isn't often since they live in Minneapolis."

At this he gave her a more approving look and his gray eyes focused on her mouth. "What is your deepest, darkest desire, Teri? What is it you want more than anything right now? Right this minute."

She went stock still. Heat crept up her neck. She couldn't speak.

He leaned close enough that she could have kissed him. When he spoke next she felt the warmth of his breath against her lips and caught the pleasant, yeasty scent of beer. "What do you want right now, Teri?" he repeated.

"I—" Her throat was so dry she could hardly get anything out. When she did, she couldn't believe the words came out of her mouth, but it was as if he was magically drawing them from her. "I want to be fucked by a stranger." A wash of heat flushed over her. She was a tough lawyer, but this—this was different.

Josh gave a nod of approval at her honesty, but his expression was still unreadable. "Just any stranger, Teri?"

Her whole body was on fire with embarrassment, arousal, and yet confidence, too. "I want to be fucked by you."

Chapter Two

ꕤ

Teri almost slapped her hand over her mouth. She'd just told a stranger she wanted him to fuck her.

"Good girl." Josh brushed his lips so softly over hers that she gasped. "You'll be rewarded for your honesty, Teri."

Before she had a chance to process that comment, he leaned back. "Tell me how you like to be fucked, Teri."

She blinked. Tried to think. Okay, time to change things up a bit. "It's only fair you tell me about yourself, first."

He gave a slow nod. "Fair is fair."

"So what are you doing here in San Francisco?" She felt a little more on familiar ground doing the interrogating. "What do you do for a living?"

"I'm in the city for a conference," he said. "I own a stock brokerage."

Ten points for Josh. "Where do you live?" she asked.

He took a swig of his beer. "Born and raised in Los Angeles."

She felt a strange sort of pleasure that they shared the same city. "Angels or Dodgers?"

Josh grinned. "Dodgers through and through."

"Humph." She tapped her manicured nails on the table. "You just lost points on that one."

He chuckled and then answered her other questions. He had two sisters, a brother and a puppy named Stix.

"What about relationships?" she asked. "Any girlfriends in the closet?"

He didn't seem to mind her straightforwardness as he gave just as direct of an answer. "I just ended a year-long relationship with Lauren and Sara."

Her eyes widened. "*Two* women?"

He shrugged one shoulder. "They're twins."

"Every man's fantasy," Teri murmured.

"But tonight you're my fantasy, Teri," he said, taking control of the conversation again, going back into his dominating role. He gave her what was most definitely a command. "Remove your underwear."

She jerked and her hand bumped into her empty martini glass, knocking it over. In a fast movement, Josh caught the glass and righted it. "Are you out of your mind?" she said in a harsh whisper.

He raised a brow, challenging her.

Okay, she could take a challenge any day of the week and turn it to her advantage.

She inched her hand up one side of her skirt to her hip, until her fingers reached the edge of her thong. Adrenaline rushed through her body at the thought of getting caught. She glanced around the bar to see if anyone could see what she was doing.

"Look at me, Teri, and don't look away again."

Her gaze snapped back to him and she met his gray eyes. Butterflies began battling the insides of her belly like crazy, and her body hummed with desire. She forced herself to watch him as she inched her underwear from her hips. She prayed the tablecloth was long enough that no one could see her move her thong down her thighs to her knees, where they promptly fell to her ankles. With her cheeks burning like crazy, she caught the edge of her thong with the toe of her high heel, and brought it up high enough that she could grasp it with her hand. It was soaking wet.

When she had it in her lap, he held out his open palm. "Give it to me, Teri."

Fine. She raised it and flung it at him like a slingshot.

Amusement flashed across his features as he snatched it out of the air. He raised the thong to his nose where she watched his chest rise as he inhaled. "You're hot for me, aren't you, Teri," he said—as a statement, not a question.

She shifted in her seat, aware of how much more naked she was beneath her dress. She waited two heartbeats before she said, "Yes."

He took her underwear and stuffed it into his back pocket. "Yes, what?"

She wrinkled her brows, puzzled. "I don't know what you mean."

He looked at her and said in a calm, matter-of-fact way, "Yes, Master."

This time Teri almost upset the whole table, the way her body jerked in surprise. "Yes, *Master*?"

"That's right, Teri." He leaned in close once again, and moved his lips to her ear. His warm breath caressed her as he said, "Tonight I'm your Master."

Master? Wasn't that something that a submissive called a Dominant in a BDSM relationship? "Are you out of your freaking mind?" she asked in disbelief.

He reached up and brushed the heavy fall of her dark hair over her shoulder, his fingers brushing her bare shoulder and causing tingles to radiate through her. "Tonight I'll be your Master, Teri. Turn over control to me and I'll give you a night you'll never forget."

"Are you a Dom?" she asked, keeping her voice steady. "Are you into BDSM?"

"That's right, Teri." He laid his hand over her thigh and stroked her bare skin with his thumb. "And I intend to fuck you in ways you've never been fucked before."

She took a deep breath. "I'm not so sure about this."

"I think you are, Teri." His hand slowly moved up her leg, pushing the silky material of her dress up to her hip.

She couldn't move for the life of her as his fingers met the crevice between her thigh and her pussy. His eyes held hers the entire time he touched her. When his fingers slipped into her drenched folds she nearly came undone.

Her entire body was trembling as he gave a satisfied smile. "You want me to fuck you so bad that you'd take me right here, right now, wouldn't you, Teri." Another statement.

"I, uh—" Jeez, where'd her brain just go?

"Yes, Master," he said calmly as he began to stroke her clit.

She could barely think as his fingers dipped in and out of her slick core and then moved back to her clit. She was sure the tablecloth covered them enough that no one could see what he was doing to her, but she was afraid anyone in the bar could read it in her expression.

"You are going to climax right here in front of all these people," he said in a firm voice. "Do you understand, Teri?"

God, she didn't want him to stop.

It was all she could do not to start moaning aloud. "Yes, Master," she whispered. Master? She'd really just called this stranger Master?

He gave her an approving smile. "Very good, Teri."

His gaze never leaving hers, Josh thrust two fingers into her pussy and she almost yelped from the exquisite feel of it. With expert movements, he stroked her wet folds, then began to concentrate on her clit, circling it, moving in slow, drawn-out movements.

She was going to lose her mind. Her eyelids began to drift closed, but his sharp voice brought her gaze snapping back to his. "Look at me, Teri," he demanded. "Watch me while I finger-fuck you."

The intense look in his icy gray eyes made the feelings build up even more and more within her. She was close, so close.

"Come *now*, Teri," he commanded at the same time he pinched her clit, *hard*.

Her body exploded. She couldn't help the moan that rushed through her lips as her hips bucked against his hand and a light sheen of sweat broke out over her skin. Her body shook as he continued holding onto her clit.

When she couldn't take any more, she said, "Josh. Stop."

He pinched harder and her body jerked again. "Yes?"

"Um—please, Master." She couldn't believe she was saying this. "Please stop, Master."

He gave her a satisfied smile and withdrew his hand from her pussy. She almost collapsed in exhaustion from the incredible orgasm she'd just had. Even the pain of him pinching her clit had made her climax even more exquisite.

Josh brought his hand to his nose and inhaled again, and she saw her juices glistening in his fingers. He slipped first one and then another into his mouth, sucking her taste from them.

What a turn-on!

"You taste delicious, Teri." He picked up a napkin from the tabletop and wiped his fingers clean. "I want to sample more of you."

Her body was completely buzzing with desire and need. He'd already given her an amazing orgasm. What else could he do for her?

Josh took her hand, catching her by surprise, and brought her up with him to stand. He picked up her little black purse and handed it to her. "We're going to my room," he said in a matter-of-fact tone.

It was as if she was in a dream. Her legs barely felt like they would support her after her orgasm and the fact that this stranger had such immediate control over her. Within fifteen minutes of meeting her, he'd had her underwear off and had finger-fucked her.

As Josh led her through the crowded hotel lounge, Teri's heart pounded, and countless thoughts raced through her mind. What was she doing? Where was he taking her? Was she out of her mind? This was a stranger! What if he was dangerous?

But that dangerous mien about him was what made her more excited. It was controlled danger that made her want to experience all that he had to offer. He was definitely a bad boy, and that turned her on to no end. Instinct told her that this man wouldn't harm her…but what if her instincts were wrong?

It was too late to back out. She wanted him too badly. She'd wanted to be fucked by a stranger tonight, and that's exactly what she was going to get.

But a Dom? A BDSM Master? What did he have in mind for her?

Rather than frighten her, the thought intrigued her. She knew about BDSM, knew that a submissive relinquished control to the Dominant. Did she want that for tonight? As a corporate lawyer, she was used to being in control. Could she turn that over to this man?

Josh had such a hard-on that he had to bite the inside of his cheek to control the need to take Teri the moment they stepped into his hotel room. Hell, he'd take her in the elevator if he didn't have other plans for her.

He gripped her hand in his as they walked across the hotel lobby. He looked down at her and gave her a reassuring yet dominant look to let her know exactly what her place was in this night's relationship.

"You'll have a safe word, Teri," he said as they reached the bank of elevators. "If at any time you want me to stop, you say the word and this night ends."

She cleared her throat. "Safe word?"

"Master," he reminded her with a low rumble.

Okay, the game was on. She could do this. "Yes, er, Master."

"Choose a word, Teri."

They reached the elevators and Josh pressed the up button while Teri looked as if she was trying to think of a safe word.

"Negotiations," she finally said.

He nodded as the elevator door dinged. "Negotiations it is."

Even though there would be no negotiations tonight.

The elevator was empty, to Josh's satisfaction, and it was glass-walled. He pressed his hand to her lower back ushered her into it as he let his palm slide down the silky dress over her ass. She gave a startled little gasp and he squeezed.

When the door closed behind them he pressed the button for the thirty-first floor. He pushed her up against the wooden bar just below the windows that looked out at the night view of the San Francisco skyline and she gave a little cry of surprise. His body was flush against hers, his erect cock firm against her backside.

As the elevator started to move, Josh shoved her skirt up to her hips, completely baring her ass.

She tried to tug it back down. "Someone could see!"

"That's your first punishment, Teri." He forced her skirt back up. "You fought me, and you didn't refer to me as Master."

The tough-as-nails lawyer went still, and he wondered if she was about to say her safe word. But instead she gripped the wooden bar as the elevator whooshed upward.

"Pinch your nipples, Teri," he commanded as he slipped his fingers into her wet pussy from behind.

In the reflection in the glass he saw the slight curve of her lips and her heavy-lidded eyes. "Yes, Master," she said as she brought her hands to her breasts and began tugging at her nipples, pinching and pulling at them.

The elevator came to a stop and dinged, and Josh casually looked over his shoulder to see that they'd arrived at his floor. He let her skirt slide down her ass, but not before he gave one more flick against her clit.

"Oh, jeez," she whispered. As he turned her around to face him, she dropped her hands from her breasts, gave him a cocky look and said, "I mean oh, jeez, *Master*."

He almost laughed aloud. Instead he kept his expression stony. A good Dom maintained control at all times. And he was the best.

Josh took her by the hand again, and led her out onto the carpeted floor and down the hall to his luxury suite, one of the largest in the hotel. He slipped the key card from his pocket and opened the door before pushing it open and motioning to Teri to enter.

"Beautiful room," she said in an appreciative voice, "er, Master."

It had a breathtaking view of the Golden Gate Bridge, Alcatraz, and other sights. The windows were floor to ceiling and the curtains were wide open. The suite was expansive, with deep, plush carpeting, fine mahogany furniture and vases of fresh flowers.

When he had her at the center of the room he positioned her so that she was looking at him. He took her small purse from her grip and tossed it onto one of the overstuffed couches.

"Remove your clothing, Teri," he commanded.

Teri seriously thought about running for the door. God, would her body ever stop feeling like it was bursting into flames? This time prickles of heat went from her scalp to her toes and back again.

"Teri…" he said with a look in his eye that told her she was about to be in serious trouble. He'd said she'd already earned one punishment. No doubt he'd be happy to add another.

Punishments? She was *really* out of her mind to even let things go this far.

"I believe only in safe, sane and *consensual* BDSM. If you've changed your mind, say your safe word and everything ends now." He rubbed his hands lightly up and down her upper arms. "Or turn over yourself *completely* for tonight. I won't accept anything less than absolute submission. I won't negotiate with you."

For once Teri hesitated. She was used to making snap decisions, to being in control. From this point on she would relinquish that control to Josh, a Dom she didn't even know.

She'd wanted sex with a stranger and this man turned her on more than any man ever had in her life. This was her fantasy come true. And if he pushed her too far she'd say her safe word.

When she made up her mind, she made up her mind.

"Yes, Master," she said clearly. "I'm yours for tonight, as long as you promise not to push me too far."

He studied her and slowly nodded. "If I push you beyond your limits, Teri, just say your safe word."

When she started to toe off one of her heels, he placed a hand on her arm. "Leave the shoes, Teri."

"Yes, Master." She reached behind her for the zipper at the top of her buttocks, and it made a soft hiss as she pulled it down. She maintained eye contact with him as she reached up for the clasp of the dress's halter top. After a heartbeat she let the material drop. It slid down her breasts, her belly, her thighs, a caress against her skin. When it was on the floor, she was bare except for the bra and her heels.

He looked at her expectantly. She raised her chin and brought her hands up to unfasten the front clasp of her strapless bra. She let it drop to the floor.

She was entirely naked. In front of a stranger. At this Dom's mercy.

His expression was still unreadable as he slowly walked around her, his gaze taking her in from head to toe. The only sign that he was aroused was the bulge in his jeans, and that gave her a measure of satisfaction. At least she was having some effect on him.

And was he ever having an effect on her. Her nipples were diamond-hard in the cool air of the luxurious suite and her pussy was so wet her upper thighs were slick from it. She felt completely erotic standing only in her three-inch heels and nothing else, with an incredibly gorgeous man studying her body.

He finally came to stand in front of her, and his icy gray eyes focused on her. "Widen your stance to shoulder-width apart, your hands behind your back and your eyes lowered, Teri. Do not move until I return."

Despite her instinct to rebel, she obeyed. "Yes, Master," she mumbled as an afterthought.

Even though her eyes were lowered, she saw him turn away and stride across the plush carpeting to an open door. Through it she could see an enormous bed, and her pussy ached at the thought that this stranger would probably be fucking her on that bed soon.

It seemed to take forever before he returned. Her steel nerves were quickly turning to tinfoil and she was afraid her knees would give out.

And when she saw what he was carrying, they almost did.

Chapter Three

ℰ𝒮

Teri's eyes widened as her head shot up and her jaw dropped. Josh was carrying a black duffel bag in one hand—and a flogger in the other.

Now's the time to run, she shouted in her head. *That or shout your safe word.*

"You've earned a second punishment, Teri," he said as he dropped the duffel bag at her feet. "I instructed you to keep your eyes lowered."

Oh, shit.

Automatically, as if she'd done this countless times, she looked at the floor and said, "Yes, Master."

He knelt before the duffel bag, in her line of sight and she studied him while he was intent on searching the bag. He was gorgeous with his blond hair and the way his muscles rippled beneath the taut black T-shirt that he wore.

She bit her lip as she watched him draw out a black satin scarf, what looked like leather cuffs, a long silver chain with clamps on both ends and a metal-studded black collar.

Oh. My. God.

When he started to raise his head, she immediately looked at her feet. She suddenly felt so vulnerable in front of this man. She *was* vulnerable.

When he looked at her again she could see he was holding the black collar. "Tonight you are my slave, Teri." He brought the leather to her neck and began fastening it. "Tonight you are mine. Do you understand?"

Teri almost shouted "*What?*" but bit her tongue to keep from saying anything. Now he was calling her slave? She managed to get out a "Yes, Master" in a choked voice.

When the collar was firm around her neck, she had to resist reaching up to touch it. She'd seen that it had a D ring on it, and the thought went through her mind that he might intend to leash her. How humiliating that would be if he did.

Next he selected the satin scarf. Her heartbeat sped up when he brought it to her eyes and began to tie it around her head. She gasped as everything went black.

"This is part of your punishment, slave," he said as he tightened the scarf, just enough that it was secure and so that it wasn't hurting her. "You have lost the right to see what it is I'm about to do to you."

"What are you going to do to me, Master?" she asked, the words barely coming out in a croak.

"Did I give you permission to speak, slave?" His fingers grasped her nipple and pinched so hard she yelped.

"No, Master."

"If you speak again without permission, I will be forced to gag you as well, slave."

Her cheeks burned fiery hot, but she didn't open her mouth. A gag was the last thing she wanted.

Blindfolded and unable to see, she found her other senses seemed magnified. She could smell his clean scent of man and aftershave, and felt the heat of his body close to hers. When he moved away she knew it immediately, even though he wasn't touching her. She heard him kneel and imagined him picking up one of the things he'd laid out on the floor and then he was standing close to her again.

"On your knees, slave."

She barely remembered to keep her mouth shut as she followed his instructions. Her high heels wobbled as she tried to kneel with her hands behind her back. Josh held her elbow and with his help she got to her knees.

"That's a good slave," he murmured as he moved behind her. The next thing she knew he had taken her wrists and had fastened leather cuffs around each, then hooked them together so that she couldn't move them.

Teri felt a moment's panic. She'd thought she was vulnerable before, but now she was bound and on her knees on top of being naked and blindfolded. For what seemed the millionth time she asked herself what she'd gotten into.

While at the same time she realized she'd never been so aroused in her entire life. Her breasts were hard and aching, her pussy so wet and slick that she caught her own scent.

"You are here to please me." He moved from behind her and she felt him kneel again in front of her. "Anything that I do to you is for *my* pleasure, not yours. Do you understand?"

When I get my hands untied—

Teri started to answer, but remembered his instructions in time and just nodded.

"As your Master, I know what's best for you, slave. I know what you need and I'll take care of you."

Teri licked her dry lips and said nothing.

She couldn't help a gasp when something clamped down on her nipple. The pain was incredible and tears wet her eyes behind the blindfold. But to her surprise the pain began to turn into an intense sort of pleasure.

Blinded as she was, she couldn't see what it was, but at the sound of a chain rustling she realized what the silver chain and the two clamps on it were for, just before a clamp bit down on her other nipple.

This time she did shout out in pain and her eyes watered even more. And again the pain blended into the strange sense of pleasure. Incredibly her arousal grew and she wanted his cock in her pussy so badly she could taste it.

"Shall I add another punishment, slave?" he said in that dominating tone that told her she was about to be in big trouble if she didn't shut her mouth.

She shook her head.

"I may punish you anyway, Teri." He tugged on the chain linking from one nipple to the other and she had to bite her lower lip hard not to cry out. "You'll now take a position of complete subjugation."

Teri didn't have a chance to wonder what he meant before he held one hand to her belly and pressed down on her back with his other while he guided her down. He positioned her so that one cheek was to the floor, her breasts were brushing the carpet, and her ass high in the air. He moved behind her and pushed her knees farther apart so that her thighs were spread wide and her pussy and ass were completely bared to him. Her hands were still cuffed behind her back, and there was no way in hell she could move. And she couldn't see a damn thing.

She thought about shouting her safe word, but she was so turned on that she was sure she could come with a brush against her clit. Maybe he'd drive into her and fuck her just like this. The thought alone nearly made her writhe.

When he had her situated, he moved away from her and she heard rustling noises, like he was digging in his duffel bag. In the next moment he was behind her and pressing something long and hard inside her pussy—a dildo or a vibrator.

This time she bit the inside of her cheek to keep from crying out in surprise and pleasure.

"You've been a very bad girl, Teri." His warm hand rested on her ass and he began squeezing one butt cheek and then the other. "You will learn to obey me in every way. To do as I wish *when* I wish. Do you understand?"

Teri nodded, her cheek rubbing against the carpet with her movement.

"Very good, slave." He moved away again and she heard a squishy sort of sound. "I'm giving you your two punishments at once. Be careful that you don't earn another." Something cool and slick pressed against her anus.

He couldn't. He *wouldn't*!

He slid something deep into her anus. It stretched her. It hurt. It burned. But like the clamps on her nipples, the pain became pleasure. She felt so incredibly horny, so full, that she couldn't imagine being anywhere but here at this very moment. How she wanted him to fuck her just like this.

"Soon my cock is going to be in your ass instead of the plug, Teri," he said as if he heard her thoughts. "Have you ever been fucked in the ass before? You may respond."

Her throat already felt rusty as if from disuse. "No, Master."

"Good. Now for your punishments." He moved away again and Teri felt real fear rise up within her. "The blindfold, the cuffs, the nipple clamps, the dildo, the butt plug and now the flogger shall be suitable," he said.

Her whole body went tense.

"I'm going to teach you a lesson now, slave." He pressed something firm yet soft—a ball—against her lips. "This is a gag ball to help you hold back your screams."

Her heart was going like crazy as he forced the ball into her mouth. How could she shout her safe word now?

Then he pressed a piece of cloth into her hand. "As you cannot speak, slave, I've given you a scarf. If at any moment you want me to stop and end this night, drop the scarf. Do you understand?"

Some relief trickled through Teri even though her fear was at its highest for the evening. She nodded.

He again trailed the flogger over her ass. "When I say it will end, Teri, I mean it will end. The moment you drop the handkerchief, the moment you say your safe word, you will return to your hotel room."

Teri felt a strange sense of loss at that thought. Like she wanted this. Needed this. She was so close to coming, with her pussy and ass filled, her nipples aching from the clamps, her body wide open and exposed to him in this position.

"Relax, slave," he murmured as he rubbed her buttocks. "It's going to hurt a lot more if you tense up."

She tried to relax like he instructed, she really did, but her whole body was like a coiled spring.

"One more thing, slave." He reached under her and pulled on the chain between the nipple clamps and she gave a moan behind the gag ball. "You may not come without my permission."

The flogger tickled her ass as he trailed the soft strands over her skin. The feel of it was soothing and erotic.

But then one lash hit her, then another. She shouted her surprise, but it was muffled by the ball. They burned, but not too badly, and she felt herself growing wetter.

A lash landed harder this time against her ass and she screamed against the gag ball. This one *really* burned. It hurt so bad tears flooded her eyes behind the blindfold. She almost let go of the scarf that she was gripping tight in one hand. Another lash fell, this one right at that spot between the butt plug and the dildo. Again the burn, but this time pleasure hummed along her skin, too.

"Will you behave now, slave?" he said as another lash hit her.

She nodded. Yes, yes, yes! She'd do whatever he wanted of her.

But he flogged her over and over, each lash landing in a different area, never the same place at once. She couldn't believe the pleasure that came from the pain. How could it feel so good? The need to climax was building up so intensely within her that she clenched her pussy tight around the dildo as if that might keep her from coming.

But the more lashes that fell, the more she needed to reach orgasm. She wanted to beg him to stop, but the gag ball was in her mouth, and she couldn't tell him she was so close to climax.

Her legs trembled so badly she was afraid they might slide out from under her. Surely he knew she was close.

He landed another lash to that place between the dildo and the butt plug and she lost it.

Her orgasm rocketed through her body. Her channel clenched and unclenched around the dildo, and her anus throbbed around the butt plug. Fire licked her body and she trembled so badly that her legs did give out and she slipped so that she was flat on her belly. Her body continued to buck and shake until finally the last wave vanished.

God, it was the best orgasm she'd ever experienced in her life.

Josh moved before her, and yanked off her blindfold. The light seemed so bright now.

She squinted and blinked. When she rolled just enough to see his handsome face her heart nearly stopped beating at his angry expression.

"You were a very bad girl, Teri." He reached beneath her and tugged on the chain that pulled on her nipple clamps, causing her to cry out behind the gag ball. "Now you'll receive a *true* punishment."

Chapter Four

ℬ

When he was out of Teri's range of sight, Josh smiled in satisfaction. She was the perfect submissive. He didn't know anything about this woman other than the fact she was a corporate lawyer, she had family in Minneapolis and lived in Los Angeles, and the fact that although she might be new to BDSM—she was born for it.

Josh reached around and removed the gag ball from her mouth and she gave a shuddering sigh of relief. He slipped the slick dildo from her pussy. He considered taking out the butt plug, but decided to keep her on edge. She had another punishment in order, and he planned to make it one she'd never forget. Hell, this night was one she'd never forget and neither would he.

He left the leather cuffs on her wrists as well, keeping her arms bound behind her back. He helped her ease up from the floor onto her haunches. Her green eyes were dilated, her lips wide and inviting, and one cheek was red from being against the carpet.

And her back, thighs and buttocks were covered with his marks. Light pink stripes that looked beautiful against her pale skin.

He tugged on the silver chain between the clover clamps, and she bit her lip hard to keep from crying out. Her engorged nipples needed circulation and he unclamped one after the other. He knew she'd feel a moment of intense pain before pleasure and relief. The watering of her eyes and the intensity of her expression told him he was correct.

He brushed a tear from her eye with his thumb. "Remember, you always have your safe word, Teri."

She nodded, but said nothing.

His slave for the night was so beautiful and his cock was so damn hard. He stood in front of her, unfastened his belt and opened his jeans to set his cock and balls free. Teri's eyes widened and her lips parted.

"Let's see how good you give head, slave." Josh gripped her hair and brought her to his erection. He forced himself between her lips and slid to the back of her throat. She gagged a little, but began swirling her tongue along his length and applying suction. Damn, but her mouth felt so good around his cock. "Yeah, that's it, slave. I'm going to fuck your mouth before your next punishment."

Josh kept his grip on her hair, keeping her still as he thrust his cock in and out of her mouth. He was careful not to go too deep, not wanting to hurt her. The pressure, the need to come was unbelievable. "Look at me," he demanded when she lowered her gaze.

She brought him closer to peak as he watched the wide green eyes that were focused on him. Seeing his wet cock sliding in and out of her beautiful lips brought him that much closer to climax. To have this powerful woman on her knees before him was an aphrodisiac in itself.

He fucked her mouth faster, the climax building within him so great that he ground his teeth. "I'm going to come on your breasts, Teri," he said and pulled his cock out of her mouth just before he lost it. His balls drew up and intense sensation burst from his sac to the head of his cock. His fluid jetted onto her breasts. His body jerked as each spasm of his climax rolled through him.

When he had spent himself, he was breathing hard and a bead of sweat trickled down the side of his forehead. He wiped it away on his shoulder then tucked his cock back into his jeans and zipped up. He took Teri by her upper arms and drew her up to stand before him.

At that moment he wanted to kiss her so badly, to taste her mouth as much as he wanted to taste her pussy. But he was waiting. Making her wait.

"Did you enjoy sucking me off, slave?" Josh said as he trailed one of his fingers through the sticky fluid on her breasts.

She nodded and he could see the honesty in her eyes.

He gripped her by the arm and led her to the bedroom. She looked so incredibly sexy, naked and in only high heels, his collar and the leather cuffs.

After he wiped his fluid from her chest, he said, "Lie on your belly on the bed, slave. And don't move."

Josh had to help her scoot up so that she was facedown in the middle of the bed. He paused to admire his handiwork again and could just imagine how the sting on her backside was making her feel. No doubt her orgasm had left her feeling raw and on edge, and anything he did to her now was going to make it even more difficult for her not to come a second time without his permission.

He left her on the bed to move to his special suitcase full of tools of what he considered to be his craft, in addition to what he'd had in the duffel bag. He was an artist when it came to BDSM, turning his slaves into works of art, and no matter where he traveled, he took a good many of his tools with him—in case he went to a BDSM club and met a beautiful woman looking for a Dom.

The leather straps he needed were neatly folded to one side of the suitcase. When he returned to Teri, her eyes widened at the sight of the long strips of leather that had buckles on one end and clamps on the other. He didn't choose to enlighten her. Instead he proceeded to fasten each of the leather straps around the lower legs of the bed. It wasn't a four-poster, of course, so he needed another method of restraint.

To her credit, Teri remained quiet as he worked, but he saw how hard she was breathing by the movement of her back. He smelled her rich musk and the scent of her skin mixed with her perfume of orange blossoms. Her dark hair was loose and wild around her shoulders and her green eyes were wide as she watched him.

After he was done attaching the restraints to each leg of the bed, he grabbed a couple of ankle cuffs. Starting with one ankle, he cuffed her, then hooked a leg restraint to it and tightened it so that she would not be able to move. In moments he had her other leg fastened. After unhooking her wrists, he moved them from behind her back to fasten them to the leather straps at the front bedposts.

When he finished restraining his new plaything, he stopped to look in satisfaction at her beautiful body spread out upon the bed. Her legs were spread so wide that her folds and clit were well exposed to him, as well as the butt plug that was still up her ass.

"Good girl," he murmured as he rubbed her flogged ass with his hand and felt her tremble beneath his touch. Her skin was smooth to his callused palm, but he felt the warmth from the welts he had raised. Just touching her and seeing her that way made his cock grow hard again.

He turned away from her and headed for the suite's bar and refrigerator.

Teri didn't know whether to laugh or cry. All she knew was that she was being erotically tortured, she'd had the most incredible orgasm of her life, she'd just given him head and it had turned her on to see him spill his fluid on her chest. And now here she was, strapped facedown on the bed, spread-eagle. She was just as open and vulnerable as she had been when he had her on her knees, face to the floor and blindfolded.

Her skin tingled when Josh walked away, his footsteps muffled by the carpeting. How was he going to torture her next? Would he whip her this time? Oh, God, would it hurt?

What he'd done to her so far—it had been incredible. She never would have believed she'd enjoy sexual pain, but she had. It had actually been *pleasurable*.

She'd wanted to fuck a stranger, and she'd definitely gotten more than she'd bargained for.

When Josh came back, he came up beside her to where she could see. He was carrying an ice bucket and a bottle that looked like champagne. He set the champagne bottle and a cork remover on the nightstand, along with a few foil packets.

Her heart thudded. He wasn't planning on fucking her just once.

He took the ice bucket with him as he moved behind her and out of her range of sight. "You're going to tell me about yourself, slave," Josh said as the bed sank beneath his weight. He was sitting between her splayed thighs. "I want to know everything about you while you receive your punishment."

Well, that was the last thing she'd expected. "Yes, Master." She licked her lips as she anticipated what he was going to do next. "What would you like to know?"

"How about your childhood, Teri?" he said just before she felt something so cold against her ass that she had to choke down a cry.

It had to be ice that he was stroking her buttocks with. The freezing chunk of ice contrasted with the burn she still felt from the flogging. It gave her a different sort of pain and pleasure.

"I—" She gasped as he circled the butt plug with the ice and paused at the sensitive area between her pussy and her anus. "Um, I was born in San Diego."

Cold water from melted ice dripped down her body. "Tell me about your family."

Well, what could it hurt? If they could be this intimate, she could share a little about her history. "My dad left me and my mom and sister when I was just a kid," she said, "and I never saw him again. I lived in San Diego until I was eighteen and went to UCLA, and my mom passed away just a couple of years later."

She paused and made a hissing sound as he stroked the crevice between her thigh and pussy with the ice. "What next, Teri?" he asked.

"When I-I passed the bar exam, I went straight to work for the firm I'm with n-now." She was having a *really* hard time talking the way he was trailing the cube down the inside of one thigh, to the back of her knee and down her calf to her ankle. "I, um, do a lot of traveling, Master."

Josh slipped off her high heel just before he ran the ice cube along the arch of her foot. She couldn't help the giggle that spilled from her lips, or stop herself from jerking her ankle against the restraints. She thought she heard amusement in his voice when he added, "Now I know you are ticklish." He moved to her other foot, flipped off her shoe, and ran the ice down her arch, causing her to giggle and squirm again. "Very ticklish. I wonder where else you are?"

She wasn't about to tell him that. Not until he said, "Tell me, Teri. I'll know you're lying if you do. Where are you ticklish?"

Ah, man. "My knees and my underarms, Master."

"Very good."

She heard the shift of ice against ice in the bucket and then he was applying a bigger piece to her leg. She shivered from the cold, and her body ached so badly to be fucked. This waiting, the way he was drawing it out, the ice freezing and biting her skin and melting—all of it was driving her crazy.

"What about *you*, Teri?" he asked as he reached the inside of her other thigh.

"Well…" Jeez, what was there to her other than her job? "I don't really have any kind of social life. I don't know my neighbors, and like I told you, I don't have any pets." Her voice shook as he reached the lip of her pussy. "I guess I'm boring, Master."

"Oh, I think you're anything but, Teri," he said just as he pressed an ice cube against her clit.

Teri cried out at the extreme sensation of ice against her sensitive flesh. *Oh. My. God.* Her clit was on fire, it was so cold. He held it there and the fire turned into a cold numbness that had her trembling.

"What makes you tick, Teri?" He forced the ice tighter against her clit. "Not your job, not material things. What's inside of you?"

She was having a *real* hard time focusing on his question. When the words finally came out, they surprised her. "I-I'm outwardly forward, but inside I'm really hesitant. I don't make friends easily."

"Why do you think that is, Teri?" he said.

For some reason it felt freeing to tell this stranger her deepest feelings. "It's because I'm afraid of…rejection."

He moved the ice cube away from her clit and her muscles went slack with relief. She heard the ice bucket again, and then he stuck a large, smooth piece right at the entrance to her pussy.

Oh, God. Again the sensitive flesh around the opening was on fire and hurriedly becoming cold, then numb. Her pussy clenched and unclenched around the ice.

"You're afraid of commitment, too, Teri," he stated as he pushed the ice in deeper. "That's why the thought of fucking a stranger appeals to you."

That familiar heat rose to her cheeks despite the cold. She swallowed as she fought off the sensations the ice was creating in her body. It was barely inside her, yet she felt it all the way to her belly.

"I guess so, Master," she mumbled. "I travel too much, and, well, it's just easier this way."

"You don't have to worry about anyone leaving you, or dying on you, isn't that right, Teri?"

The bluntness of his statement overwhelmed her. Was that why she shied away from relationships? Because she'd been hurt too many times?

"Teri..." he said with a strong note of warning in his tone.

"Yes, Master," she said quietly.

"Good girl." He moved the ice from her pussy up to her anus where the butt plug was still filling her. "Would you like me to fuck you now, Teri?"

"Yes, Master." Teri shivered again from the cold of the ice.

"I'm not finished with your punishment."

Chapter Five

ꟷ

Josh got up and moved away and Teri almost banged her head against the bed in frustration. This man was drawing out her erotic torture the same way he was drawing out the darkest thoughts from the depths of her soul.

When he returned he was out of her line of vision still, so she didn't know what he had planned this time. He removed the butt plug and she felt an aching emptiness. But then he shoved something much larger into her anus, and she screamed in surprise and pain.

She choked back a sob as her body conformed to the larger butt plug, and it didn't surprise her this time when she began to enjoy the sensation of it being deep in her ass. Even the burning from its entry didn't bother her after a few moments.

Josh came up beside her and grabbed the bottle of champagne from the nightstand, opened it and raised the bottle over her back. Slowly he poured it along her spine, over her buttocks and down into the folds of her pussy.

Teri's reaction was immediate. She cried out and thrashed against her bonds from the feel of the champagne bubbles and the cool fluid. She moaned and shivered as Josh began to flick his tongue along her spine, slowly licking up the champagne.

She discovered she had another ticklish spot—right at the base of her spine. The feel of him lapping up the fluid made her squirm.

He grabbed the end of the butt plug in his hand and thrust it in and out of her ass a few times as he moved his mouth close to her folds.

Teri was trembling all over from the feel of his tongue along her skin, the butt plug fucking her ass, and now his mouth so close to her pussy.

"Mmmm, champagne and woman," he said just before he buried his mouth against her pussy.

"Josh!" she cried out as his tongue began to lap her folds. He paused and she hurried to say, "Master, I mean Master."

He gave an approving rumble and began licking and sucking at her folds. He paused only long enough to say, "Don't come without permission, slave. Remember that."

Teri moaned. She was so close, so turned on, so out of control. She jerked against her restraints and writhed beneath his tongue. She'd get so close and then he'd back off before starting the torture again, as if he sensed her body's needs. The smells of sex, of champagne, of Josh's masculine scent enhanced every sensation.

The pain of the flogging, the ache from the nipple clamps, the intense feeling of the butt plug—all of it added together to make her completely crazy with desire.

She was so sure, so sure she couldn't take it anymore when he finally stopped. Sweat rolled down her cheeks, she was covered in perspiration, and the sheet was damp and cool against her skin from the melted ice. Her whole body trembled.

He moved to his suitcase again and this time he brought back a leash and clipped it to the D ring on her collar then let the leather lie along her back, nestled in her ass crack. He stood at the head of the bed, by her face. His icy gray eyes studied her as he unfastened his pants again and released his cock and balls. *Damn*, did he have a nice cock—she'd really enjoyed giving him head.

He tore open one of the foil packets and sheathed his erection with it. Her anticipation grew as he moved behind her and between her splayed legs. She felt his hands at each ankle just before he released the restraints. Her legs were free.

"On your knees," he commanded, but he helped her at the same time. Her arms were still stretched out, and one cheek was against the bed.

When her ass was high in the air she trembled with excitement. He was finally going to fuck her. She'd finally feel him deep inside her pussy.

He removed the butt plug and tossed it onto the floor. Before she had a chance to take a breath, he drove his cock into her ass.

Teri screamed. Fire, burning, then pleasure as he began to pump in and out of her. He grabbed the leash and forced her head up as he fucked her ass. In the position she was in it was uncomfortable having her head pulled up, but she was so lost in the moment she didn't care. He fucked her long and hard, reaching a spot inside her that she'd never known could be so pleasurable.

"That's it, slave." Josh slammed his hips harder against hers, his balls slapping her. "Take my cock. Take me deep inside your ass."

She moaned and squirmed feeling the need to climax so badly she could hardly stand it.

It took all Josh had to pull out before he came. Damn, this woman was sexy. She just might be what he'd been missing. He'd had lots of sexy women before, but intuition told him there was something special about Teri.

He released the leash and let her head loll forward. She was breathing hard and her body glistened with sweat.

After Josh climbed off the bed and disposed of the condom, he unfastened the wrist restraints and removed her cuffs. The only thing he left on her was his metal-studded collar.

"On your back, bend your knees and keep your legs open wide," he ordered.

Teri obeyed, and when she was settled he took the opportunity to view her beautiful body. Her skin was flushed, her green eyes dark with desire, her brown hair in a silken mass against the white sheets.

He left her for a moment then returned with two champagne glasses. He reached for the champagne bottle, poured what was left into the glasses. But rather than offer one to Teri or take a drink himself, he moved between her thighs and slid the neck of the bottle into her pussy and started fucking her with it.

She cried out and grasped the bed sheet with her hands, her knuckles whitening.

"Do you like this, slave?" Josh asked, keeping his eyes always on Teri, watching her for any signs of discomfort. "Do you want me to keep fucking you with the bottle?"

"Yes." Teri moaned with every impact of the champagne bottle. "But I'd rather have *you* fuck me, Master."

Frankly, he couldn't wait any longer. His control had been tested to the limit. He tossed aside the bottle and it landed with a thump on the carpet. In just a matter of moments he'd stripped out of his clothing and stood at the foot of the bed, his cock hard and ready to fuck her.

Teri took in Josh's naked, athletic body. He was muscular, fit, and so damn good-looking. She took all of him in, from his blond hair, to his ice-gray eyes, broad shoulders, trim hips and athletic thighs.

Her pussy was drenched from all the erotic torture and her nipples still ached from the clamps. Her backside burned from the flogger, yet she felt chilled from the ice. It all combined to make her so incredibly horny that all she could think about was Josh's cock in her pussy.

Josh took a moment to sheathe himself with another condom and then he was back between her legs. He drew her down so that her ass was resting on the edge of the bed and her knees bent close to her chest. Her breathing quickened as he pressed his hips between her thighs and his gray eyes held hers.

He lowered himself so that his hands were braced to either side of her shoulders, and his face was close to hers. "You make a very good slave, Teri." He brushed his lips lightly over hers, and it tickled her lips when he said, "Have you enjoyed being my plaything?"

"Yes, Master," she whispered just before his mouth took hers.

After all they had done together tonight, this was the first time he had kissed her. And God, what a kiss. It was a gentle exploration, not the forceful domination that she'd expected. He tasted so good. Of male and champagne, and her, too. He bit her lower lip, just hard enough to make her sigh.

When he rose up he kept his gaze fixed on hers. He positioned his cock at her entrance, sliding in just a fraction, just enough to make her squirm in anticipation. She needed him deeper, needed him *now*. He hooked his arms under knees, raised her up high, and drove his cock into her pussy.

Teri cried out at the exquisite sensation of him thrusting in and out of her. The way he was holding her, the way he was looking at her, this was not a Dom and his slave. This was a man and a woman.

He fucked her long and slow and she gripped the sheets to anchor herself. He filled her so perfectly, so thick and so long.

She drew closer and closer to climax.

"Squeeze your nipples," he said in a husky voice that didn't sound like a command. It sounded more like desire, like he needed to see what she looked like when she touched herself.

Teri brought her hands up to her breasts and cupped them before she pinched her nipples and gave a loud moan. They were still sore from the nipple clamps, but the added sensation of her squeezing them while she was being fucked made her wild for her orgasm.

Higher and higher she climbed. It was like she was flying. She was ready to beg him to let her come. He fucked and fucked her, harder then harder yet. Faster and faster yet.

When her thighs started quivering in his arms and she knew she was almost to the point of no return, Josh thrust even harder into her. "Come for me, Teri," he said. "Yes, baby, come for me."

Her orgasm slammed into her like a tidal wave. It was like she was being turned inside out and then back again. Josh kept pumping in and out of her until he shouted and his cock throbbed inside her. Every pulse of his cock matched the contractions inside her channel.

Finally, he released her legs and withdrew his cock. He tossed the spent condom aside, then caught her up to him so that her thighs were clamped around his waist and he was carrying her to the side of the bed. With a groan of male satisfaction, he rolled them both onto the bed and arranged them so that his body spooned hers. She snuggled into his embrace and gave a long, relaxed sigh.

Being fucked by a stranger had never felt so good.

Chapter Six

ꕥ

Teri grabbed her two-piece fitted suit for the final day of negotiations. During the week she'd spent her days negotiating contracts—

And her nights at Josh's mercy.

After the second night together they had moved all of her things to his room, and she had given complete control over to him—in the bedroom. She wasn't a lifestyle sub and didn't think she could be. But God, how she loved it in the bedroom.

While she fastened her garters, Teri relived that first night they'd been together, after they'd fallen asleep. They had awoken during the night and Josh entered her, treating her gently like a fragile object, even though he knew just how rough she'd enjoyed it. After she came in yet another spectacular orgasm, they snuggled together once again.

Only this time they talked into the early hours of the morning.

By the time they had each ended up spilling their hearts and souls to one another, Teri had been drained. She fell asleep, still in his arms, and happier than she could remember being in a long time.

Teri smiled as the skirt of her suit slid over her naked ass. She'd taken to not wearing underwear while spending these wonderful days with Josh. She felt wicked when she was making presentations and handling negotiations in a roomful of mostly men. As always she was a professional—tough, and sometimes intimidating. But underneath, her pussy remained damp and she couldn't wait to get back to the hotel and Josh.

She put on the fitted suited jacket and frowned as she slipped the last button through its hole. Tomorrow she was scheduled to fly to New York City. Tonight would be her last night with Josh.

Would he want to see her again, when she was in Los Angeles?

She'd only known the man a week, but she hated the idea of not seeing him again. At the thought she accidentally jabbed her scalp with the clip as she put her hair up.

Tears moistened her eyes from the pain and she let the clip drop to the countertop in the suite's opulent bathroom. She gazed into the mirror, seeing this time a woman who was well-rested and very satisfied. Had it been only a week ago that she'd stared at her reflection knowing she needed something else in her life?

"Teri," came Josh's voice from the bedroom, jarring her from her thoughts.

Her heart beat a little faster at the sound of his voice, and it pushed aside any thoughts of sadness at their parting.

When she reached the bedroom, her heart thudded even more. Josh was holding a bouquet of yellow roses with sprigs of baby's breath. Her favorite color. Instead of a dominant look on his features, he looked almost boyish, hopeful.

She took the roses from him, inhaled their sweet fragrance then looked back at Josh. "Thank you," she said, and then noticed he was holding a long, flat, navy blue velvet box.

Her pulse rate kicked up. Josh took the bouquet from her trembling hands and set it on the vanity table. When her hands were free, he placed the velvet box in them.

"Open it," he said in a husky voice as she stood and stared at it.

She swallowed and lifted the lid, and caught her breath. Inside was what looked like a choker made from triple strands of fine gold. Gold and diamond bars were positioned around the choker, holding the three strands together.

When she raised her head, her gaze met his gray eyes. She'd never seen the look on his features that he had right now. Uncertainty.

"I want to see you again, Teri." He reached up and cupped her face in his hand. "Whenever you're at home in L.A., I want to be with you and to give us a chance to get to know one another better." He dropped his gaze to the choker. "This is a collar I had specially designed for you. If you agree to continue our relationship, I would like you to wear it."

Without even giving a moment's thought, Teri flung her arms around Josh's neck. "Yes," she murmured against his chest. "Yes to everything."

He drew back and took the box from her hands. While she watched, he slipped the collar from the box then set the box aside. He brought the collar to her neck, and she lifted her hair so that he could fasten it.

It settled around her throat perfectly. He turned her so that she was facing the vanity mirror and she brought her fingers up to trace the strands. "It's beautiful, Josh."

He took her by the shoulders and brushed his lips over hers. "*You're* beautiful."

Josh maneuvered her so that she was sitting on the edge of the bed. She was already in tune with his thoughts and hiked up her skirt to reveal her bare pussy. At the same time he unzipped his slacks and released his cock.

He slid into her wet channel, fucking her in a way that he'd never fucked her before. Slow and sensual, with a need and a sweet urgency.

His thrusts became deeper and harder and she rose up to meet every plunge of his cock.

Her orgasm came out of nowhere. She gave a cry and her body trembled beneath his. He thrust into her several times more before groaning with his own release.

The moment they could both catch their breath, Josh smiled at Teri. "You've just earned another punishment."

Teri smiled back. She couldn't wait.

About the Author

ꕤ

National bestselling author Cheyenne McCray is the award-winning author of sixteen books and six novellas. Among other accolades, Chey has been presented with the prestigious Romantic Times BOOKclub's Reviewers' Choice Award for "Best Erotic Romance of the Year."

Chey has been writing ever since she can remember, back to her kindergarten days when she penned her first poem. She always knew one day she would write novels, hoping her readers would get lost in the worlds she created, as she did when she was lost in a good book. Cheyenne enjoys spending time with her husband and three sons, traveling, and of course writing, writing, writing. Visit her website at www.cheyennemccray.com

Why an electronic book?

We live in the Information Age—an exciting time in the history of human civilization, in which technology rules supreme and continues to progress in leaps and bounds every minute of every day. For a multitude of reasons, more and more avid literary fans are opting to purchase e-books instead of paper books. The question from those not yet initiated into the world of electronic reading is simply: *Why?*

1. ***Price.*** An electronic title at Ellora's Cave Publishing and Cerridwen Press runs anywhere from 40% to 75% less than the cover price of the exact same title in paperback format. Why? Basic mathematics and cost. It is less expensive to publish an e-book (no paper and printing, no warehousing and shipping) than it is to publish a paperback, so the savings are passed along to the consumer.
2. ***Space.*** Running out of room in your house for your books? That is one worry you will never have with electronic books. For a low one-time c ost, you can purchase a handheld device specifically designed for e-reading. Many e-readers have large, convenient screens for viewing. Better yet, hundreds of titles can be stored within your new library—on a single microchip. There are a variety of e-readers from different manufacturers. You can also read e-books on your PC or laptop computer. (Please note that Ellora's

Cave does not endorse any specific brands. You can check our websites at www.ellorascave.com or www.cerridwenpress.com for information we make available to new consumers.)

3. ***Mobility***. Because your new e-library consists of only a microchip within a small, easily transportable e-reader, your entire cache of books can be taken with you wherever you go.
4. ***Personal Viewing Preferences.*** Are the words you are currently reading too small? Too large? Too... *ANNOYING*? Paperback books cannot be modified according to personal preferences, but e-books can.
5. ***Instant Gratification.*** Is it the middle of the night and all the bookstores near you are closed? Are you tired of waiting days, sometimes weeks, for bookstores to ship the novels you bought? Ellora's Cave Publishing sells instantaneous downloads twenty-four hours a day, seven days a week, every day of the year. Our webstore is never closed. Our e-book delivery system is 100% automated, meaning your order is filled as soon as you pay for it.

Those are a few of the top reasons why electronic books are replacing paperbacks for many avid readers.

As always, Ellora's Cave and Cerridwen Press welcome your questions and comments. We invite you to email us at Comments@ellorascave.com or write to us directly at Ellora's Cave Publishing Inc., 1056 Home Avenue, Akron, OH 44310-3502.

Kate Hill
Elemental Desires
Lora Leigh

Cerridwen, the Celtic Goddess of wisdom, was the muse who brought inspiration to storytellers and those in the creative arts. Cerridwen Press encompasses the best and most innovative stories in all genres of today's fiction. Visit our site and discover the newest titles by talented authors who still get inspired - much like the ancient storytellers did, once upon a time.

ELLORA'S CAVE
ROMANTICA PUBLISHING

Your G.U.I.D.E. to
Type 1 Diabetes Management

Achieve world-class A1Cs,
sleep better, & live more!

Illustrated for easy learning

MATTHEW J. COLLINS

T1D since 1997, low 5% A1C

Written & illustrated by Matthew J. Collins, Type 1 diabetic.

www.T1DPro.com
www.T1DPro.com/blog

ISBN: 987-1-7342640-0-5
EBOOK ISBN: 978-1-7342640-1-2

First Edition

For my daughter, Martina, and my wife, Bárbara.
You are the reasons I will always do my best to keep my blood sugars tightly controlled. Thank you for your support.
Les amo mucho!

Special thanks to my mom and dad, Dorie and Jeff Collins, for being the best parents a T1D guy could ask for. I love you both and owe a great deal of my success to you.

SUPPORT YOUR LOCAL CHAPTER OF JDRF AT WWW.JDRF.ORG
A portion of author royalties is donated to JDRF.

Table of Contents

Diet

Exercise

The "Free" 8 Hours

Closing Thoughts

First Things, First

Type 1 diabetes (or, T1D[1]) is serious. But it doesn't have to dominate your life. World-class blood sugar control is 100% possible by combining basic technology and healthy routines. To help give you confidence, I've tried to demystify a few common doubts T1Ds and parents usually have before diving into the world of Type 1 diabetes management.

Will I need an entire week to read this book and learn the methods for tight blood sugar control?

No. I wrote this book in response to requests from the T1D community, specifically to get you the answers you need as quickly as possible, with a no-nonsense approach. The purpose of this book is to help you achieve the best quality of life possible with a quick and easy manual directly from my point-of-view. The book covers my perspective on how to manage T1D—based on my experience.

I've been living with T1D for 21 years, with A1Cs in the low 5% range. T1D Pro could have easily been five hundred pages detailing examples of every topic I've learned about along the way. But I know you don't need an encyclopedia; instead, you need concise and relevant information. And you need it now!

To accomplish this, I outline the principles of the best T1D management practices as straightforwardly as I could. I provide a few case studies, as well, to clarify why specific topics are essential.

---

[1] T1D is an acronym for Type 1 Diabetes. AKA "Type 1."

Will tight control cost me a fortune?

No, not necessarily. Insurance certainly helps. But, depending on your setup, prices will range from inexpensive to very expensive. And I do mean *very* expensive, so choose wisely. To help you do this, I've included insights at the end of each chapter to highlight my T1D management system.

Do I need Einstein's IQ to achieve good results?

No! Through observation and consistent routines (which you'll learn in Chapters 2-5), I've been able to achieve near-perfect blood sugars for the past six years—with no severe lows. I'm certainly no Einstein, and you needn't be either.

Do I need a top-rated endocrinologist[2] to achieve tight control?

Nope, not that either.

While excellent medical teams can serve you well, I realize accessing them in remote parts of the world can be challenging. To assist, this book helps clarify your options for world-class control.

Tight sugars, everyone.

~ Matt

---

[2] Endocrinologists are doctors specializing in the endocrine (hormone) system in the body. They'll be your primary physician for T1D.

My Story

"I never dreamed about success. I worked for it."
~ Estee Lauder

Gunnison, Colorado
Age thirty-four (nineteen years post-diagnosis)

Splash!

All my senses were on fire. Every small movement or noise could be my next delicious dinner over the campfire. What didn't occur to me was whether my small fly rod would be able to handle a monster trout. My hiking friend, Craig, swung his camera into focus in anticipation of either me falling into the icy, high mountain lake or the unlikely event of one of us landing this beast of a fish.

It was early July 2017 in the Gunnison Range of Colorado. Vast swathes of snow still covered the mountains near our absurdly high altitude (12,000') campsite. Earlier in the summer, my buddy and I had decided to take a mini-backpacking trip, four days—and eighteen round trip miles of hiking, with a 6,000-foot elevation gain—to reach one of the best high-alpine fishing lakes in the world.
This was one hell of a climb.

Anyone who's ever hiked at altitude knows how tough it is. You feel weak, sometimes confused, maybe even a little sick—similar to the feeling of having low blood sugar. But carrying a

60 lb. bag with a tent, food, clothes, and fishing gear…umm, I mean diabetic supplies, was a whole other story.

So, how on earth could I, a Type 1 diabetic, make this happen?

"Matt, do you think you can handle this trip? I know you're a Type 1 diabetic and all. It's okay if you want to go on an easier route," said Craig.

"The chance to catch the biggest fish in Colorado? Let's go…It'll be a piece of cake," I replied. The pun was intended.

Slurp, slurp, slurp.

Now, the fish were taunting me. They were devouring something from the surface of the water, but I couldn't quite make out what it was. I needed to think. I needed to 'diagnose' the situation. I looked down at my fly box and grabbed my go-to fly in cases like this: The Royal Wolf, which is made to look like one thing to a fish…irre-sis-tible!

I peeked down at my Apple® Watch to check my sugars…108 mg/dl. Nice. A perfect blood sugar level. Just as I did this, a thought came to me:

> *What in the world would I be doing right now if I hadn't taken the time to understand Type 1 diabetes? What would this trip be like with sub-par A1Cs and constant blood sugar fluctuations?*

Just as quickly as the thought had arrived, it disappeared. And right when it did…Boom!

"Fish on!" And this thing was HUGE!

Thirty minutes, and about a hundred pictures later, I landed the biggest trout of my life, and all because I was able to control my sugars well enough to make the epic trip in the backcountry of Colorado. I was booming with excitement; a moment I'll cherish for the rest of my life.

My name's Matt Collins and I've been a Type 1 diabetic since 1997. At the time of writing this book, I'm thirty-six years old, married to the love of my life, Barbara—a veterinarian from Santiago, Chile. We spend most of our days in Miami, Florida with our—at the time of writing, in mid-2019—one-year-old daughter, Martina, and our dog, Bellota.

During the week, I work full-time for a major medical device company and play tennis competitively in the evenings. For vacation, we typically pack up the family (poodle and all) and fly to wherever we've scouted out the year before. Our most recent trip was to Tokyo, Japan during cherry blossom season (I highly recommend this).

For work, I'm on planes from Miami to (name just about any location in Latin America) about twice per month. Needless to say, I'm traveling a whole lot. Overall, life is good—despite T1D.

Why I wrote T1D Pro

In the winter of 2015, I started my Instagram account (@matt_t1d) to post tips and insights related to blood sugar control. Having several years of a solid understanding of the disease under my belt, I wanted to share what I had learned. I didn't think much of it at the time, wrongly assuming most T1Ds already knew everything I was delivering. What could I possibly share that could help anyone else?

To my surprise, though, within just a few months, hundreds of people all around the world started to follow my account because the global conversation related to blood sugar management *wasn't* being widely communicated. As my account grew, I started receiving requests from newly diagnosed T1Ds (and their parents) to document my methods for blood sugar management.

Since the first request, in January 2018, I've been carefully organizing my methods into what has evolved into the first edition of this book. I'm going to continue to document our T1D community's progress, which will further develop into future editions.

Full disclaimer: This is *my* process. Sponsors and companies do NOT influence my process or recommendations. I'm neither paid nor rewarded by any of the companies whose products I use.

Why you need this book!

So, here's where I get to brag a bit.

All of my activity is great. But in reality, it's all for naught if my blood sugars aren't super tightly controlled. You see, most T1Ds are unable to experience everything life offers because their blood sugars aren't well controlled. I, too, was one of these people until I discovered this reality—from the point of diagnosis, for T1Ds, blood sugar dictates both the feasibility and quality of everything we do. Yep. I do mean everything. Sports, emotions, social activities, behavior, school, travel—the whole shebang.

Before realizing this, I had missed way too many important moments in my life. Everything up to the point of good blood sugar control was marginalized due to less-than-optimal control. I had misunderstood too many important lectures in business school. I'd missed too many good nights of sleep. How many more home runs could I have hit? How many more fish could I have caught? Was I low during my wedding? Yikes...Enough was enough.

It was time for me to take control. And, that's exactly what I did.

With my new commitment to blood sugar excellence, and through careful observation and a bit of self-experimentation, I started to achieve near-perfect blood sugars and have kept it that way for the past six years. This, in turn, has led to what I consider, the highest quality of life I've had since being diagnosed in 1997. If only I'd discovered the truth sooner.

But, what does near-perfect blood sugars even mean? For me, I've been able to achieve A1Cs in the low 5.0%, with an average 'time in-range' of about 95% consistently. As a result, I've been able to travel the world, start a family, and achieve personal goals I'd never thought possible since being diagnosed twenty-one years ago.

Who needs T1D Pro?

T1D Pro best serves two primary audiences:

- T1Ds ready to take control and achieve world-class A1Cs, and
- Parents of newly diagnosed T1Ds

I firmly believe new T1Ds deserve the most attention since there is very little simple-to-understand information specifically about blood sugar control methods. And with this book, you have a chance to dramatically improve your child's quality of life or your own.

What you'll learn in T1D Pro

After analyzing all the inputs allowing me to achieve my success as a T1D, the same themes kept resurfacing. To keep this book as simple as possible, I narrowed down the most critical topics using the acronym GUIDE:

- **G**lucose Visibility
- **U**nderstanding
- **I**nsulin
- **D**iet
- **E**xercise

For better learning, however, the order of this book will read as UGIDE so you can cover *Understanding* first; a few basics of T1D need to be covered before everything else makes sense.

After that, we'll dive into *Glucose Visibility,* which is—in my opinion—the most essential tool for managing blood sugars. Finally, we'll close with two variables and another vital tool every controlled T1D must master; *Insulin, Diet,* and *Exercise.*

Now, put your learning caps on and prepare for *tight sugars*!

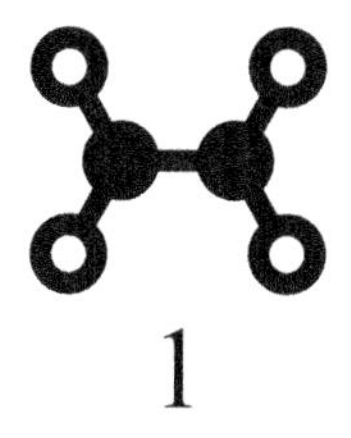

1

Understanding

"*Understanding brings control.*"
~ Bonewitz

"*Understanding can overcome any situation, however mysterious or insurmountable it may appear to be.*"
~ Norman Vincent Peale

Author's note: If you're already familiar with the basics of T1D I recommend skipping to the 'Goals' section at the end of this chapter. If not, start here.

So, what is T1D?

Simply put, T1D (or Type 1 diabetes) is a chronic condition in which a person's pancreas does not produce any insulin. Insulin is the hormone—created in the islet cells of your pancreas (or not, in our case!)—that regulates the amount of blood sugar in the bloodstream. Insulin acts as a bridge, allowing sugars in the bloodstream to move to the body's cells. It's only because of insulin that the body can use the sugar from food (aka glucose from carbohydrates) for energy.

Insulin needs to be administered by T1Ds to prevent blood sugar levels from rising too high (hyperglycemia). If insulin *isn't* present, blood sugar levels can quickly run wildly high and create all kinds of problems in our bodies.

At the moment, there's no cure for T1D, but as you'll see in this book, you can manage it very well with medical devices, insulin, and a robust set of sugar-controlling habits and behaviors.

FYI—there are two types of diabetes, Type 1 and Type 2. In this book, we're only talking about Type 1. For your knowledge, though, Type 2 diabetes occurs when the pancreas does make insulin, but the body doesn't *utilize* it properly (...unlike Type 1 diabetes in which our pancreas doesn't produce insulin at all).

But, so what? Why do you care that Type 1 diabetics can't produce insulin? Why is this important?

To understand this, you must first grasp a few basic concepts of what it means for you to be T1D and how your inability to produce insulin impacts your life. At the end of the chapter, I've provided recommendations around blood sugar management goals as a T1D, which lay the foundation for the methodology we'll be discussing in the rest of the book.

The basics - what's supposed to happen...

Let's begin by looking at what's *supposed to* happen.

For non-diabetics, the digestion process begins with chewing, swallowing, and breaking down food into a form that can be used for energy. During this process carbohydrates are converted to simple sugars and absorbed into the bloodstream.

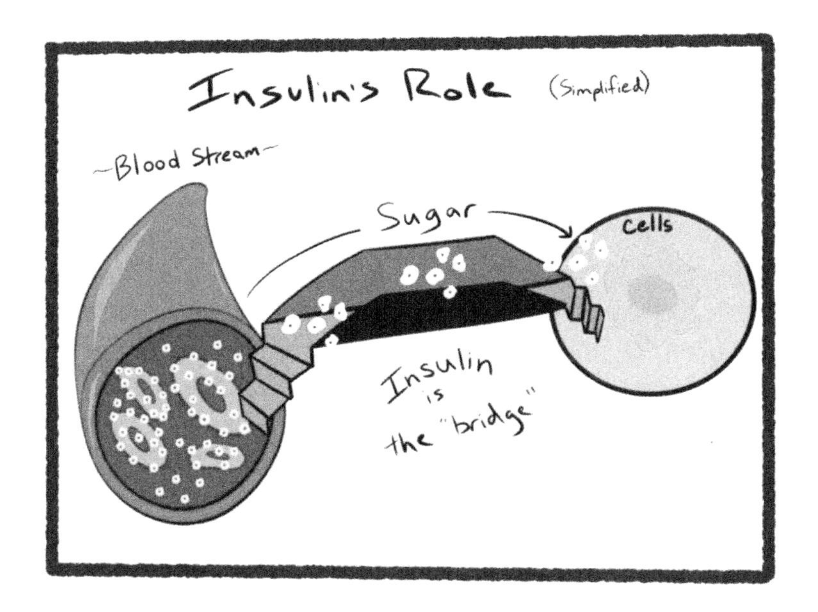

For *non-diabetics*, insulin[3] is then released from the pancreas' islet cells to enable sugars to travel from the bloodstream to the cells. Their cells are happy, and they might feel more energetic as a result of eating. All is well.

Remember; this is what's *supposed* to happen—and does happen—*for people who don't have Type 1 diabetes.* But with Type 1 diabetes, things are different. Here's how the process looks when you have T1D.

---

[3] Insulin is a hormone that acts like a bridge for opening the door to your cells. Insulin unlocks your cells' 'doors' in order to receive the sugars from your blood, thus lowering the amount of sugar in your blood, and energizing the cell.

Type 1 diabetic digestion of sugar

(Keep in mind, what's outlined below assumes the T1D is *not* aware of their condition and *not* managing with insulin.)

When a T1D eats, the process is the same as for a non-diabetic, until the broken-down sugars reach the bloodstream. When sugar reaches a T1D's bloodstream, their pancreas is unable to create or release insulin.[4] As a result, the sugar in the bloodstream remains in the blood, and blood sugar levels rise. If this continues for an extended period, the T1D's cells do not receive any sugar at all, potentially leading to life-threatening consequences.

Remember, cells *need* sugar to survive. Sugar serves as their preferred source of energy. But if cells can't receive energy from sugar in the blood, they'll look for other sources of fuel. In the case of unmanaged T1Ds, cells will take energy from the body's fat supply, and in extreme cases, from lean mass. When this happens, the body is in a state called diabetic ketoacidosis. Often, the T1D will lose weight, and if left untreated, diabetic ketoacidosis can lead to coma and death.[5]

Understanding A1C

Another basic concept you need to understand is the A1C test. As we'll discuss in Chapter 2, while being aware of your blood sugar levels throughout the day is essential for successfully managing T1D, it's also critical to get a general snapshot of your control over a longer period of time.

To do this, the medical community (and I!) recommend getting a test called an HbA1C, or A1C. An A1C is a measurement that conveys the percentage of hemoglobin in

---

[4] Simplified for easy understanding.

[5] https://www.mayoclinic.org/diseases-conditions/diabetic-ketoacidosis/symptoms-causes/syc-20371551

blood that is coated with sugar. Think of an A1C as your blood sugar report card. This report is generated via a simple blood test every three months to give you an idea of your control over that time.

A non-diabetic typically has an A1C between 4.7-5.6% (This is how we convey A1C in the US. It may be different if you're from outside of the US). At the time of writing this book, the global average of T1Ds' A1Cs is 8.6% , but improving quickly as access to medical devices and better insulin improves. If A1C levels are high it means, on average, the person had higher than normal blood sugar levels and need to work on lowering them. If A1Cs are lower it means, on average, the person had a lower than normal blood sugar levels and may need to watch out for low blood sugars. Either way, by knowing A1C levels, it's easier to make informed decisions about T1D management plans.

So, what changes blood sugar?

In the life of a non-diabetic, zero thinking is required to maintain perfect glucose levels. Everything happens automatically. Even better, when non-diabetics eat something with carbohydrates—another name for food with sugar—the exact amount of insulin needed is automatically released to the bloodstream, and as a result, blood sugar levels remain normal (between 80-120 mg/dl).

On the other hand, with a non-insulin producing pancreas, a T1D's life becomes an intricate balancing act. We T1Ds must stabilize a range of variables to optimize blood sugar levels. The two primary variables are insulin and diet (food and drink).

As a general rule, food with carbohydrates contains sugar, and when eaten—if you have T1D—will cause blood sugars to start rising if left untreated. Insulin, as discussed earlier, is the hormone that's supposed to be released by your pancreas to lower blood sugar levels. But T1Ds don't make any insulin. So, at a basic level, our job as a T1D is to figure out a way to perfectly balance the amount of sugar (carbohydrates) and insulin—to maintain the proper amount of sugar in the blood at all times.

But this can prove to be complicated. Give too little insulin (or eat too much), and blood sugar levels will remain high. Give too much insulin (or eat too little), and blood sugar levels will dip low. Thus, a balancing act is always in play.

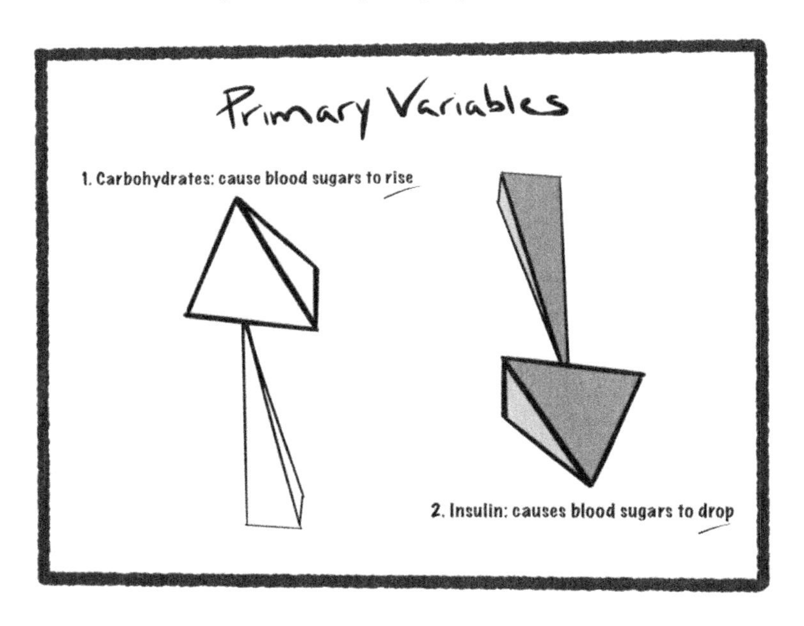

The scales and graphs below illustrate the primary variables of T1D when they're out of balance. In Example A, this T1D has either not used enough insulin or has eaten too many carbohydrates. As a result, they will experience 'high blood sugar' as seen in the graph. In contrast, in Example B, they've either used too much insulin or haven't eaten enough carbs. The result is a 'low blood sugar.'

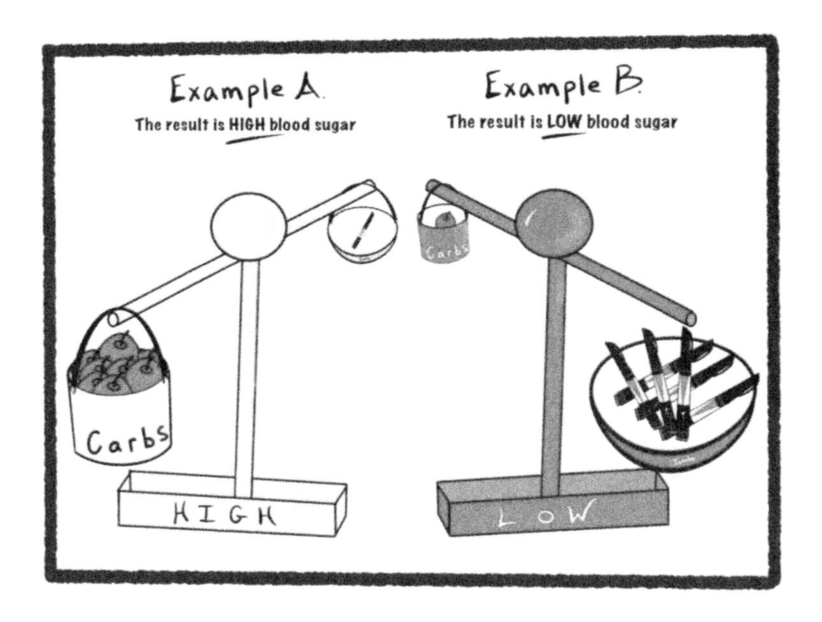

Sounds tricky, right? It certainly is if you're not aware of how to manage the variables. To make things easier for you, I outline exactly how I manage T1D, and the relationship between insulin and food, in Chapters 3 and 4, entitled 'Insulin' and 'Diet.'

Blood sugars affect everything

At this point, you might be wondering why it matters if blood sugars go high or low, and how that affects you day to day.

To best describe the importance of maintaining tight control, I've invited a T1D friend of mine, Chris, to give his personal account of what happens when he's too low (a term used to describe blood sugars are below 70 mg/dl) or high (when blood sugars are above our desired range; typically 150-180 mg/dl).

I found his reflection on the matter to be very much in line with mine. Here's Chris:

"When I'm too high, I feel lethargic, slow, and agitated. When I'm too low, I feel like I'm drunk...literally. I start sweating from adrenaline. I feel confused and can hardly speak. It's a scary feeling.

"As a real estate agent, I need to be in control at all times to give my clients the best experience possible. But, if I'm either high or low, I can't do that. To be my best, I have to maintain tight control. Otherwise, I could end up passed out on a seller's floor!

"I like to play basketball on the weekends and always make sure to have my blood sugars on-point before and during the game. If my blood sugar drops, you can be sure my game will suffer. I'll feel slow and tired, and before I know it, I've lost three games. It's not a good feeling. If I'm high, I'll probably suffer just as much due to the uncomfortable feeling. It's just not fun.

"The only way for me to sell the most houses, and win the most basketball games, is for me to stay in control of T1D. That's the ***only*** *way."*

Chris' point about blood sugars impacting all aspects of his life is not to be taken lightly. It's very easy to forget just how important it is to maintain good blood sugars. The truth is, our blood sugars affect the quality of sleep, sports, school, work, relationships, and yup…even sex. Everything.

Even with new gadgets and new insulins, it's common for T1Ds to suffer from poor, or complete lack of sleep, due to poor blood sugar management. But, we're going to change that.

Low and high blood sugar

I'm going to repeat myself here to make the point - even with new gadgets and new insulins, it's still common that T1Ds suffer the short-term, and sometimes even the long-term consequences of T1D due to poorly managed blood sugars. This is not meant to scare you, but rather bring awareness to what *could* happen if you blood sugars aren't controlled. The more aware you are, the better you'll be able to manage T1D.

To do this, I've outlined below the most common symptoms and the consequences of low, high, and healthy blood sugars.

Low Blood Sugar

Being low (or *hypo*glycemic) is the most severe state of blood sugar. Being too low (<70 mg/dl), at any time, can quickly turn into an emergency situation since your body always needs sugar in its blood to feed the brain and vital organs. It's also, in my opinion, the most annoying state of being for a T1D.

Being low inhibits a person from doing just about everything they know how to do and can very quickly turn into a dire situation. Due to the immediate severity of low blood sugar, we'll cover the symptoms and consequences of it first.

Low Blood Sugar Symptoms

When low, people generally start sweating and feel a jolt of adrenaline, (the body's natural way of alerting itself to get energy). Typically, this is coupled with a perplexed state of mind and often the onset of an unusually pale complexion. Sometimes, the pupils in the eyes will dilate, and the person will feel hungry.

(Put me in a café when I'm low, and I feel like I could eat everything on the menu!)

Other symptoms may include central nervous system (CNS) issues such as weakness, headaches and lethargy, dizziness, nausea, and a sense of feeling floaty or lightheaded. Stress-related symptoms might also emerge, such as irritability, nervousness, and anxiety.

Low Blood Sugar Consequences

While the symptoms of being low are uncomfortable, the short term/immediate consequences of being low are dangerous, and potentially deadly. Over my twenty years with T1D, I have, without question, failed exams, struck out in baseball games, and embarrassed myself in social situations all because I was low. Luckily, I've never faced the most serious of consequences. But going low happens to most of us and must be recognized.

The long-term consequences of low blood sugar are still relatively unknown. However, in 2007, a study by the New England Journal of Medicine concluded that while low blood sugars can cause nerve cell death, it does not have any impact on long-term brain function.

High Blood Sugar

High blood sugar (or *hyper*glycemia) occurs when blood sugars rise above the normal threshold. This typically occurs when a person doesn't have enough insulin to compensate for the number of carbs consumed. Other factors, like stress and sickness, can also cause blood sugar to rise too high.

High Blood Sugar Symptoms

Having high blood sugar feels uncomfortable. No—it feels downright *crappy*. High blood sugar symptoms include increased thirst, shortness of breath, vomiting and nausea, extreme tiredness and fatigue, pain in the stomach, a fruity odor to the breath, mouth dryness, abnormally fast heartbeat, and frequent need to urinate as the body tries to rid itself of excess sugar.

High Blood Sugar Consequences

This section might be hard for you to hear. But, as a person with T1D, you must understand the consequences of being high, so you'll make the best blood sugar management decisions.

Long-term consequences of high blood sugars will start to be realized after blood sugar levels have been elevated for extended periods - weeks, months, and years on end. An easy way to know if blood sugars have been too high, for too long, is via the A1C measurement.

As described earlier, A1C is a measurement of hemoglobin in your blood that's coated with sugar. By being high for long periods of time (say, over the course of three months), it allows more sugar to coat the blood's hemoglobin, thus raising A1C levels. This is very bad for a person's health and often leads to horrendous long-term consequences, including blindness, kidney failure, and amputations of extremities. A person with high A1C levels might experience difficulties with healing as well, which is why your endocrinologist typically checks your feet sensitivity when you visit.

But why do these issues occur? The reason is easy to understand with an analogy.

Think of it this way. What happens when you put a few small, rounded pebbles down a hose? Not much. The pebbles come out the other end without damaging the hose. Smooth sailing. Now, what happens when you try to put big, sharp rocks through a hose? The hose usually tears apart, and water leaks out. A similar thing happens to blood vessels when A1C levels are higher than normal. The glycated—extra sugar-coated—hemoglobin in the blood will slowly, but surely, tear apart vessels and nerves in your extremities, especially in the most sensitive like the eyes, feet, and kidneys.

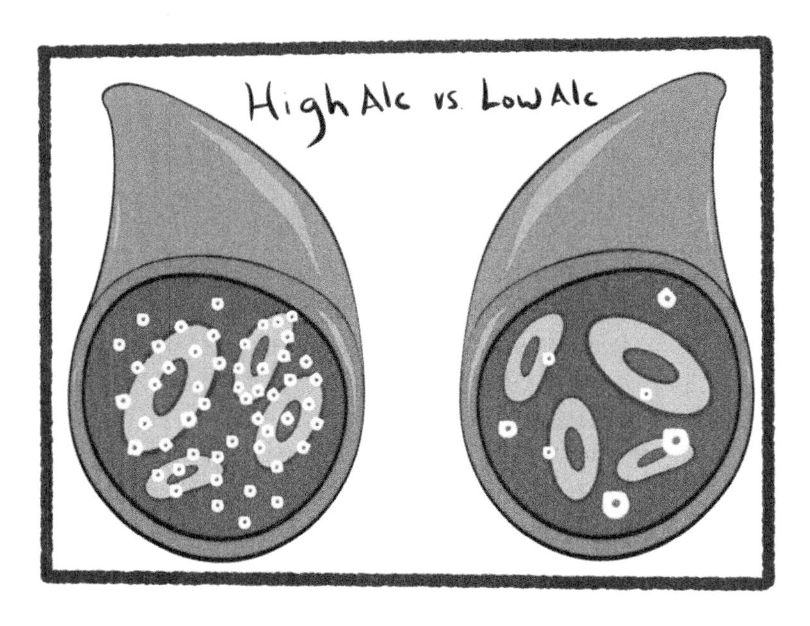

The *short-term* consequences of high blood sugar haven't been documented very well by the medical community. However, I can give you my opinion on the matter based on personal experience. Outside of heavy urination and feeling very irritable, I firmly believe that short-term high blood sugars can have a very damaging effect on nerves. I've noticed that if I go into the mid-200's, even for an hour or so, it takes me at least 24-48 hours for my sensitivity to completely recover.

Normal Blood Sugar

Believe it or not, there's good news to this story. And that is, T1Ds who can achieve normal blood sugars—80-120 mg/dl—and can routinely maintain them near there, feel exactly like they did before developing the disease. It might seem like common sense, but I've included this section to point out the fact that, yes, T1Ds can (and should) feel entirely normal with proper blood sugar management.

Before taking control, I felt "normal" about 50% of the time. Thus, I was probably in the normal range, about 50% of the time. That said, with the education and guidance you'll learn throughout this book, there's no reason you can't be in-range 80%+ of the time. I know first-hand this is possible. If I can do it, so can you!

Goals

Disclaimer:

Always consult your endocrinologist when deciding on your blood sugar targets. That said, I'm going to give you the down and dirty on the goals I've used to achieve low 5.0% A1Cs for the past five years. It's up to you to do all the necessary checks to be sure they'll suit you too.

At a fundamental level, my ultimate objective as a T1D is to maintain my sugars in the normal range at all times. (As a reminder, the normal range is 80-120 mg/dl.) But this is not realistic for me, or any T1D, 100% of the time.

Instead, I focus on the following three goals: 1) Low A1C, 2) Percentage of time in-range, and 3) Quality of life.

1) Low A1C

As a review, a T1D's A1C (or HbA1C) is a measurement that tells the percentage of hemoglobin in the blood that's coated with sugar. The A1C measurement is determined with a simple blood test every three months. The more hemoglobin in the blood that is coated with sugar as a result of high blood sugars, the higher the A1C result will be, and vice versa.

I have a personal goal to always maintain my A1C levels in 'normal range,' from 4.7–5.6%. This might sound like a tough goal to achieve, but from experience, I can tell you it's 100% achievable.

> Please note, this might even be different from what *your* endocrinologist recommends. The reality is, though, the closer you stay to the normal range, the better off you'll be in the long run when considering long-term consequences.[6]

2) Percentage of time in-range

While A1C is always going to be king, the concept of 'time in-range' is critical to understand as well.

When I was younger, my doctors and I used to think my blood sugar was in control because my A1C was relatively low. I would go into my endo appointments every three months and leave with congratulatory praise from my doctors because, at the time, A1C was the only thing that mattered.

If my A1C was low, nobody cared how I arrived there. What nobody realized, though, is that I never really felt 'normal.' I remember about half of high school and college schooling passing by in what I now know to be a state of

---

[6] As long as you don't go low. Going low while having great A1C's is hazardous and should be avoided.

groggy high blood sugar, or scary low blood sugar. I was correcting myself constantly with extra carbs and insulin. Of course, this state of being took a ton of time and energy out of me, and almost never landed me in a predictable state of *well*being—or 'in-range.'

As time went on, though, my ability to clearly visualize my sugar levels got better. I then realized a low A1C could be achieved two different ways. 1) A T1D can—as I did when I was younger—maintain blood sugar averages at a low level but have dangerously high standard deviations in blood sugar levels throughout the day. Bad idea. Or, as I do now 2) maintain blood sugar averages at a healthy level *and* have low blood sugar standard deviations.

Standard deviation stands for the variance in blood sugar numbers throughout the day. In the graph below, you can see my blood sugars were fluctuating throughout the day. In other words, I was riding the "blood sugar rollercoaster." In this example, my blood sugar levels averaged about 120 mg/dl. But, my standard deviation during the day was a whopping 80! This means my blood sugar levels ranged from as low as 40 mg/dl (120 mg/dl – 80 = 40 mg/dl) to as high as 200 mg/dl (120 mg/dl + 80 = 200 mg/dl). The result was that more than half of my day was spent either fighting a low blood sugar level with food, or a high blood sugar level with insulin.

Let me tell you; THIS IS NO WAY TO LIVE!

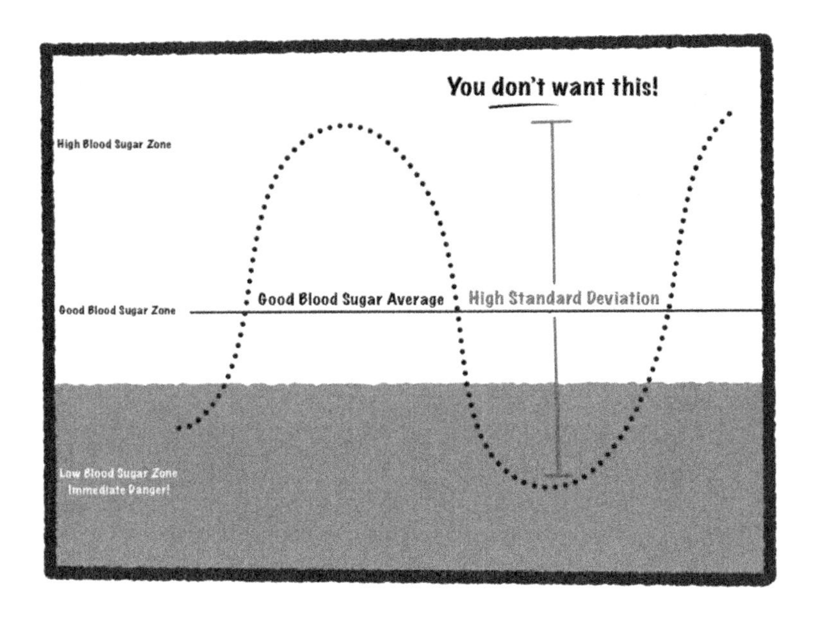

To fix this issue, I set myself a lower standard deviation target of 30. This means that with an average blood sugar level of 120 mg/dl, my blood sugar level range is narrowed from 90 mg/dl to 150 mg/dl. Therefore, my new 'in-range' blood sugar level is 90 mg/dl to 150 mg/dl. The more time I can spend *in this range*, the better I feel.

After understanding this concept, I realized that if I could spend every day with an average blood sugar of 120 mg/dl *and* be 'in-range', then I could also feel, act, and look completely normal 100% of the time; instead of just 50% as I did before. As a result, at the age of thirty-six, I'm playing the best sports of my life, sleeping better than I did before I was diagnosed twenty-one years ago, and I've been able to live my life the way I want to live it…a far contrast to my early years with T1D when each day was a challenge.

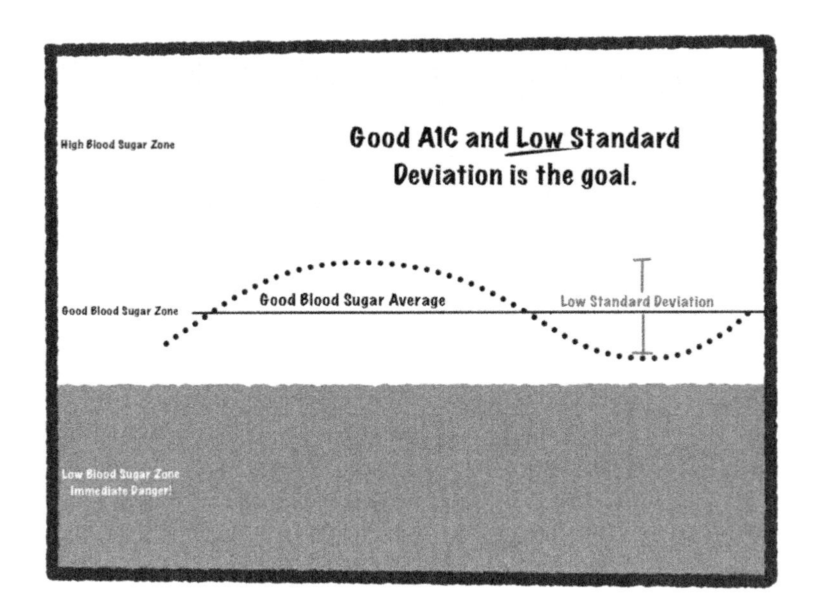

Please remember, though, that 'in-range' is a relative term since each person's target range might be different.

The actual *range* you choose is crucial to your success. For example, if you set your range too high, at 160-220 mg/dl, and your standard deviation relatively low, at 30, you're not doing yourself any favors. This equates to an average blood sugar level of 190 mg/dl. As a result, you'll risk negative long-term consequences due to having, *on average*, high blood sugar. Remember, 190 mg/dl is well above the normal target range of 80-120 mg/dl.

I can't tell you where to set your range. But as a reference, I set mine as close to normal as possible, at 90-150 mg/dl. This range gives me an average blood sugar target of 120 mg/dl and a standard deviation of 30. As a suggestion, you may want to start with a slightly wider range for yourself if you're new to the concept; perhaps try 80-180 mg/dl, giving you a larger standard deviation of 50.

You can tighten your range as you improve your T1D management.

3) Quality of Life

A lot goes into measuring the quality of one's life. But, for a T1D, I think the following two factors need to be the most carefully considered:

- *Time* spent managing T1D, and
- *Amount* of materials management— (sometimes there are a LOT)!

When thinking about quality of life, there are specific questions I ask T1Ds in my network, like: "What are your hobbies?" and, "How difficult is it for you to get up and travel on a moment's notice?"

If the answers are, "None" and "Impossible," their quality of life is probably taking a back seat to T1D management. This, in my opinion, is also no way to live.

Let me be clear. Nothing in the world matters more than your T1D management. But, if the method you choose to manage T1D ruins your quality life, you may want to consider different management methods. As you'll soon discover, there are several.

"*Much to learn you still have, my old Padawan.*
This is just the beginning."
~ Yoda to Luke Skywalker in Star Wars, A New Hope

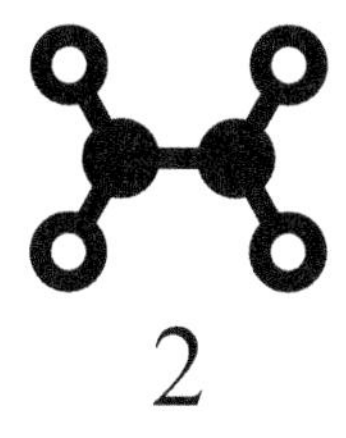

2

Glucose Visibility

"What gets measured, gets managed."
~ Peter Drucker

"Data data data. You can't make bricks without clay."
~ Sherlock Holmes

Now that you have a good understanding of T1D basics and what you're trying to accomplish, it's time to introduce what is, in my opinion, the most critical concept for achieving world-class blood sugars: glucose visibility. The notion of Glucose visibility involves knowing where blood sugars are now, where they are headed, and how they react to certain foods, insulin doses, and the plethora of other variables that could alter them.

Spot check/finger prick test

Until recently, the most popular method for checking blood sugar levels was though spot checks and finger pricks. With the spot check/finger prick method, T1Ds prick their finger, squeeze out a drop of blood, and place the blood on a test trip.

(The test strip works in conjunction with a blood sugar testing meter that calculates blood sugar levels in a few seconds.)

As you can imagine, this method is cumbersome and time-consuming. I'd even go as far as to say this method is actually a bit misleading for T1Ds since they only convey blood sugar levels at *single points in time.* They give you a snapshot of what blood sugar levels are at a particular moment. But they don't tell the entire story needed to manage T1D properly.

To understand this more clearly, imagine driving a car for an entire day on a curvy, mountain road, and having a goal to keep the speed between 70 and 80 mph. If you go below 70 mph, you crash. If you go above 80 mph, you fly off the road.

But, instead of having a normal speedometer that continuously displays the speed, you only get four read-outs of speed per day. This would be *really* difficult to do, wouldn't it? But this is what it's like trying to control blood sugars all day, every day, with just the spot check/finger prick method.

What people often forget about is that blood sugars, just like car speeds, move constantly. A lot is happening to your blood sugars between finger pricks. Even though a blood sugar meter may show a reading of 100 mg/dl—which is quite good if you remember from the goals section—blood sugars could be *rising or dropping* fast, without the T1D being aware. As a result, T1Ds who only use the finger prick method sometimes have a false sense of control. This was certainly the case for me when I managed my blood sugars using only this method.

I remember on so many occasions, feeling *horrible* shortly after an "in-range" finger prick reading, only to realize an hour later that I was actually rising or falling rapidly at the time of the check. The reality is, the only way to fully visualize blood sugars with the finger prick method is to check blood at very close intervals throughout the day; every five minutes or so. Neither practical nor fun.

The good news is there's a newer method (one that I adopted when I decided to seek optimal blood sugar control) to get a fully visible picture of your blood sugar using a medical device called a Continuous Glucose Monitor, or CGM. When reflecting on my quality of life as a T1D, moving from finger pricks to a CGM has, by far, made the most significant impact. Using a CGM has given me crystal clear visibility of my blood sugars and trends. But, most importantly, it has made T1D management, and my *life,* substantially easier.

Continuous Glucose Monitoring (CGM)

A CGM is a small device that uses an electrode underneath the skin to read blood sugars continually throughout the day. The electrode communicates with a transmitter, which sends a Bluetooth message to a receiver—or to a smartphone—about every three minutes to give maximum visibility of the blood sugar levels. If you choose to use your phone as the CGM receiver, blood sugars are displayed on an application via an easy-to-read graph of your glucose readings.

I recommend a CMG for all T1Ds looking to manage blood sugar levels actively. Since starting on a CGM in 2014, my blood sugar averages, and the related standard deviations, have been much lower. Most important, however, I no longer *feel* diabetic. I feel like I did prior to being diagnosed because my control is as tight as...well, a non-diabetic.

My work is easier, my relationships have improved, and most importantly, my quality of life is near-perfect. There are several features and benefits of a CGM that have contributed to my success, a few of which we'll cover here.

100% visibility = better management

Unlike the finger prick management system that only gives a snapshot of blood sugar levels at the time of the check, a CGM constantly monitors blood sugars and gives you a new reading every three minutes. Using a CGM is also much easier than the finger prick method. The entire "blood sugar checking" process is, basically, automated. As a result, with very little effort, I'm able to get 480 blood sugar data points per day. The impact of this kind of visibility for me is that I'm able to make better *decisions* about my management.

Think about the car analogy for a second. In this case, a CGM is similar to having a speedometer for the car that you're trying to maintain between 70 and 80 mph on a curvy, mountain road. With a speedometer, you'd know exactly where to hit the gas (eat) or pump the brakes (give insulin) at each turn to maintain the proper speed.

Trends = more predictability

The beauty of continuous blood sugar visibility is the ability to see where they're trending. This gives you the power to *predict* where they'll be in the future and make decisions *now* to achieve the best results.

The way CGMs communicate trends is by calculating the rate of change in blood sugars and displaying an arrow on the application corresponding to the rate of change. (Refer to illustration) If your blood sugar is increasing slowly, you'll see a slanting upward—diagonal—arrow. If it's rising rapidly, you'll see an upward—vertical—arrow. And if it's rising *very* quickly, you'll see two upward arrows. The same is true for blood sugars that are falling (i.e., if your blood sugar is dropping very rapidly, the application will display two downward arrows.[7])

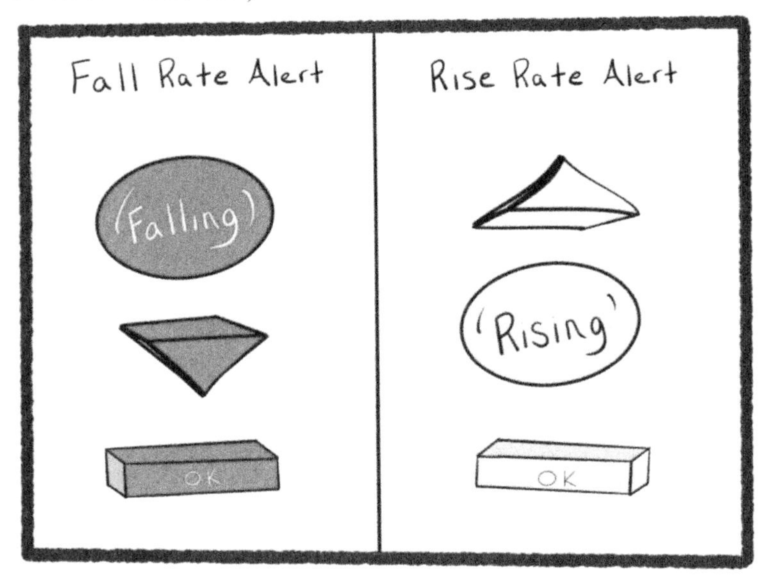

[7] This is my experience of using the Dexcom® CGM system. Other manufacturers' devices may vary slightly in their methods of displaying trends.

Alerts = fewer worries

Not only do CGMs make blood sugars visible, but they can also audibly alert you when sugars go awry. Most CGM applications include an alert system that plays sounds from the receiver or phone when high or low blood sugars occur. I use the Dexcom® system, which has an alert feature I set to notify me when my blood sugar is too high, too low, rising too fast, or dropping too fast.

On my system, I've set my low setting to 90 mg/dl and my high setting to 150 mg/dl. I think this is an excellent range to shoot for once you become used to managing sugars with a CGM. At first, you'll be a little surprised at just how much your blood sugars fluctuate. As a result, your alerts will be going off all the time if you set the range too narrowly. But, as time goes on and you become better at managing your blood sugars, you'll want to tighten your range.

Another analogy I like to give related to CGMs and alerts is that of how maps have changed over the years. For me, comparing the finger prick method of checking blood sugar to a CGM is like comparing paper maps to GPS (Google Maps). With a paper map, you have to periodically check for landmarks on the road to determine your location, whereas GPS guides you directly to your destination. They'll even alert you when you've drifted off course.

How many people get lost these days compared to the days of using paper maps? Not many.

Alerts are essential for me, and anyone who travels alone. I travel internationally for work regularly and often find myself alone in strange cities where only the front desk person at the hotel knows my name. They certainly don't know (or even care) that I'm T1D. But I still feel assured I'm going to be okay because I know my CGM will alert the heck out of me if I slip into a low blood sugar zone in the middle of the night.

Annoying? Maybe. Safer? Absolutely![8]

It's true. The alert system CAN be a little annoying at times. But it's VERY effective. Remember, the idea for the alert system isn't necessarily to make you happy, but rather to help you control your blood sugars within a specific range. And don't worry; the better you get at managing your blood sugars, the less often the alerts will sound.

---

[8] Make sure to bring chargers for your receiver or smartphone when traveling.

Some systems, like Dexcom®, have even taken their alert software a step further and have provided 'predictive low' alerts. Predictive low alerts notify users in advance of going low based on the trends the CGM shows. I think this is a *fantastic* new feature that should be taken advantage of by everyone who can.

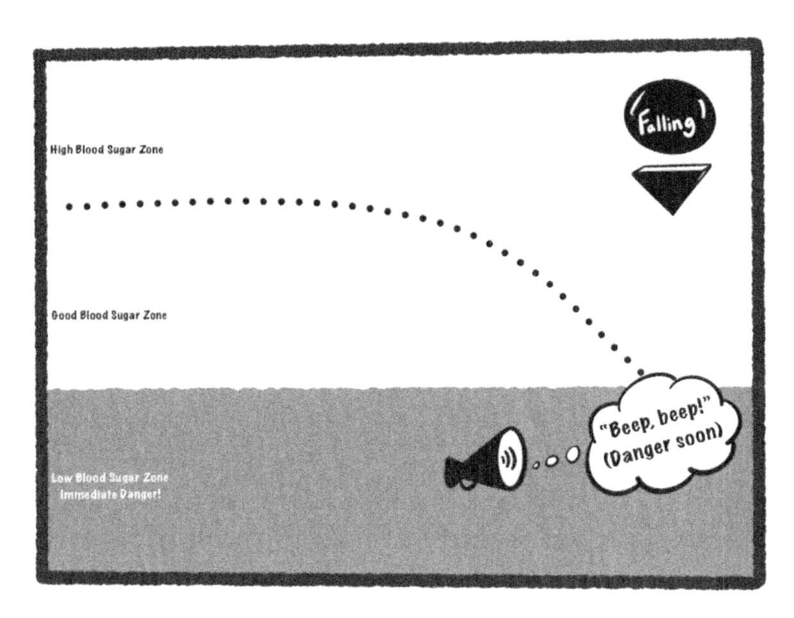

Live it, learn it

One significant benefit of CGMs that I've found is the ability to understand the *impact* of food and insulin choices by simply looking at the blood sugar graphs in the hours just after eating and giving insulin. When I first started using my CGM, more times than not, my assumptions about the way certain foods impacted my blood sugars, or my tolerance to insulin injections, was wrong. And, when first starting with a CGM, the graphs on the receiver proved it!

Sharing

Something I think could benefit T1D parents and friends is the "sharing" capability of the Dexcom® CGM system. Dexcom® has enabled T1Ds who use a smartphone as the receiver to share their blood sugar readings in real-time with anybody else with a smartphone.

(CGM manufacturers take advantage of the fact that the blood sugar data is in the cloud and use it to share the information. This could be extremely useful if your son or daughter heads to school or to a friend's house for a sleepover!) I use this feature when I'm traveling for work to share my numbers with my wife for safety reasons.

Case study – Why CGM's matter

In a recent study conducted by the American Society for Metabolic and Bariatric Surgery, (ASMBS) it was concluded that obese people in the United States are indeed very aware they are overweight—and, it's not until a life-altering event occurs that they'll begin to seek change to control their obesity. Maybe it's a matter of routine. Perhaps it's a lack of knowledge. Either way, it seems obese patients carry on day-in and day-out as if nothing bad is going to happen.

What ASMBS realized, though, is that when an obese patient finally experiences the day they can't pick up their kids anymore, walk out of the house, or have their first heart attack, things *do* change.

ASMBS sees a lot of patients at this point turn to bariatric surgery as a means of controlling their weight. But, in a lot of cases, permanent damage has already set in with the patient.

I think there are some definite parallels for our situation as T1Ds. I know from personal experience...

For fourteen years, I tested my blood sugar via the finger prick method. And, to be honest, everything seemed fine. Four times per day, I'd prick my finger, wait the five seconds for the glucometer to display my blood sugar levels, and off I went. And, that was the extent of my glucose visibility.

My A1Cs were in the mid-6.0% range, so of course, I was happy. I was satisfied because my endo was satisfied. My life did seem pretty good...because at this stage of my life as a T1D, 'pretty good' was what I was used to. 'Pretty good' was part of my routine.

It wasn't until my major life-altering event occurred that I changed my blood sugar management. When I was twenty-nine years old, I made a trip to Michigan to visit my grandmother in her nursing home with the rest of my family. It was 3:00 p.m., two hours after my last meal, and I began to feel a little "tired."

Maybe I'm just tired from traveling. Maybe I'm low, I thought. *Let me check myself to make sure.*

97 mg/dl.

Cool. I'm not low, just tired - Famous last words.

The next thing I remember is me flailing hysterically in the parking lot of the nursing home, passing out, and nearly cracking my skull open on the pavement. Nobody understood what was going on. All my family knew was that I had just checked my blood sugar and got a "good" finger prick reading. What nobody realized, though, is that blood sugars can change rapidly and I was crashing fast. I can't imagine what was going through their heads.

"Is Matt just going crazy? Is he just sad to see Grandma in the nursing home?"

Nope. I was trending dangerously low and didn't realize it because I had minimal glucose visibility via the finger prick method.

Looking back on the situation, I'm lucky to be alive. Just as I passed out, my older brother, JD, grabbed me and gently lowered me to the ground, called 911, and revived me with juice and a shot of glucagon. Thank God. Given different circumstances, I could've been unconscious in the street with no-one around to revive me.

(Which reminds me, if you don't already have a medical alert bracelet, get one! There are hundreds of vendors who sell them.)

Shortly after this event, I decided the risk of not having perfect visibility of my blood sugars far outweighed the perceived burden of wearing a CGM. So, the following Monday, I called my local Dexcom® rep and ordered their CGM system. Since then, everything has changed for the better. I never again experienced awkward social situations due to unknown low blood sugars. I never again had to wonder why at certain times things seemed so easy, and at other times the same task nearly impossible. I never again feared solo adventures.

Perfect glucose visibility also certainly helped me lower my average glucose levels *and* standard deviations. This, in turn, helped me reduce my A1C to the low 5% range. But, the real impact for me is that it made my *life* better. I finally realized how much easier work and sports could be. I had forgotten that sleeping through the night was a possibility!

Everything changed. For the first time since being diagnosed, I didn't feel 'pretty good.' I felt great!

...or at least, I didn't feel *diabetic* anymore because my control became so good as a result. Needless to say, for me, the CGM was a total game-changer.

If you find yourself wondering, 'Is a CGM right for me? Is this going to a pain in the butt to wear?' I'd strongly urge you to reconsider. I believe glucose visibility is the cornerstone of managing T1D. And the rest of T1D management becomes much easier because of having a CGM.

I highly recommend getting your hands on a CGM prior to an adverse event occurring. Don't wait until you find yourself in an uncomfortable situation due to unknown high or low blood sugars. The reality is that it only takes one bad episode like this to land in a hospital for the night, or even worse. Again, don't wait. Take action now and get the glucose visibility you need and deserve.

My Setup, as of September 2019[9]

At the time of writing T1D Pro, I'm using the Dexcom G6® CGM. I have used a variety of CGMs in the past and like Dexcom® the best. A company based in San Diego, Dexcom® has one sole focus: "to offer more value than any other glucose monitoring provider in the Continuous Glucose Monitoring market." I couldn't agree more.

I currently use my iPhone® as my primary receiver[10]. I also have an Apple® Watch version 2.0 that serves as my

[9] See Appendix A for a complete list of T1D Pro recommended products. I'm looking forward to your inputs as well!

[10] The receiver is where you actually see the glucose readings. Dexcom® provides you with a separate plastic receiver. That said,

secondary receiver. If I have my phone available, I can see my sugar levels on the Dexcom® app, or on the phone home screen. If I don't have my phone available, but it's still in the vicinity, I can also quickly glance at my watch where my glucose is displayed. This makes it very convenient during meetings or school to be able to see blood sugar levels without making it look like I'm playing a game on my phone.

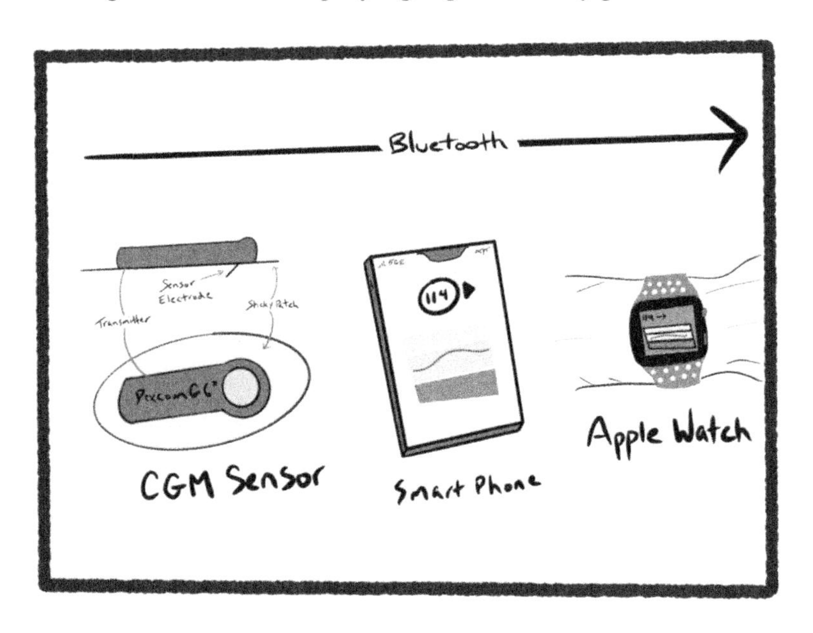

The settings I keep on the Dexcom® application are crucial. Remember, CGMs like Dexcom® alert you when your sugar levels are rising or dropping too quickly, or when you are too high or too low. All of this is easily adjusted in the application on your smartphone or the receiver.

I like to minimize the things I carry. To do this, I allow the Dexcom® system to communicate with my iPhone® so it can serve as my receiver. The way this works is that the CGM transmitter sends a Bluetooth message to the iPhone® and the blood sugars are then displayed on the Dexcom® application.

I have my settings as follows:

Low: 90 mg/dl
High: 150 mg/dl
Urgent Low Soon: On
Rise Rate: 2 mg/dl/min
Fall Rate: 2 mg/dl/min

I also keep the 'scheduled' alert active for evenings. The scheduled alerts allow the user to have separate alert settings for different times during the day. In my case, I keep a slightly higher 'High' setting for the evenings to give myself a little bit of leeway during the evenings, so I can sleep without an alert going off all night. To do this, I set my High alert for 170 mg/dl from 10:00 p.m. to 7:00 a.m. every day.

If you're interested in trying Dexcom®, head over to www.Dexcom.com to check out their products. If Dexcom® doesn't work for you, there are a variety of options out there. Do a little research and find one that suits your needs. The bottom line is; get a CGM and start using it ASAP!

T1D Pro tip

If you want to take glucose visibility to another level, download an app called Nightscout X.

Through this app, you can enable electronics in your house (like your TV or other displays) to show your CGM readings throughout the day. I have not needed to do this yet. But it sounds like an exciting idea. If you have tried this, I encourage you to share your experience on www.T1dPro.com.

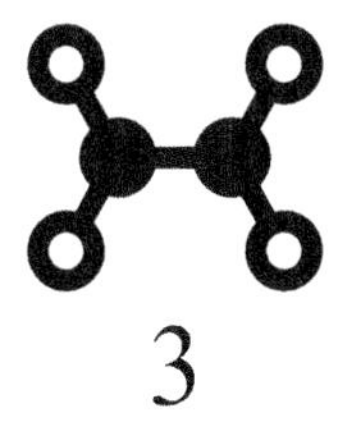

3

Insulin

"Whenever you find yourself on the side of the majority, it is time to pause and reflect."
~ Mark Twain

There are two primary variables every T1D needs to balance; insulin and food. In this chapter, I'll discuss insulin's role in T1D management and the popular methods of insulin delivery, followed by a step-by-step thought process to help you choose an insulin management system. And, as usual, I'll end with a review of my insulin delivery setup and why I chose it.

Insulin's role

If you recall from Chapter 1, insulin is a potent hormone that allows our cells to utilize sugars in our blood for energy. When a non-diabetic person eats something, the carbohydrates consumed are broken down into simple sugars, which are then absorbed into their bloodstream. At this point, the non-diabetic person's body calculates the *exact* amount of insulin required to maintain blood sugar levels somewhere between 80-120 mg/dl.

The problem we're faced with as T1D's is we *don't make any insulin*. Luckily for us, though, in the early 1920's, a physician named Dr. Banting successfully produced synthetic insulin for therapeutic use for Type 1 diabetics. Since then, several major pharmaceutical companies have manufactured and sold synthetic insulin.

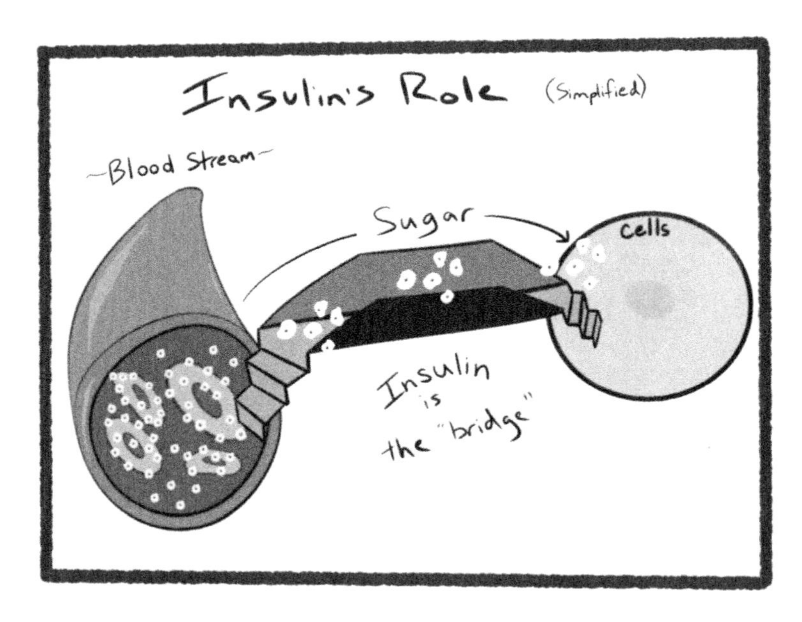

Types of insulin

It's our job as T1Ds to figure out how to administer proper amounts of insulin to maintain blood sugars at optimal levels. To do so, it's vital to understand the different types of insulin involved in the process.

Fast-acting insulin

As previously discussed, when a non-T1D eats carbohydrates, insulin is released to enable glucose to enter their body's cells. The insulin released after eating is what we refer to as 'short-term,' or 'fast-acting' insulin. Fast-acting insulin is what is used to control and balance blood sugars after ingesting food. It begins to work three to fifteen minutes after injecting and stays active in the body for about three hours.

The rule for using fast-acting insulin is simple: Every time you eat carbohydrates, you'll typically have to give fast-acting insulin to balance your blood sugar. (Note: if you have low blood sugar levels before eating, or don't consume *any* carbs during the meal, it may not be necessary to give any fast-acting insulin.)

Basal insulin

Throughout the day, the body goes through a variety of activities that make blood sugars rise *without* eating any carbohydrates.[11] Therefore, the simple act of being alive—even though you're not necessarily eating—requires the body to release a continual volume of insulin. The steady release of insulin to manage blood sugars in the neutral state is called basal insulin; sometimes referred to as *background insulin,* because it's managing your blood sugar in the background between meals.

To help you understand this better, think of our car analogy in the illustration below. Along our journey from point A to point B, we might have to stop at red lights. Even when the car is at a stoplight, gas is required to keep the engine running in the idle state. If too much gas is given, though,

[11] Stress, hormones, menstruel cycles etc.

you'll flood the engine. If too little gas is given, the car will conk out. But with the perfect amount of gas, your car stays puttering along smoothly until the light turns green.

Similarly, with basal insulin, if you give too much, you'll be sinking low all day. If you don't give enough, you'll be fighting high blood sugars all day. Finding your correct basal rate sets the foundation for everything else you do with your diabetes management. It makes your "engine" run smoothly all day long.

Insulin delivery methods

All T1Ds need to administer insulin to survive. *How* you do that is a matter of personal choice. I don't think 'one size fits all'. So, instead of trying to persuade you to use one method or the other, I've outline what I believe are the major pros and cons of each. At the end of the chapter, I'll, once again, describe my set-up and why I chose it so you can make the best decision for you or your child.

(Please note that sometimes, endocrinologists will steer you toward a particular method of insulin delivery. Please always listen carefully and consider their suggestions. But, keep in mind, the method of choice for you or your child is still *yours*.)

Pumps

Insulin pumps are small (pager-sized), computerized medical devices that work to deliver insulin for diabetics. What makes pumps unique is the *way* they deliver insulin and the *type* of insulin needed - just one!

Insulin pumps act similarly to the way a non-diabetic's body manages blood sugar, by continuously releasing precise amounts of fast-acting insulin throughout the day. The continuous delivery of fast-acting insulin serves as a pump's 'basal rate.' When a T1D using a pump eats, an insulin delivery of the same fast-acting insulin is given to process carbohydrates. The delivery of fast-acting insulin to cover carbs is also referred to as a 'bolus.'

➢ *Pump pros*

For as long as I can remember, insulin pumps have been the popular choice for endocrinologists and patients. T1Ds around the world swear by them because of their automation and functionality.

One of the most powerful features of pumps is the ability to deliver very precise doses of insulin, giving T1D's the power to zero-in basal rates to meet individualized, ever-changing needs. Some pump manufacturers even allow users to select fractional units to fine-tune insulin delivery even further.

Some pumps also work in conjunction with CGMs and can adjust basal rates in real-time. This is an extremely powerful tool that can be utilized to minimize the time required to recover from a low blood sugar event or avoid them altogether. It's only a matter of time before pumps will be able to automatically manage high blood sugars as well. (This would be considered a fully closed-loop system with no user interventions required.)

Another advantage of pumps is they're (somewhat) discreet. I know a lot of people get nervous about injecting insulin with needles in public. With a pump, giving insulin merely looks like you're texting someone. Nice!

But, as with anything else, while there are some clear advantages of pumps, they're not the insulin delivery system of choice for everyone. As I stated before, just because it's the popular choice for many, doesn't mean it has to be the choice for you.

- ***Pump cons***

There are, indeed, some serious risks and considerations to watch out for when deciding to use a pump. I've listed them below.

1) Infusion Site Failure

Head over to Instagram and type in #pumpproblems and you'll see hundreds of posts about infusion site failures. Here's the lowdown on what's happening.

For the pump system to deliver insulin to subcutaneous[12] tissue, a small plastic tube needs to be inserted just below the skin. Sometimes—more than I am willing to deal with—the plastic infusion sites fail as a result from getting clogged or bent. At this point, stop and remember that the infusion site is

---

[12] Tissue just below the surface of the skin.

the *only* insulin delivery vehicle for pump users. That means if the infusion site is broken or damaged, *no* insulin is being received. No basal or fast-acting insulin at all!

The result is that blood sugars will most likely spike very high, very quickly. And, when trying to correct the high blood sugar via a pump with a bad infusion site, blood sugars might continue to rise because (once again) *no* insulin is being received. I've been in this situation before and it's infuriating.

2) Tubing Issues

Tubing also poses a serious risk, especially for small children.[13] Most active people will, undoubtedly, get their pump cords stuck on doorknobs, seatbelts, or tangled with belt buckles and other things that could rip out the infusion site. Not good.

3) Battery Failures

Most pumps rely on battery power. As we all know, battery life is notoriously short - yet another risk factor to deal with.

4) Insulin Reservoir Capacity Problems

Consider the annoyance of running out of insulin in the middle of the night. Good luck getting eight hours of sleep that night!

5) Product Management Blips

This one hits home hard for me as a traveler. Consider managing the a) pump hardware, b) pump batteries, c) infusion sites, d) insulin cartridges...and e) insulin. Forget just one item, and the pump system is rendered useless and you could find yourself in a very difficult situation.

---

[13] Some pump companies do offer tubeless pumps.

6) Comfort

Pumps are about the size of a pager and weigh about 5 oz with batteries and insulin. Depending on the model you choose, they can cause serious discomfort while sleeping or being active (think about contact sports).

Keep in mind, when wearing a pump with a CGM, the pump is an *additional* piece of hardware physically attached to the body (CGM + Insulin Pump). For a young kid—or anybody active, for that matter—this could prove to be quite cumbersome.

7) Cost

Last, but not least, pumps are expensive. Even if your insurance covers part of the pump, you're probably looking at a few thousand dollars/year out of pocket for pump supplies.

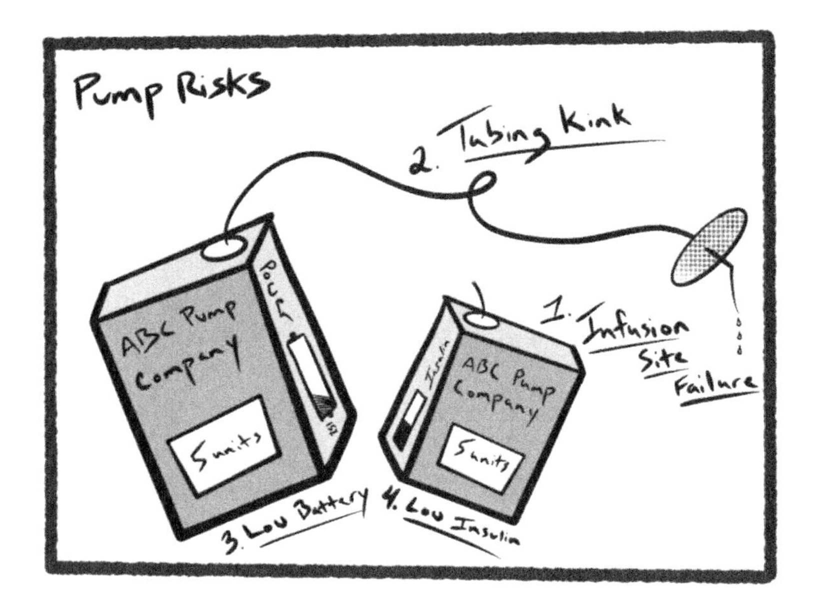

Manual Daily Injections (MDI)

The Manual Daily Injections—or MDI method—has been around since the discovery of insulin. At a basic level, MDI is exactly what it sounds like. With the MDI insulin delivery method, you inject insulin several times throughout the day; once to administer basal insulin, and again after every meal. With MDI, you'll deliver insulin with either syringes or insulin pens.

➢ *MDI pros*

One of the things people like the most about MDI is the fact you don't have to wear anything at all to deliver insulin. Unlike a pump that requires physically attaching something to your body, with MDI you just have to carry your insulin syringes or pens.

The only physical piece of hardware worn in this case is your CGM.[14] The benefit many MDI users experience, as a result, is better mobility and freedom of motion. When using the MDI system, there are very few activities you'll have to second-guess for fear of disrupting insulin delivery.

---

[14] With the pump, you would wear two pieces of hardware: your CGM, and the pump.

Another positive feature of MDI is that basal rates are delivered at only *one* point during the day—and that's it! One and done. The basal insulins that MDI T1Ds use are engineered to slowly release throughout the day. So, instead of having to rely on a physical device to constantly administer basal insulin twenty-four hours per day, with MDI, you administer one shot of basal insulin and you're done! You then have nothing to worry about until the next day at the same time.

The last, but sometimes overlooked, benefit of MDI is product management. With MDI, there are very few medical products you need to deal with. All an MDI user needs to manage is their insulin and syringes. Or, if you're using insulin pens, then it's just insulin pens and pen needles. That's it! No batteries, cables, infusion sets, or cartridges. This makes spontaneous activities a heck of a lot easier.

➢ ***MDI cons***

While MDI is the simpler option, nothing's perfect. There are three key drawbacks with MDI that I've listed below.

1) Inability to alter mid-day basal rates

Unlike pump users, you won't be able to alter your basal rates throughout the day. Not a huge deal for most people. But, if your schedule changes a lot, this might be a useful feature of the pump that isn't available for MDI users.

2) Remembering to administer basal rate

An obvious downside to MDI management is you'll have to *remember* to give your basal rate at roughly the same time every day. Some people do forget! You'll also have to remember to take your insulin with you when you leave your house since there's nothing physically attached to you.

3) Injection phobia

Unlike a pump, where insulin can be delivered discretely, with MDI you'll have to take out your needles and pens in public, clean your injection spot, and inject. This can be off-putting for some.

Mastering insulin management

Now that you have the basics covered and understand insulin's role and delivery methods, it's time to hone your skills to achieve the best outcomes. Through 21 years of experience as a T1D, I've narrowed the thought process of mastering insulin management down to four easy steps.

Step 1 – Select an insulin delivery method

As we discussed earlier, this is a matter of personal choice. But as you decide between using a pump or MDI, I encourage you to consider things often overlooked by many when going through this process.

The first decision criterion I recommend considering is your tolerance for risk. If your risk tolerance is high, and you're comfortable handling the occasional pump blips, then you might be comfortable with a pump. I, personally, would be very annoyed if my pump site failed or my battery died at an inconvenient time, causing my blood sugars to skyrocket.

Not surprisingly, my risk tolerance is very low. For that reason, the pump was not the right option for me. That said, for others, the ability to change basal rates on the fly and not having to remember a daily basal rate injection far outweigh the risks. Again, it's a matter of personal choice.

Lifestyle is another criterion to consider. I live a reasonably spontaneous life. When I need to pack for a trip, I usually only have an hour or two to gather my things. All things considered; I know I'm more likely to forget one of the several supplies needed for a pump than someone who lives a simpler, more predictable life. If I had a job that didn't require me to travel several times per month, the pump may have been a better choice. I would have more time to manage my supplies and make the pump system work properly.

Last but not least, functionality is the final criterion to consider. I have several T1D friends who rave about their pumps' ability to give delayed boluses to cover appetizers at social events (very cool feature), and the ability to automatically alter basal rates to prevent low blood sugars (another very cool feature).

If these things are essential for you, I encourage you to investigate using a pump. If not, then MDI might be a better option. Do your research and talk to other T1Ds and pump salespeople to identify your options. There's no right or wrong choice - just the choice that suits *you* best!

Step 2 – Dial in your basal rates

Understanding and mastering basal rates will solve the majority of your headaches when managing insulin as a T1D. All the time and money spent trying to achieve better blood sugars will all go to waste if your basal rates aren't correct. Once you nail your basal rates, the rest is quite simple[15].

Recall that basal insulin is the insulin that manages blood sugars in the neutral state. With perfectly administered basal rates, it's like putting blood sugars on autopilot, unless new variables are added (food and fast-acting insulin). It doesn't necessarily mean blood sugars will be in the desired range. It just means they won't be changing. If basal rates are *incorrect*, however, you'd typically see blood sugars rising or falling throughout the day.

A particularly easy way to know if your basal rate is correct is by viewing your CGM during the night, since this is typically a 7-9 hour window that's free from variables.

To test if your basal rate is correct during the night, here's what I recommend:

- Eat dinner early. 6 p.m. at the latest, or at least four hours before going to bed. Eat a very low-carb dinner, i.e. salad with very few garnishes and very little dressing. This will minimize the amount of insulin needed to cover the dinner carbs.

- If you've decided on MDI as your insulin delivery method of choice, go ahead and give your current basal rate. (Your current basal rate is probably one that was prescribed to you by your physician but might not be perfectly *dialed in* yet.) If you're on a pump, there's

[15] In my opinion.

nothing you have to do at this point since basal insulin is already running its course via the pump.

- Check your blood sugars on your CGM to make sure your numbers are within range. Ideally, you won't have to give any fast-acting insulin at this point. The goal is to go to bed and sleep for eight hours without having any extra carbs, fats [16], or insulin running through your system.

- Now, go to bed. Sleep through the night, and in the morning check your overnight readings/graph on your CGM. What I want you to observe here is the *slope* of the blood sugar line. If the slope is close to zero—or a flat line—you know your basal rates are probably correct. If your slope is positive (pointing upward toward the right, meaning your blood sugar was rising steadily throughout the night under the influence of zero carbs or fast-acting insulin) you might have to increase your basal rate. If the slope is negative (pointing downward toward the right, meaning your blood sugar was dropping steadily throughout the night), then you may need to lower your basal rate. The goal here is to get as flat a blood sugar line as possible.

Once you've achieved a flat line on your CGM readings, you'll know you have discovered the correct basal rate.

---

[16] Fats cause blood sugar spikes a few hours after eating. This is because fats decrease a T1D's insulin sensitivity. For fatty meals, you'll typically have to give fast-acting insulin at the time of eating, and again a few hours later. Best to avoid fatty meals when dialing in your basal rates.

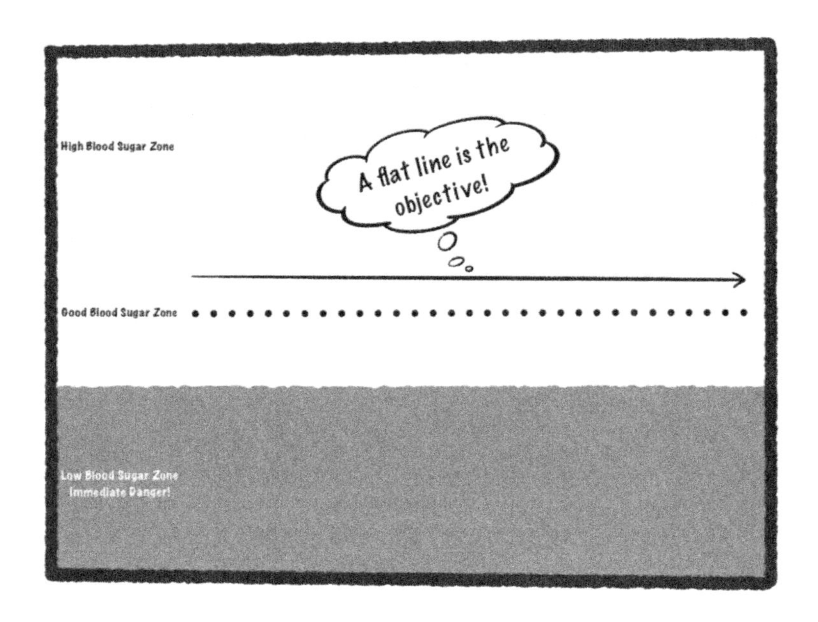

An important note here is that I'm not interested in what your blood sugar numbers during the night were, just as long as they didn't *change* dramatically overnight. For example, if my blood sugar was 100 mg/dl when I went to bed and I woke up near 100 mg/dl, then I know I'm giving the proper amount of basal insulin. It means that my "idle state" was stable. But, if I went to bed at 100 mg/dl and woke up at 50 mg/dl, I would have evidence to suggest my basal rate was probably too high and would need to decrease it.

This may take several weeks to master. It took me almost a month. Also, it's important to note that basal rate requirements may change from time to time depending on activity and stress levels.

Step 3 – Understand your insulin-to-carb ratio

Now that you have your basal rates dialed in to ensure steady blood sugars in the "idle state," we need to discuss how to properly calculate the fast-acting insulin you'll need when consuming carbohydrates.

Recall from Chapter 1 that when T1Ds eat, carbs are digested and converted into simple sugars, which end up in the bloodstream but can't make their way to the cells...because T1Ds don't make insulin. Therefore, it's *your* job when eating carbs to administer fast-acting insulin to allow sugars in the bloodstream to access the body's cells.

But, it's critically important to administer the *right* amount. Give too much, and you'll 'go low,' causing serious immediate problems. Give too little, and you'll 'go high,' contributing to serious long-term health problems.

You can master the ability to give perfect amounts of fast-acting insulin by understanding something called the "insulin-to-carb ratio." The insulin-to-carb ratio is a term that's used to understand exactly how many carbs can be processed with **one** unit of insulin.

To understand this better, I'll explain using myself as an example. My insulin-to-carb ratio is 1:20, or one unit to twenty grams of carbohydrate. This means that for every unit of insulin I inject, I can eat twenty grams of carbohydrates and maintain steady blood sugar levels. If I eat forty grams of carb, I would need to give two units of insulin; three units for sixty grams of carb, and so on.

To figure out your insulin-to-carb ratio, you'll have to experiment a bit. I recommend starting simple. I advise figuring out insulin-to-carb ratios in a similar state as you did when dialing in basal rates; with as few variables as possible.

Here's the plan I recommend:

- Start this exercise when you wake up in the morning assuming you haven't yet eaten anything or given any fast-acting insulin in the past three hours.

- The first thing you're going to do is test your blood sugar at the beginning of the experiment. Write this number down.

- Next, (assuming your preliminary insulin-to-carb ratio is 1:20, like mine) give one unit of insulin and eat twenty grams of carbs. Remember, at this point, you're going to be using the insulin-to-carb ratio you *think* is correct for *you*. (For example, if you think yours is 1:40, then give one unit of insulin and eat forty grams of carb. If you think your is 1:10, then give one unit of insulin and eat ten grams of carb.)

    - I usually don't eat foods in packages. But, for this exercise, consuming foods in a package containing the exact amount of carbs you desire gives the precision needed for best results.

- Now, WAIT three hours without giving any more insulin or eating any more carbs.[17] After three hours have passed, check your blood sugar again.

- If you end up high three hours later, you'll know that you'll need to adjust your insulin-to-carb ratio to reflect a smaller amount of carbs. (The opposite is true if you end up with low blood sugar afterward.)

- Keep repeating this process until blood sugars before starting are close to the blood sugars after completing the three-hour waiting period. When they're close, you'll know that you have arrived at your optimal 'insulin-to-carb ratio.'[18]

---

[17] If you see any symptoms of hypoglycemia, please stop the experiment and EAT!

[18] With some people, their insulin-to-carb ratio might change throughout the day. Pay close attention to your CGM to see if this

Once you've landed on your perfect insulin-to-carb ratio, eating is a piece of cake (pun intended). Now all you'll have to do is know what you're eating, do the math based on the amount of carbs you plan to eat, dial it up, and inject.[19]

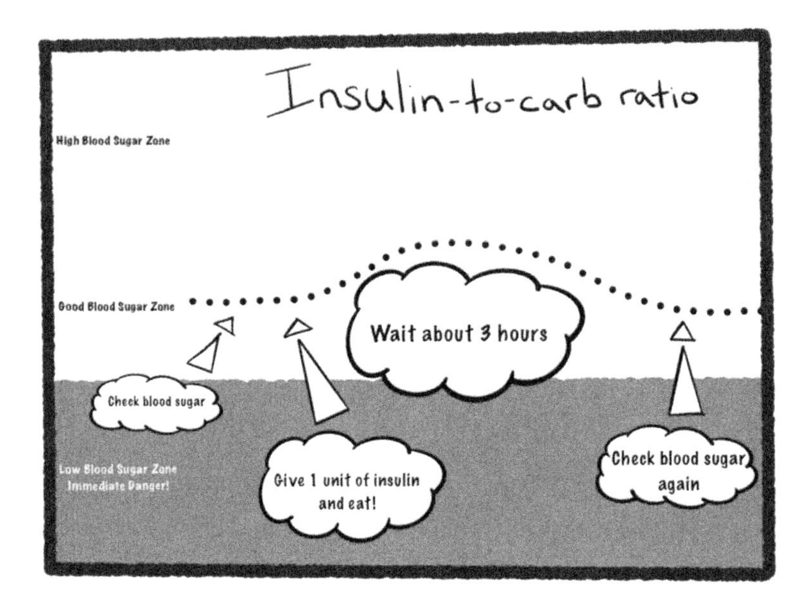

Step 4 – Understand your correction factor

Correction factor is a term used to describe how far blood sugar will drop as a result of giving **one** unit of insulin. This is extremely useful when trying to correct high blood sugars. To understand this concept better, I'll once again use myself as an example.

---

is the case. This is another example of how powerful the visibility of your sugars really is. Without a CGM, understanding these changes wouldn't be possible.

[19] Sometimes, the math won't work out perfectly for MDI users. You might end up with a need for half units of insulin. Some pen manufacturers do not allow for half units. Most pumps and basic syringes will allow for fractional unit increments.

My correction factor is 40 mg/dl for every one unit of insulin; or 1 unit:40 mg/dl. This means that for every unit of insulin I give myself without eating food, my blood sugar should drop around forty points. So, for example, if my blood sugar is high—let's assume it's 200 mg/dl—I would correct it by giving two units of insulin. The logic here is that I'm trying to get my blood sugar back to the 'normal range'; somewhere around 120 mg/dl. To lower my blood sugar to 120 mg/dl would require an *80 mg/dl* drop from 200 mg/dl. Since my correction factor is 40 mg/dl per unit of insulin, then I would require *two* units of insulin.

'Food' for thought

As you can see, the insulin-to-carb ratio and correction factor are relatively simple concepts to understand. One helps you dose insulin properly when eating. The other enables you to correct high blood sugars. But *both* start with understanding the effects of taking just **one** unit of insulin.

Because of this, it's worth noting that, sometimes, there is a transitive relationship between the denominators[20] of both ratios; the numbers representing grams of carbohydrate and mg/dl. In other words, it stands to reason that by reworking your insulin-to-carb ratio and correction factor, you should be able to realize how much your blood sugar will typically rise as a result of eating a specific amount of carbs – without using insulin. (This may not be consistent across the board due to food types and other variables. But it's worth understanding the logic.)

Using my numbers as an example, I can eat twenty grams of carbs for every unit of insulin I give; and for every unit of insulin I give without eating, my blood sugar will fall forty

[20] The number on the bottom of the ratio.

mg/dl. If we take insulin out of both equations, I can then conclude that my blood sugar will typically rise about forty mg/dl for every twenty grams of carbohydrates I eat.

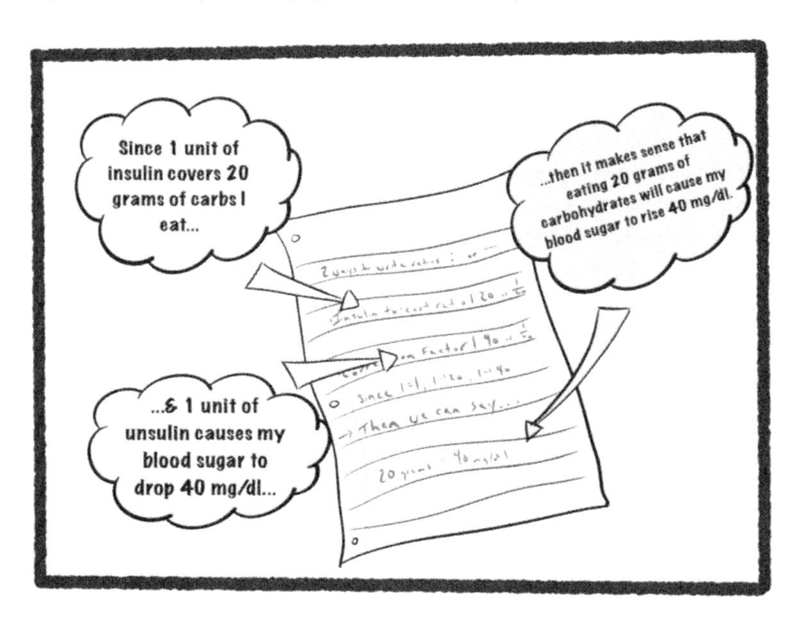

T1D Pro tip

If you have dialed in your basal rate insulin and you're following your insulin-to-carb ratios and correction factors well, but are still experiencing high blood sugars, there may be a culprit. And, the culprit could be the fact that insulin is incredibly sensitive to the elements and sometimes goes bad. If it was shipped in warm temperatures or mishandled along the way, there's a risk the insulin you received is no longer active. If this is the case, I always throw away both my basal rate and fast-acting insulins and start fresh. More times than not, this little tactic solves the issues at hand. If you're a pump user, make sure your infusion site is connected well, and everything is working correctly.

Case study – Insulin and math

Understanding the concepts behind insulin-to-carb ratio and correction factor is simple, but what happens when my blood sugar is high (or low), *and* I want to eat. Math is what happens.

As an example, let's assume my blood sugar is somewhat high at 200 mg/dl, *and* I want to eat 40g of carbs. For this example, I want my blood sugars to be 120 mg/dl 3 hours post-meal.

What do I do?

In cases like this, I'd have to calculate the insulin to cover my carbs (insulin-to-carb ratio) AND the insulin I'll have to give to correct the high blood sugar (correction factor). In my case, I would give 2 units to cover the 40g of carbs (since 1 unit covers 20g of carbs, and I'm eating 40g) plus 2 units to correct the 80 mg/dl overage (since 1 unit brings my blood sugars down 40 mg/dl), for a total of 4 units.

I'll admit it. The math can get downright ugly sometimes. To make life easier, though, I've started using apps like "Insulin Calculate" that you can program with *your* insulin-to-carb ratio and correction factor and will automatically figure out the correct doses of insulin you need to return to the normal range. Believe me, it's well worth checking out apps like this to avoid scrambling with back-of-the-napkin math!

My setup, September 2019[21]

For me, simplicity and risk are the most important criteria to consider when choosing an insulin management system. For this reason, I use the MDI method of insulin delivery via insulin pens. As I stated earlier, though, you might find that a pump suits you better. It's just a matter of choice.

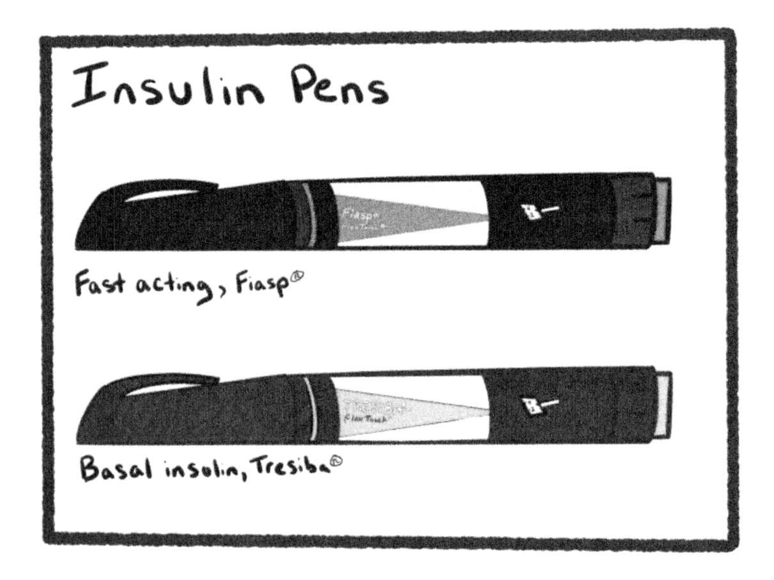

[21] See Appendix A for a complete list of T1D Pro recommended products. I'm looking forward to your inputs as well!

Today I use what I believe to be the best insulin on the market, Tresiba®, for my basal insulin and Fiasp® for my fast-acting insulin.[22]

Tresiba®: The unique molecular design of Tresiba® allows it to work around-the-clock for a slow and steady release of basal insulin for twenty-four hours.[23] This feature is rare in the world of basal insulins. Most of them only cover 18-22 hours of the day, which by definition, would leave part of the day open with no basal insulin on board. With Tresiba®, I am covered the entire day.

I usually give my Tresiba® basal shot around 11:00 p.m., or about the time I go to bed every night. As a result, remembering to give my Tresiba® has become part of my routine.

With one shot, I'm covered for the rest of the day. Nothing to worry about. No cables, batteries, or infusion sites, just my single shot. As we discussed earlier, the only risk is if I *forget* to give this shot. (FYI—it's happened exactly ZERO times in 6 years. So, in my opinion, the risk is minimal.)

Fiasp®: Fiasp® is NovoNordisk's® new version of NovoLog®[24] that was designed to be ultra-fast-acting. To accomplish this, they added vitamin B3 and amino acids.

With the addition of these two ingredients, Fiasp® begins working in as little as 2.5 minutes.

But why is this important? You see, when T1Ds used to give fast-acting insulin, it usually took much longer for the insulin to begin working with previous insulin brands. The

---

[22] Please note, I do not receive remuneration from either of these brands. This is for informational use only.

[23] https://www.tresiba.com/about-tresiba/how-tresiba-works.html

[24] Confused? NovoNordisk® has virtually owned the fast-acting insulin market for years. NovoLog® was one of them. To keep their patent on certain fast-acting insulin, they had to make changes to their previously patented insulins. In this case, they did a nice job!

issue with this is that very few people know what their meal is going to look like fifteen minutes *before* eating. How many carbs will it have? How much insulin should I give? I very rarely had the right information.

Now, with Fiasp®, NovoNordisk® claims that it's safe to give insulin as late as twenty minutes *after* eating![25] This is a huge advantage for me as someone who eats out quite often and doesn't necessarily see my meal before eating it.

Be careful if, you too, decide to use Fiasp® because it does works *very* fast! You may experience a few low blood sugars if you're not prepared to eat quickly after injecting.

FYI: My insulin-to-carb ratio is 1:20. So, I give one unit of Fiasp® for every twenty carbs I eat.

[25]https://www.fiasppro.com/content/dam/novonordisk/fiasppro/Downloads/Fiasp_Patient_Brochure.pdf

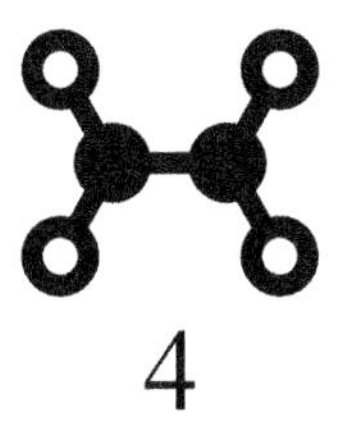

4

Diet

"*The right decisions are always the hardest to make. But, they must be made in order to live the life you deserve.*"
~ Trent Shelton

"*Our life is frittered away by detail...simplify, simplify.*"
~ Henry David Thoreau

We've arrived at the part of our journey where we need to discuss the second, and often harder to manage primary variable; diet. Food can be tricky to manage because...well...it's so darn delicious and hard to resist! Believe me, I understand and face the same challenge.

Not only are we surrounded by a culture that pushes fast-food advertisements 24/7, but it's now increasingly more challenging to eat responsibly due to peer pressure in social situations. The sad truth is, for uninformed T1Ds, the fast-food norm only sets us up for failure.

If this sounds familiar for you and your family, you're not alone. I regularly consult with T1Ds around the country with whom I discuss a variety of T1D topics. The purpose of these discussions is to learn how they manage their blood sugar and determine where

I can help the most. More times than not, the initial conversation looks something like this:

Me: "Do you have a CGM?"
T1D: "*Yup.*"

Me: "Do you have a good understanding of your insulin basal rate requirements and insulin-to-carb ratio?"
T1D: *"Absolutely. I have them down perfectly."*

Me: "Um...what do you usually eat?"
T1D: *"Yesterday I ate Cinnamon Toast Crunch for breakfast, hamburgers for lunch, and pizza for dinner. I have no idea why my sugars bounce around all day, and I wake up super high after going to bed at 110 mg/dl."*

Me: Face-plant in hand.

In this chapter I'll teach you the right way to think about food and how to eat the foods you love, while ensuring we meet our goals—A1C, time in-range, and quality of life.

Food as a variable

Dr. Joel Hoomans from Roberts Wesleyan College claims humans make up to 35,000 decisions per day.[26] The number increases with increased levels of responsibility. These decisions include what to wear, where to go, and what to say.

For T1Ds, there are even more. Our decisions include an additional list ranging from insulin doses to CGM placement, and, of course, what to eat! Each of these food choices will inevitably impact blood sugars. Remember, a simplified way to think about food's role in our effort to balance blood sugar levels looks like this:

[26] https://go.roberts.edu/leadingedge/the-great-choices-of-strategic-leaders

The more carb-rich food eaten, the more insulin needed to balance glucose levels. And, vice versa. The fewer carb-rich foods eaten, the fewer units of insulin required to cover the carbohydrates.

As a result, I think the best way to think about food is as a *variable.* To understand this better, we'll use our car analogy once again. For this case, though, we'll need some ground rules for our car:

Let's pretend we're on a race between the cities of 'Morninglandia' and 'Eveninglandia.' But, it's not a typical race where the fastest car wins. The objective here is to see who can maintain a constant speed of 75 miles per hour. (Similar to our objective to maintain consistently good blood sugar levels.) We're equipped with a speedometer (like our CGM), gas (like our insulin), and a map.

On the map, there are two routes, both taking us from Morninglandia to Eveninglandia and are exactly the same length. Route A is straight. Route B, however, requires crossing big hills and valleys.

Which route do you think is the best option? Route A, of course, as it has far fewer variables!

While this example illustrates a simple point, it's important to remember the principle as it relates to food and blood sugar management; minimizing variables minimizes opportunities for blood sugar fluctuation. This is essential with our conversation about food because there are a lot of things to consider. While our decisions about *what* to eat are necessary, *when to eat it* also plays a critical role in blood sugar management.

For that reason, I've outlined my philosophy on diet in this chapter to give you the best insight about my habits when eating at home and on the road. (Remember, I travel all over the world for work. Lots of good—and bad—choices out there!)

My diet philosophy

I love food, and I really enjoy the varieties the world has to offer including Italian pastas in the streets of Rome and fresh tuna from Tokyo's famed fish market. All with good blood sugars. My last trip to Santiago, Chile was for ten days, where I averaged 105 mg/dl and a standard deviation of 23 mg/dl. Not bad for a city that lives on empanadas.

The *way* I'm able to maintain proper blood sugar levels *and* eat the foods I enjoy is with a method that I coined ***The Right Food at the Right Time*** **(RFRT for short)**.

Think of RFRT as a page ripped out of 'The Book of Common Sense.' Generally speaking, I think it's an excellent idea to eat a low-carb diet. But, I know if I find myself in Istanbul, I'm certainly going to eat their famous Lamb Gyro with bread. To do this successfully as a T1D, though, there's a *right time* to do so. I've outlined below the logic I use to eat the foods I love and still maintain quality blood sugars.

RFRT Rule #1 - I start my day with a low-carb breakfast

As a rule, I never eat a lot of carbs in the morning. I have way too much going on from 8 a.m.-12:00 p.m. to be dealing with fluctuating blood sugars. For this reason, cereals, pancakes (except for keto pancakes), and oatmeal are all out because they're packed with a LOT of carbohydrates, and they represent a variable that I don't want to handle in the morning.

Instead, I eat two organic eggs with avocado and coffee. This choice of breakfast consists of very few carbohydrates. And, *for me*, I only need one unit of insulin to make sure I'm steady until lunch.[27] As a result, my blood sugars tend to stay in the low 100's mg/dl throughout the morning. That's a solid 5-6 hours of perfect blood sugar. A great way to start the day.

RFRT Rule #2 - If I really want carbs and fats, I'll eat them at lunch

Here's the logic. If you're going to eat pizza, pasta, or empanadas (like I do on occasion), they have to be balanced with larger amounts of insulin. But, balancing a lot of carbs and insulin can be challenging. It's tough to nail a fast-acting dose of insulin to compensate for a *lot* of carbs. The odds of being 100% correct, every time you inject fast-acting insulin to cover carbs, is almost zero – even with a solid understanding of your insulin-to-carb ratio.

The question is, then: Do you really want to be rolling the dice before going to bed or first thing in the morning? I don't. I, for one, don't like the feeling of dialing up large amounts of

---

[27] It's important to note your insulin dosage might be different than mine, depending on your carb-to-insulin ratio. It's also worth noting that this book wasn't designed to tell you how to eat pancakes. It was designed to help you or your child achieve near perfect A1Cs based on my experience!

insulin to cover large quantities of carbs right before I climb into bed or start my day.

Instead, I choose to use the *mid-day* window of opportunity to eat my heavy carbs (if at all). When I eat carbs at lunch, I have enough time before dinner and bed to correct myself if necessary. For this reason, lunch is the only meal where you'll find me eating pasta plates in Italy or empanadas in Latin America.

Limiting my carb intake to mid-day is the only way to guarantee I'll have a good morning and sleep properly through the night.

RFRT Rule #3 - I eat a low-carb, low-fat, and low-protein dinner before 8:00 p.m.

Eat dinner before 8:00 p.m.: I generally like to eat dinner before 8:00 p.m. Here's why. I go to bed around 11:00 p.m. every night. That means, whatever insulin I give (very little at dinner) and carbs I eat (very few at dinner) will have balanced out by the time I lay my head down at 11:00 p.m. Most fast-acting insulins last around three hours in the body, peaking sometime during the first few hours. This means if I'm done with dinner around 8:00 p.m., and have already given my insulin, then I'm usually able to go to bed three hours later without any variables actively running through my body.[28]

Avoid high amounts of carbs: This is similar to Rule #1. Decreasing the amount of carbs decreases the amount of insulin needed to cover the carbs, thus increasing my odds of stable blood sugars before bed. Minimizing variables before sleeping is definitely the way to go. Fewer variables = more consistent blood sugars = better sleep.

Avoid high amounts of fats: This one's tricky. Fatty foods don't always come hand-in-hand with carbs (though, they

[28] Except your basal insulin running in the background.

certainly do with pizza). But fatty food is hard to deal with as a Type 1 diabetic. This is because fats tend to make T1Ds more insulin resistant two to three hours after consumption.[29] The result is that most T1Ds tend to go high a few hours *after* eating fatty foods, like pizza. So, an inquisitive T1D might say, why not eat pizza at 8:00 p.m., give your fast-acting insulin to cover the carbs at 8:00 p.m., and then another injection later on in the evening to cover the effects of the fat?

It's a decent idea. And, admittedly, I have done this on occasion. But, remember, I've had T1D since 1997 and know exactly how my body is going to react. If you're a parent of a new T1D, or just trying to figure out how to bring your own blood sugars into range for the first time, my recommendation is to avoid fatty foods at dinner altogether. Like I covered earlier, eat them at lunch so you'll have plenty of time to hop off the blood sugar rollercoaster before going to bed.

Avoid high protein dinners: Some protein is okay. I, occasionally, like to have a small steak for dinner, or a few pieces of chicken with a salad. But, large amounts of meat can wreak havoc on blood sugars due to something called gluconeogenesis.

Gluconeogenesis is a process in which your body converts protein to glycogen. Your body can do this with small amounts of protein and not affect blood sugars. But, with large amounts of protein, I always notice a steady increase to my blood sugars after I go to bed.

---

[29] This can vary by person.

T1D Pro tip

Whatever you do, avoid anything containing the ingredient 'high fructose corn syrup,' also known as corn sugar. High fructose corn syrup is a manufactured, more quickly absorbed sweetener made from corn syrup. Over the past few decades, high fructose corn syrup has worked its way into our diets at a staggering rate. If you're living in the US, go into your cabinets and look at how many products contain some sort of corn syrup. You'll be amazed.

High fructose corn syrup causes insulin resistance, obesity (due to an increase in appetite), and high blood pressure. The result when I eat something containing high fructose corn syrup is that my blood sugars tend to run higher than usual, and I actually *feel* hungrier than I did before, which causes me to want even more of it. It's a vicious cycle.

Do yourself a favor and clear your kitchen of any food or drink containing high fructose corn syrup[30].

My diet plan[31]

For this section, I've just listed a few ideas that match my diet philosophy, with a few bonuses to help satisfy all the sweet-toothed folks out there. As requested, I will commit to taking pictures of my meals and posting them on Instagram at either @matt_t1d or @t1d_pro. Bon Appétit!

[30] High Fructose Corn Syrup goes by several different names. Do your research when in doubt!
[31] See Appendix A for a complete list of T1D Pro recommended products. I'm looking forward to your inputs as well!

Breakfast:

- 90% of my breakfasts consist of two organic eggs cooked any way, avocado, salsa, coffee, and water. (Notice that I don't eat a lot of, if any, fruit at breakfast.)

- Occasionally, I'll mix it up with keto pancakes. I was hesitant to put pancakes on the list until I found a company called Birch Benders®[32] that sells a "just add water" keto pancake mix at Wholefoods and various other supermarkets. Each pancake comes out to about 2 grams of carb because they're made with almond flour as opposed to wheat flour. They also have Keto syrup, which I will try and report on soon!

- I'll also occasionally eat organic, unsweetened yogurt. This is the "riskiest" breakfast for me due to the carb content. Most yogurts have about 15-20g/serving, which can spike your sugars if you don't give insulin to counter the effect. Careful with this one. Yogurt mixed with the improper dosage of insulin could ruin your entire morning.

---

[32] www.Birchbenders.com

Lunch:

- Tuna salad is my go-to lunch. I love tuna. It's a nice way to add some delicious protein to what could otherwise be a boring salad. I use an organic salad dressing, or sometimes just a dab of oil and lemon.

  (Lemons are amazingly flavorful and contain very few carbs.) No chips. For a drink, I'll always include sparkling water. I love the LaCroix [33] flavored sparkling water.

  I do not think Diet Coke/Sprite/anything like this is good to drink. They all contain ingredients like Sucralose which mess up your digestive tract and cause gut issues too.

- Chicken Soup. I mean, who doesn't love chicken soup?

- Sushi. Go nuts! It's lunch, after all. :)

[33] www.lacroixwater.com

Dinner:

- Low carb/zucchini "pasta" is a favorite that my wife taught me. And, it's super simple to make. Think of your favorite pasta. Now, instead of traditional noodles, replace them with zucchini noodles you make using a chef's knife, vegetable peeler, or Julienne Peeler. Then add your favorite meat and sauce, and voilà. Low carb zucchini "pasta" is yours to enjoy!

- Bowls - This is one I absolutely LOVE. Someone should open a restaurant centered around this entire idea.

  The concept is simple: Add easy to make, low carb, but delicious ingredients together with soy sauce, salt, and pepper. The bowls I like to make include cooked shrimp, Avocado, a healthy dose of green lettuce, radishes, soybeans (these are great).

- Sushi...but instead of sushi with rice, I eat sashimi to keep my carb count low. Warning: *Some* sashimi contains a lot of fat, which can cause your blood sugars to rise throughout the night. Select carefully for this option.

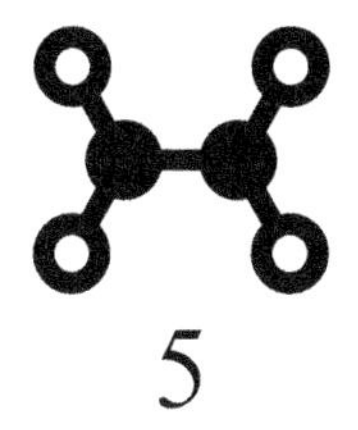

5

Exercise

"Good things come to those who sweat."
~ Anonymous

"When it comes to health and well-being, regular exercise is about as close to a magic potion as you can get."
~ Thich Nhat Hanh[34]

Exercise is one of the most overlooked tools regarding T1D management. Perhaps this is due to other important factors taking priority, like insulin and diet, or rapidly declining activity levels around the world, making exercise seem more like a chore than a tool. But in my opinion, exercise is absolutely critical to successful blood sugar control. In my experience, exercise has been the "great equalizer" helping me to achieve world-class A1Cs and a high percentage of time in-range, when combined with proper insulin and diet management.[35]

In this chapter, we'll cover why exercise is so important, the effects it gives you as a T1D, and my typical exercise plan

[34] Vietnamese Buddhist monk
[35] This statement has not been evaluated by the FDA.

for the week. We'll finish the chapter with a case study to explore best practices for exercise.

(It's important to note that the section on my exercise plan is a bit more detailed than previous chapters since there are so many things to consider when beginning.)

Why exercise?

I should start by giving some credit where credit is due. When I was diagnosed in 1997, I was completely unaware of the positive effects exercise has on blood sugars. It wasn't until I met with my endocrinologist at the time, Dr. Bernard Degnan, that I was permanently converted to an exercise enthusiast for the purpose of maintaining better blood sugar control.

I vividly remember one of my first visits to his office, when Dr. Degnan actually wrote ***"exercise"*** into my original management plan. He effectively *prescribed* exercise to me, which I thought was a brilliant move. (Thank you, Doctor Degnan! I will never forget your recommendation or your help!)

At this visit, Dr. Degnan explained to me that every T1D needs to exercise for at least one hour every day, to maintain optimal blood sugar levels.

"*But, why*?" I asked.

His answer was simple:

"Exercise helps increase your insulin sensitivity," he said. "It just makes your entire system work *better*. Think of exercise like adding oil to your car. Add oil to your car at the scheduled times, and your car will burn gas more efficiently. As a result, your car will work better and last longer. The same is true for you and the relationship between exercise and the efficiency of your insulin."

"If you exercise every day, you'll make the best use of your insulin. And, as a result, you should have better blood sugars. Makes sense?"[36]

I nodded my head, 'yes'—and have built exercise into my daily routine ever since.

Here's what I've learned

It wasn't until I had my first CGM and perfect visibility of my sugars that I *understood* the effects of exercise on my blood sugar. Here are two observations worth sharing.

Exercise increased my insulin sensitivity

Dr. Degnan was right. After exercising, I notice that my insulin requirements can decrease by as much as 20%! So, why does this matter?

Another way to think about insulin sensitivity is to understand that after exercising, I need far *less* insulin to cover the *same* amount of carbohydrates eaten before exercising. In other words, I'm able to decrease one of my primary variables. And, remember: fewer variables = more consistent blood sugars.

The magnitude of the effect is related to the *length* and *effort* of exercise

The more strenuously and longer I exercise, the longer the effects will be on my blood sugar. If I engage in my usual activity of playing a set of tennis, I notice my insulin sensitivity increases for about twenty-four hours. If, however, I was to race in an Iron-Man triathlon, I would probably see raised levels of insulin sensitivity for a more extended period.

---

[36] Remember, this was in Detroit...aka "Motor City".

To keep things consistent, I try to build a similar duration and stress level into my daily exercise routine. Whether I'm vacationing in Europe or working in Sao Paulo, Brazil, I always find a way to break a sweat at least once, the same time, the same way, every day. It sounds tough...and it is. But, trust me when I say it's worth it.

What I want you to gather from this is that exercise—if managed correctly—can absolutely be the "great equalizer" for you too. I build exercise into my daily routine, and I recommend you do the same.

But why does exercise work to help T1Ds maintain better glucose levels? Let's take a quick look.

(There are 100 different resources you could find on the internet to give you some variation of this. I encourage you to dive in further to learn as much as you can. I've simplified the explanation for easier understanding.)

How exercise increases insulin sensitivity

Understanding exercise and insulin sensitivity begins with something called 'glycogen' and its relationship with our muscles and glucose.

Glycogen is a complex form of glucose that is stored in our muscles to support activity that will happen later.[37] Think of glycogen as our bodies' primary source of energy reserves used to fuel muscles. When people exercise, muscles are stimulated to look for sources of energy so they can continue to grow and move the body as needed. In doing so, muscles burn the best available and closest source, glycogen.

[37] https://en.m.wikipedia.org/wiki/Glycogen

But, as muscles deplete their storage of glycogen, they then look for the second most accessible source of energy in the body to replace the depleted glycogen; sugar in the bloodstream. In other words, for muscles to grow during and after a workout, they require energy (or sugar). And, the harder and longer the exercise, the more glycogen muscles will need to support the activity.

This process continues as long as the muscles need to rebuild and grow properly. Hence, the duration and intensity of the workout have a direct impact on the length and effect on insulin sensitivity. The longer and harder the workout, the longer and harder muscles will look for energy (first from glycogen, then from sugar in the bloodstream) to complete the rebuilding process.[38]

[38] This is an extremely simplified explanation of how this works.

Types of exercise and their effects on blood sugar

While all exercise is undoubtedly helpful for managing blood sugars throughout the day, it can sometimes pose a bit of a challenge. This is because different types of exercise have different effects on blood sugars. To get an idea of the effect that different types of activity have on blood sugar levels, I've outlined my experience below.

Aerobic

Aerobic exercise is a type of activity involving long bouts of continuous motion, like running or riding a bike. For me, aerobic exercise poses the most serious threat of hypoglycemia during the workout. This is because aerobic exercise causes the body to look for glycogen in the muscles *quickly*, and as a result, causes blood sugars to drop fast. For this reason, I always make sure I'm prepared with food when I go on runs or do any aerobic exercise.

Anaerobic

Anaerobic exercise is best described as motion involving resistance, like lifting weights. For me, anaerobic exercise causes blood sugars to rise slightly during the activity. This is because anaerobic exercise is—while also healthy—very *stressful* for the body. Under this stress, the body might release hormones which could cause blood sugars to rise. (Keep in mind, for you this might be different. Still carry food with you during anaerobic exercise!)

Mixed exercise

Mixed exercise is exactly what it sounds like; a combination of aerobic and anaerobic activity with some continuous motion and resistance. Most sports involve a blend of both aerobic and anaerobic movement where you're typically moving a lot and experiencing a bit of muscle resistance.

Think about sports like tennis. In tennis, the players continually chase after balls to return to their opponent (aerobic). But they're also forcing their muscles to do a lot of work as they position themselves to hit the next winner (anaerobic).

T1D Pro tip

Try to stay *consistent* with the type and timing of exercise. I realize this is a tough tip to live by, especially if you're younger and don't have a consistent schedule yet. Life happens. I get it. But, it's essential and has helped me stay as well controlled as possible. Here's a quick case study of a composite character I'll call Jill to explain why consistency is important. I've used round numbers to simplify.

Case study – Exercise consistency is key

Jill typically works out every day to increase her insulin sensitivity throughout the week. She works out at the same time, 4:00 p.m., during the week and weekend to maintain consistency. Her exercise of choice is tennis. She likes tennis because it gives her both aerobic and anaerobic movements making it ideal for her to control her blood sugars during and after workouts. Jill knows that playing tennis for one hour will give her a slight boost in insulin sensitivity for around twenty-four hours.

But, on this particular weekend, Jill decides to change her exercise activity *and* timing. On Saturday, instead of playing tennis at 4:00 p.m., as Jill typically does, she decides to go for a ten-mile run in the morning. And, on Sunday, she decides to lift weights at 10:00 p.m.

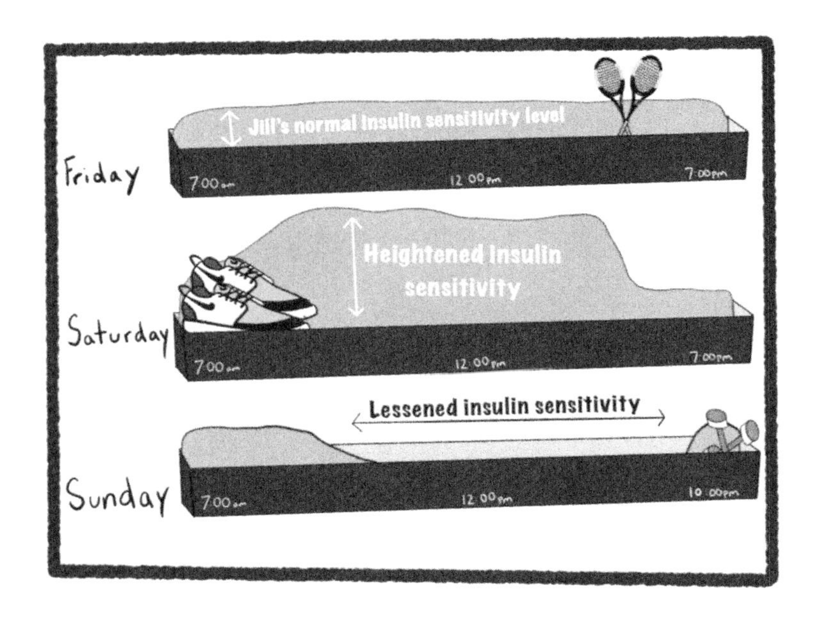

Because of the change in timing and type of exercise, Jill would have different levels of insulin sensitivity than from what she's used to. Here's a day by day summary of the effects that changing her exercise routine have on her blood sugar.

Friday night

- Jill played tennis, as usual, Friday afternoon at 4:00 p.m. This is her normal routine. She can plan on her normal increase in insulin sensitivity until about 4:00 p.m. on Saturday. As a result, we assume she slept well Friday night.

Saturday morning during the workout

- Since Jill is changing both her timing of exercise routing—Saturday morning, instead of 4:00 p.m. — and the type of exercise — purely aerobic, instead of a mixed workout, Jill would probably crash low at some point during her run if she isn't prepared with carbs. The "shock" to her system of going from a mixed workout routine to an aerobic workout, combined with the fact that her insulin sensitivity is now *double* (until 4:00 p.m.), would most likely cause her blood sugars to crash. (See illustration)

Saturday mid-day/early afternoon

- The "doubling" of her insulin sensitivity would continue until about 4:00 p.m. on Saturday.[39] The result would most likely be that Jill would be in more danger of hypoglycemia until that time. Jill would notice on her CGM readings that if she ate something and gave her usual dose of insulin on Saturday mid-day, her blood sugar would probably fall shortly after. I've been in this situation before, and it's super frustrating. Jill would probably end up eating all day, consuming massive amounts of calories, to keep her blood sugars out of the dangerously low zones. So much for the workout!

Saturday night/early Sunday morning

- Now that the effects of her Friday tennis match have worn off, Jill might be just fine during this. However, since long runs are not her normal exercise routine, she may suffer poor blood sugar control Saturday night. It's somewhat unknown since long runs aren't typical for her.

[39] Under the assumption that her run gave her an insulin sensitivity of twenty-four hours as well.

In this case study, Jill decides not to work out until late Sunday night. At 10:00 p.m., she chooses to hit the gym and lift weights.

Sunday mid-day/afternoon

- By Sunday morning, the effects of Jill's Saturday morning run have, most likely, worn off. By mid-morning, she's no longer experiencing insulin sensitivity. As a result, she may experience higher than usual blood sugars until the next time she exercises (at 10:00 p.m.)

The takeaway

- Jill just spent a whole weekend exercising in a futile way—making her life and T1D management much harder. She experienced lows on Saturday and highs on Sunday. She certainly didn't start her new week feeling refreshed and was probably left wondering what went wrong. Not fun.

  The takeaway for you is that while exercise is incredibly important for all T1Ds, I recommend thinking carefully and strategically about exercise. Just a little more planning and forethought can prevent negative patterns from taking hold.

———

My exercise routine[40]

I'm a morning person. For that reason, I like to work out in the morning and have done so consistently for years. As a result, I've been able to build a predictable routine of breaking a sweat at the same time every day.

I enjoy competition and sports like tennis, more than solitary activities like running or lifting weights. I'm fortunate that my exercise of choice is one that combines both aerobic and anaerobic activity. This makes it relatively simple for me to manage blood sugars during the exercise. As discussed, tennis is a combination of constant movement and resistance, allowing me to have the best workout experience possible as a T1D.

If you're considering something similar, most team sports like football, baseball, basketball, soccer, volleyball, and lacrosse fall into the same category as tennis. Keep in mind, though, that sports like swimming are going to be much more aerobic than others. And, gymnastics will be more anaerobic.

To appreciate the level of detail that goes into a good workout, I'll walk you through my 3-step pre-exercise routine.

Step 1 - I minimize my variables before working out

My day usually starts at around 7:30 a.m. when I wake up and eat breakfast. If you remember from the previous chapter, I'll eat two organic eggs with avocado and coffee every day for breakfast...without fail. This is a perfect meal before working out since it's loaded with protein and gives me the energy I need to push through my tennis match. It's also great because it requires little to no insulin.

[40] See Appendix A for a complete list of T1D Pro recommended products. I'm looking forward to your inputs as well!

Take a look at the actual food: Eggs, very few carbs. Avocado, very few carbs. Coffee (with Stevia), very few carbs. Long-story-short, I've *minimized both of my variables* (food and insulin) while still eating something that gives me the energy I need to compete.

Step 2 - I double check by blood sugars

Before leaving for my tennis match, I'll always doublecheck my blood sugar levels on my CGM to make sure I'm stable. If I happen to be falling slightly—visible via my CGM—I'll eat about ten grams of carbohydrates to make sure I don't go low during the workout.

If I'm trending up on my CGM, I'll typically try to give just a half unit of insulin to make sure I don't continue the upward trend. ***Be careful here, though***. I don't recommend giving large doses of insulin before working out.

Step 3 - I prepare

I always carry food with me. This is imperative. Whenever you choose to exercise, regardless of the type of activity, *always carry food.*

Also, keep your insulin with you if you administer your insulin with the MDI[41] method. It's never a good feeling when you begin an exercise routine and start seeing your blood sugar rising on your CGM. If you choose to correct yourself, I recommend administering your correction factor at a significantly discounted rate from what you'd typically give.

For example, let's pretend my blood sugar crept up to 200mg/dl during exercise. Instead of giving my standard *two* units of insulin to correct myself, I would give *one*, knowing I'll be far more susceptible to going low during exercise if I gave my usual dose.

---

[41] Multiple Daily Injection

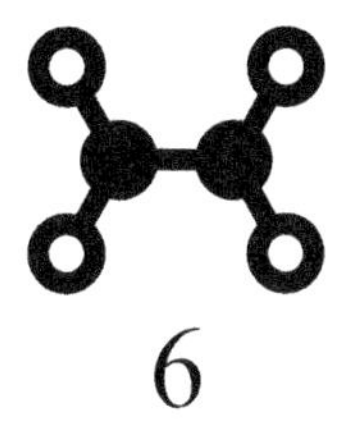

6

The "Free" 8 Hours

"Sleep is the golden chain that ties health and our bodies together."
~ Thomas Dekker, 16th Century English dramatist & writer

"Proper sleep has helped me get to where I am today as an athlete, and it is something that I continue to rely on every day."
~ Tom Brady, NFL Quarterback

Copying my model to ensure solid nighttime blood sugars may make the biggest impact on your A1C, and maybe even on your overall quality of life.

The importance of sleep

Think about sleep from a 'percentage of the day' standpoint. About a third, or 33%, of your life is spent under the covers. Sleep is so important that in some parts of the world, like Australia, they've acknowledged it by erecting a massive three-sided statue in Sydney, signifying the optimal way to spend a day: eight hours to work, eight hours to play, and of course, eight hours to sleep. And, from a blood sugar perspective, if you're able to control 33% of your day entirely in-range, there's a good chance A1Cs will improve!

Quality sleep also helps T1Ds control blood sugars during the day. It's estimated that a 'tired' T1D requires as much as 30% more insulin during the day to maintain the same blood sugar levels as a well-rested T1D. In other words, a lack of sleep means a T1D needs to introduce *more* variables into their daily routine.

In my experience, more variables usually mean blood sugars will be less steady, which will cause me to lose more sleep. It's a hamster wheel a lot of T1Ds step onto. In fact, on average, T1Ds in the United States lose over 500 hours of sleep per year due to poor blood sugar control! It's a cycle that has plagued generations of T1Ds and hasn't slowed.

This was the case for me as well until I started studying the effects of my routines via a CGM.[42] After a few months of carefully noting my bedtime preparations, and studying the blood sugar graphs the following day, I was able to design a foolproof evening routine I swear by. You won't catch me any day of the year, at any location on earth, where I'm not strictly adhering to this routine. It's that important.

My design for 8 hours of sleep

Nighttime sleep is a time that's completely free of the temptation of eating carbs or giving insulin. In other words, it's an eight-hour chunk of time where zero variables should be at play. It's a time where you can, and should, win every day, free from worry.

[42] Continuous Glucose Monitor

The secret to a good night of sleep starts with the choices you make *before going to bed*, including when to eat, what to eat, and how to prepare the bedroom. So, without further ado, here's how I design my evenings for a good night's rest.

I eat a low-carb, low-fat, and low-protein dinner before 8:00 p.m.

Sounds a little bit like the Diet chapter, right? That's for a good reason. It's the same concept. In case you forgot how this works, I've summarized the logic here for you to reference again.

Eat dinner before 8:00 p.m.: I generally like to eat dinner prior to 8:00 p.m. Here's why. I go to bed around 11:00 p.m. every night. That means, whatever insulin I give (very little at dinner) and carbs I eat (very few at dinner) will have balanced out by the time I lay my head down at 11:00 p.m. Most fast-acting insulins last around three hours in the body, peaking sometime during the first few hours. This means if I'm done with dinner around 8:00 p.m., and have already given my insulin, then I'm usually able to go to bed three hours later without any variables actively running through my body.[43]

Avoid high amounts of carbs: Decreasing the amount of carbs decreases the amount of insulin needed to cover the carbs, thus increasing my odds of my blood sugars staying stable before bed.

Avoid high amounts of fats: This one's tricky. Fatty foods don't always come hand in-hand with carbs (though, they

---

[43] Except basal insulin running in the background.

certainly do with pizza). But fatty food is hard to deal with as a Type 1 diabetic. This is because fats tend to make T1Ds more insulin resistant two to three hours after consumption.[44] The result is that most T1Ds tend to go high a few hours after eating fatty foods, like pizza.

Avoid high protein dinners: Some protein is okay. I like to have a small steak for dinner occasionally, or a few pieces of chicken with a salad. But, large amounts of meat can wreak havoc for you due to something called gluconeogenesis.

Gluconeogenesis is a process in which your body converts protein to glycogen. Your body can do this with small amounts of protein and not affect blood sugars. But, with large amounts of protein, I always notice a steady increase to my blood sugars after I go to bed.

I double-check my basal insulin rates

As an MDI insulin user, I give my basal insulin at night around 11:00 p.m., right before I go to bed. One thing I consider, though, when giving my basal insulin is whether or not I did anything unusual from an exercise standpoint. If my exercise for the day consisted of my normal activities, then it’s business as usual for my basal insulin. But, if I worked out for a remarkably long time, or did something extraordinarily strenuous, I might consider lowering my basal rate by a 5-10%.

I prepare my bedroom

If you follow the recommendations for dinner and basal rates carefully, you’ll undoubtedly sleep better in the future.

---

[44] This can vary by person.

Occasionally, though, you still might wake up from random lows or highs. Yup, even I wake up from time to time. But I've been able to reduce the negative impact on my sleep by *preparing* my bedroom appropriately. To do so, I keep three things within arms' length of my bed:

1) **My CGM receiver**

My phone serves as my CGM receiver. So, every night before I go to bed, I make sure to keep my phone next to me plugged into a charger. Remember, it won't do me any good if the battery dies in the middle of the night.

2) **My fast-acting (Fiasp®) insulin pen (for the rare occasion)**

For those occasional mid-night highs, I have set my CGM to alert me quickly. To correct the high, I'll check my blood sugar level, quickly do the correction factor math, and administer my insulin. At first, this might take a bit more time because, for some, it'll be the first time doing the math. Once you do it a few times, the correction factor calculations will come to you more naturally.

3) **A 12oz bottle of orange juice (for the rare occasion)**

Placing food near my bed turned out the biggest time saver me, and a great way to treat midnight lows. I used to get up in the middle of the night and walk to the fridge, where I'd eat random leftovers. This took upwards of ten minutes to complete. Not fun at 3:00 a.m. So, to accomplish the task at hand; raise my blood sugar quickly and predictably in a way that didn't fully wake me up; I decided small bottles of OJ were the best solution. (It's also one of the most economical ways to solve midnight lows as well.)

A few years ago, I found listings on Amazon® for 24-packs of 12oz bottles of OJ that are delivered to my door in two days with Amazon Prime®. This has been an absolute game-changer. A few times per year, all I have to do to ensure quick corrections of midnight lows is scroll over to the Amazon® app on my phone, order a 24-pack of OJ, and voilà... two days later, I have the final item I need to ensure a solid night of sleep.

~ Sweet dreams. :)

Closing Thoughts

"Success is neither magical nor mysterious. Success is the natural consequence of consistently applying the basic fundamentals."
~ Jim Rohn

"The advanced level is mastery of the basics."
~ Ray Mancini: Zen, Meditation, & the art of Shooting: Performance Edge - Sports Edition

---

At the beginning of the book I mentioned that Type 1 diabetes is a serious and potentially life-threatening condition. That's true. But I hope you've been able to arrive at the same conclusion I did a few years ago, which is, T1D *doesn't* have to degrade your quality of life if you're well controlled. And, that being well controlled is absolutely achievable.

Will you have to spend a little more time than your non-T1D peers to prepare for school, work, sports, and social activities? Absolutely. Will there be days where you feel discouraged? Sure. But by applying the principles we've discussed here, you can absolutely enjoy a healthy and full life with an A1C that's in the normal range.

If you've been paying close attention, you'll have noticed my entire philosophy of T1D management is focused around two ideas: controlling variables and implementing tools to control blood sugars. Let's spend a few minutes to review both.

Variables

In Chapters 3 and 4, we discussed two primary variables that you need to consider: insulin and diet/carbs. The insulin discussion focuses on how to choose delivery methods and understanding both basal rate and fast-acting insulin.

This second variable we discussed is diet, or food. As a review, my general attitude toward food is to choose wisely regarding *what* to eat and *when* to eat it. The choices you make around food can—and will—make or break your day.

But, remember, the effects of how well you manage your variables (insulin and carbs) will be amplified based on how well you implement your tools.

Tools

In Chapter 2, we discussed the first of two tools, a Continuous Glucose Monitor and the power of non-stop glucose visibility.

If you remember from Chapter 2, do whatever you can to get a CGM and use it!

For top-notch control of your blood sugar, a CGM is essential. If you're still having second thoughts about it, though, I encourage you to connect to the DOC[45] on Instagram or Facebook, or on the blog at www.T1DPro.com to understand the pros (many) and cons (few) of wearing a CGM. I also try to give a transparent account of my experience with Dexcom's® CGM on my personal Instagram account, @matt_t1d. Feel free to ask questions!

---

[45] Diabetic Online Community

The second tool we discussed was exercise. Remember, exercise is essential for T1Ds, but needs to stay consistent. I encourage you to make an effort to do *something* active every single day. You'll definitely notice the improvement in your insulin's performance and the steadiness of your blood sugars. It's not always the easiest thing to do, but absolutely worth it.

The takeaway for you regarding tools is for you to *use* them. It's ineffective to read about them, know about them, or talk about them—you must *use* them! There's no easier way for you to gain control of T1D and maximize the effectiveness of insulin and food, than by using the modern tools available.

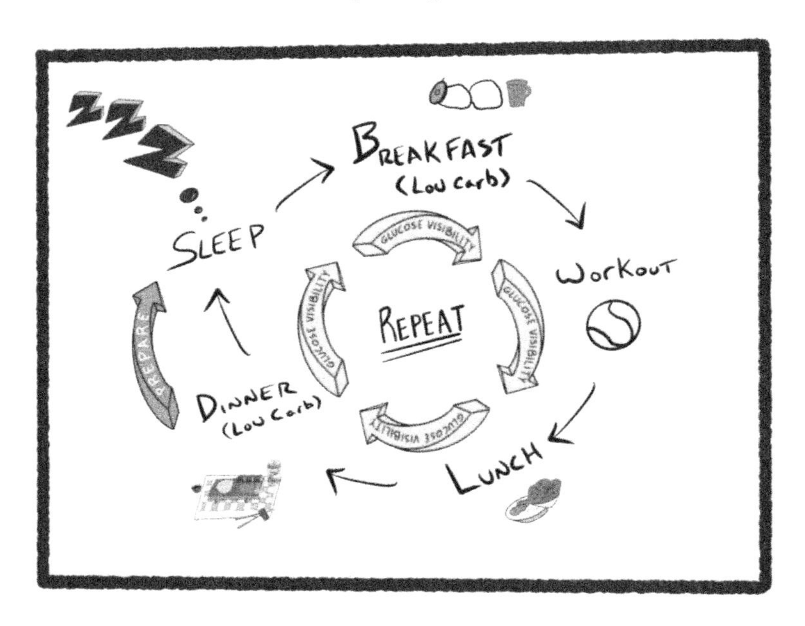

Other things to consider

While we didn't cover these in detail, there are a few additional variables that, in my experience, can alter blood sugars and can be a hassle if you're left unaware. Below are three I feel require the most attention.

Heat

Heat's a tricky one. Two things can happen to a T1D whose outside on a hot day.

If your body begins to get dehydrated, the sugar in your bloodstream will become more concentrated, and blood sugars will rise. When this happens to me, I make sure to *hydrate* appropriately. To maintain good blood sugars (and overall good health), it's always a good idea to drink plenty of liquids—plain water is best—when dealing with the heat.

Heat can also lower your blood sugars, especially if fast-acting insulin has been given. This is because blood vessels dilate when it's hot, causing insulin to be absorbed much more quickly. The result is that you'll become much more insulin sensitive. To avoid sharp drops in blood sugar, always carry food with you when it's hot out.

Sickness

Being sick is no fun, especially for the T1D community. This is because, generally speaking, people become very insulin resistant[46] when sick. To fully understand the details of sick day management, I encourage you to work closely with your endocrinologist. But, to give you a flavor of how I deal with being sick, here's an outline of the changes I make in my routine.

I cut out all carbs: I make life as easy as possible when I'm sick and cut out one of the primary variables completely; carbs. If I'm able to eat, I stick to a diet high in vegetables and protein. (If you're a parent reading this, please stay away from junk food thinking it'll make your child feel better. Trust me; they're not going to feel any better when their blood sugar spikes, *and* they're already sick.)

---

[46] Unable to use the insulin given.

I watch my blood sugar like a hawk: This goes without saying. If you have a CGM, check it and check it often, on your phone or receiver. If you do not have access to a CGM, I'd recommend checking your blood sugar every hour at a bare minimum.

I usually increase my basal rate insulin: To combat the insulin resistance that typically accompanies being sick, I give myself about 10-20% more basal rate insulin. This does two things. The first is that if I can't eat any food, I know my "fasting blood sugars" will stay healthy. The second is that if I can eat something, I know the effects of eating my veggies and protein on blood sugar should be minimal. If they do start to rise, I know just a small amount of fast-acting insulin will be enough to cover me. (Don't overdo this one. Please consult with your physician before making any insulin dosing changes.)

Stress

Of all the variables mentioned, stress might be the one that goes the most unnoticed, simply because it's woven into the fabric of our everyday lives. But, make no mistake, stress can be devastating for blood sugars.

Stress causes blood sugars to rise by activating your liver to release glucose. This happens because the body thinks it needs the extra shot of energy to cope with the stress. However, this will only cause more anxiety as blood sugars begin to rise.

Whenever I start feeling stressed about anything, I try to remember what's truly important in my life; family, friendship, and health. I manage my stress by chatting with my family and friends as much as possible. I encourage you to do the same. And, if you don't have anyone to share with, please feel free to use the blog at www.t1dpro.com/blog as a resource!

The last thing I'll leave you with is a reflection on what you're really trying to do when it comes to Type 1 diabetes management. And, that is to maximize your quality of life *with* great blood sugars. One day, maybe not too far in the future, we *will* have a cure.[47] Until that day, it's our job to stay laser-focused on maintaining our health so that when the cure finally does arrive, we're as healthy as we were prior to T1D.

To help each other along the way, please use the T1D community and share what you've learned. I also invite you to reach out directly to me with questions, comments, and suggestions using the addresses below. I'll do my best to stay in touch. Best of luck to you all!

...and as always,

Tight sugars, everyone.

Ways to contact me:
Personal IG: @matt_t1d
T1D Pro IG: @t1d_pro
Email: matt@t1dpro.com
Website: www.t1dpro.com

[47] I encourage you all to support JDRF, as they focused on finding a cure as opposed to just management.

Appendix A

As promised, here is a consolidated list of products I currently use in my T1D management. I encourage you to visit www.T1DPro.com to share your thoughts on any new products you've found helpful.

Glucose Visibility

My Setup, September 2019

- CGM: Dexcom G6® continuous glucose monitor.
- https://www.Dexcom.com
- Receiver: I use an iPhone® X as my primary receiver, where I run the Dexcom® app. The Dexcom® app is where you will see your blood sugars and adjust alerts and settings.
- https://apps.apple.com/us/app/Dexcom-g6/id1209262925
- Secondary Receiver: I also use an Apple® Watch that connects to the Dexcom® app to see my blood sugars.
- https://www.apple.com/watch/
- Finger prick glucose monitor: You should always have a backup meter on hand. I use the SideKick® All-in-one Glucose Meter. I love the SideKick® monitor because the actual meter sits right on top of the test strip case, thus eliminating the need to carry a meter AND test strips separately. Here's a link to their Amazon® page.
- https://www.amazon.com/dp/B07K36LM21/ref=cm_sw_em_r_mt_dp_U_EKNBDb8Z97EF3

Insulin

My Setup, September 2019

- Fast Acting Insulin: NovoNordisk's® Fiasp®
- https://www.fiasppro.com/
- Basal Insulin: NovoNordisk's® Tresiba®

- https://www.tresiba.com/
- Pen Needles: BD Ultra Fine™ Micro Pen Needles
- https://www.bd.com/en-us/offerings/capabilities/diabetes-care/pen-needles/bd-ultra-fine-micro-6mm-pen-needle

Diet

My Setup, September 2019

- Keto Pancakes: Birch Benders® Keto Pancakes
- https://birchbenders.com/products/keto
- Zero carb, naturally flavored sparkling water: La Croix®, any flavor
- https://www.lacroixwater.com/

Exercise

My Setup, September 2019

- I've been using the Apple® fitness app quite a bit. I like being to track the progress of my tennis matches etc. with the app.
- https://support.apple.com/en-us/HT204523

Other

My Setup, September 2019

- Bedtime setup: 10z orange juice bottles for low blood sugar. 6-foot power cord for my iPhone®.
- https://www.amazon.com/dp/B001AQTUK4/ref=cm_sw_em_r_mt_dp_U_01NBDbYBBPH5X
- https://www.amazon.com/dp/B07PHSF8DP/ref=cm_sw_em_r_mt_dp_U_82NBDb0XJ05ZP
- Insulin Travel Bag: REI® Co-op Go Box Cooler, Small. I LOVE this bag. It's waterproof, insulated, and small. Perfect for packing insulin on quick trips.
- https://www.rei.com/product/797876/rei-co-op-go-box-cooler-small

Appendix B

Bonus material: Here's a checklist of the products ***I*** take when traveling for work. Keep in mind, my trips are typically less than a week. Depending on the length of your journey, you may need to adjust. Also, if you're a pump user, you'll need to remember to take backup pump supplies.

I've designed this in logical order to make the best use of time when packing.

☐ Insulated carrying case for insulin

☐ 1 ice pack

☐ 2 NovoNordisk's® Fiasp® (fast-acting) Pens[48]

☐ 2 NovoNordisk's® Tresiba® (basal insulin) Pens

☐ Handful of pen needles **(don't forget these!)**

☐ Handful of alcohol swabs

☐ 2 Dexcom G6® sensors[49]

☐ 1 backup Dexcom G6® transmitter

---

[48] Why2? Just in case something goes wrong, it's always good to have a backup. When I arrive at my destination, I like to put the extra insulin supplies in the fridge.

[49] It's very important to have backup CGM supplies.

☐ iPhone® (to serve as your Dexcom G6® receiver)

☐ iPhone® chargers

☐ Apple® Watch

☐ Apple® Watch charger

☐ 1 Glucagon

☐ Food for the flight → I like fruit since it's easy to carry on airplanes

☐ Original Dexcom G6® receiver (the one they provide that can be used in leu of your phone if something goes haywire with your phone.

☐ Original Dexcom G6® receiver charger

☐ Finger prick glucose monitor (if you forget this, it's not the end of the world. They're usually sold at every larger corner drug store.)

T1D Pro tip

If you're flying, go on the airline's website and make sure to order the diabetic meal (or any special meal for that matter). 99% of the time, they'll serve you first!

~Safe travels

Printed in Great Britain
by Amazon